Tangled Expectations

TANGLED SERIES

SOPHIE ANDREWS

 Created with Vellum

Content Note

Tangled Expectations is a *fast* burn between a divorcée and a hopeless romantic. Be aware this is a surprise pregnancy romance with a traumatic birth experience, so please read with care.

For the mom who puts on a Disney movie and hands their kids a bowl of goldfish so you can ignore them for an hour and read...me too.

CHAPTER ONE

Wes

We were off Canal Street in the middle of Little Italy at a bar with velvet seating and insanely overpriced drinks. I balanced my gin and tonic on my leg, ankle crossed over knee. "What are you guys up to this weekend?"

Bronte tucked her dark hair behind her ear. "We're going to see a show."

"And bum around," Chris said, dropping his arm around her shoulders.

Once upon a time, Chris "CJ" Cunningham had been Hollywood's "bad boy" actor, but his life had slowed way down since he'd married Bronte, a girl I'd known since we were neighbors as kids. With his career fully on track and in order, in part due to my guidance, we were finally able to open up a production house—Booksmart Productions—like we'd been talking about for years. It had always been my dream to make my *own* movies, not simply to work on everyone else's. Now, it was finally my turn to earn my credit—Wes Isaacson, *executive producer*.

I tipped my chin to Bronte. "Feel good to be done with work?"

She was on summer vacation from her gig teaching middle school. "Oh yeah. The next ten weeks will be blessedly quiet."

All three of us directed our attention to the restaurant, as if to prove it was not quiet. The city was alive with the start of summer. More people on the streets, more music pouring from bars and shops, more heat.

I re-rolled the sleeves of my shirt. Chris had always made fun of me for wearing starched button-downs and slacks every day, but I was the brains behind our operation, and I dressed the part. If Paul Feig could wear three-piece suits on set, the least I could do was get my clothes dry-cleaned for meetings.

"So, uh…" Chris started, his knee bouncing, the single tell of his nerves. "You think they went for it?"

They being the suits at Columbia, which was the second-largest film studio in the nation and a bit pie in the sky to make a deal with. But an old college connection who worked in the marketing department there set up the meeting for Chris and me to pitch them *Turning Leaves*. It was a best-selling book about a father and son reuniting after a lifetime apart, told in dual timelines, and we'd won the film rights.

"I don't know for sure, but… Yeah, I think they were into it," I said, although I refused to allow myself to celebrate. I wouldn't until I got the *Yes* call.

Bronte rubbed her hand along Chris's thigh. "You've been holding that question in all night, huh?"

"I was trying to be cool about it." He let out a reluctant laugh.

I sipped my drink. "Hey, even if Columbia passes, it's not the end. I'm going back to LA in a few weeks, so I can put out some feelers. You want to come with?"

Chris slanted his eyes to Bronte. "Not this time."

When they'd gotten together, they had bought a house in Studio City with a plan to spend their summers in Los Angeles, but that only lasted three years. I had tried to convince them to keep the real estate and rent it out, like I did with a few properties, but it was a no-go. They were permanent East Coasters now.

Bronte cleared her throat, toying with her wedding rings. "We're going to try again."

I cocked my head, not understanding until Chris added, "For a baby."

A few months ago, Chris had called me in near tears after Bronte miscarried. One of Bronte's dreams was to have a big family, like the one she grew up in, and after trying for a while, she'd finally gotten pregnant, only to lose it weeks later. They were devastated.

I leaned forward. "Is that what this is? A little weekend away before you get to it?" When Bronte's cheeks pinked, I clapped in understanding. "Or it's *to* get to it, yeah?"

Chris pulled Bronte in close to him as her neck and face flushed red.

"Well, what are you still doing here?" I gestured to the door. "Get to it."

"Nah." He polished off the last of his drink. "We're here to hang out with you."

I checked my watch. It was still early, a few minutes after eight o'clock, but... "We're finished with our drinks. No use staying here when you guys have better things to do." My lascivious grin had Chris chuckling. "Let me quick hit the head, and I'll walk out with you guys."

I got up to use the facilities, but on the way back, my eyes snagged on a woman, sitting a few feet behind Chris and Bronte. I hadn't noticed her before, though I couldn't ignore her now. She was crying.

Chris must have noticed where I was staring because he sucked in his cheeks like he was straining not to smile.

The bastard.

"What?" Bronte toggled her attention between her husband and me. "What's funny?"

Chris's shoulders shuddered in silent laughter.

"What?" Bronte repeated, giggling this time as if she couldn't not laugh when Chris did.

He lowered his voice, explaining, "Don't look, but there's a woman behind us who's crying. Wesley here can't ever say no to a crying woman. He's got to talk to her or help her. It's some weird compulsion. His kryptonite."

Bronte's eyes took on a saccharine gleam. "Aww, Wes, really?"

I wanted to say no, but what Chris so aptly articulated was the truth. Crying women were most definitely my kryptonite.

"That's sweet," she cooed, then swiftly backtracked, sticking her finger in the air. "On the other hand, you shouldn't be approaching random women who're crying. That could be intimidating." On the sly, she peered over her shoulder, pretending to search for something in her purse. "She seems really upset."

"Christ, Bunny," Chris said with an amused smirk, "don't tell him that. Now he really won't be able to walk out of here without checking on her."

"No." I tossed back the rest of my gin and tonic, prepared to walk straight out of the bar. "No. I'm good. Let's go."

Chris escorted Bronte in front of him, around the table, and I stared at the exit. Like I was a fighter, I kept my eyes on the prize.

And I lasted all of three seconds before my gaze dipped to the crying woman, who now held a glass of red wine in one hand and used a napkin to dab her eyes with the other.

But I wouldn't stop.

Absolutely not.

One foot in front of the other. I could practically hear the *Rocky* theme song in my head.

Then the woman let out the tiniest sniffle, and *fuck*.

"Hey, I'll catch up with you guys later," I said, and Chris acknowledged me with a hand in the air, his laughter trailing after him.

I stuck my hands in my pockets, trying to appear as nonthreatening as possible as I approached the woman's table. "Excuse me? Can I help you with something?"

She shook her head, careful to keep her wall of thick hair covering her face as she wiped at her nose. "I'm fine, thank you."

But the telltale hiccup of a breath gave her away. As if I needed more evidence she was, in fact, *not* fine. "I couldn't help but notice you're crying and..." I tilted my head, hoping she would look up at me. When she didn't, I went on. "I don't know what you're going through or what happened, but I'd like to help if I can."

"What?" She sniffled, taking the sting out of what she probably hoped to be a good barb. "You some knight in shining armor?"

"No." I glanced around at all the other patrons minding their own business, as if they couldn't see or hear this woman. Maybe they couldn't. Maybe this really was my horrible super-power. "But I doubt you're going to find whatever you're searching for in this bar."

Finally, she lifted her face to me, her dark hair parting to reveal splotchy cheeks and dark eyes outlined with slightly smudged makeup in the corners. A ghost of a frown touched the left corner of her obscenely pouty lips when she huffed. "You have no idea what I'm searching for."

I narrowed my eyes, allowing my gaze to travel to her dress, the same color as her wine, highlighting her golden skin and fan-fucking-tastic rack. "No, I don't. But maybe that was the point." I shrugged as if I was some poor, unknowing victim and not a willing participant. "Maybe this was your plan all along. To get dressed up and come here, acting all downtrodden so some schmuck like me would get caught up and buy you a few drinks to dry your tears."

One dark brow rose as her eyes cleared of tears. "Are you always so sweet to strangers?"

I grinned. "I try to be."

That earned me a laugh, so I took one step closer. "What's wrong? Can I help?"

Her lips were painted a rosy color, and they pursed for a moment. "Unless you can rewind to me agreeing to go on this date and getting stood up, then no."

"I'm sorry." I chanced another step next to her table. "That sucks."

She blew out a breath from that mouth I couldn't stop staring at. "It was my first date."

I jerked my head back, and she snorted a laugh, motioning to the open seat next to her. "Since my divorce."

"Ah." I sank down into the chair, angling it toward her, and leaned back against the arm. "In that case, can I buy you another drink?"

She lifted her glass and downed the rest of her wine before plunking it on the table with a sigh. "Be my guest."

I swiped a palm over my mouth, refusing to find amusement at her distress, but she was adorably rumpled. I gestured to the server and ordered her another wine and a gin and tonic for myself, putting it on my tab. Then I extended my hand. "I'm Wes."

She wrapped her fingers around mine, her nails painted pale pink. "Margaret." Then she tipped her head back and forth. "I mean Maggie. You've seen me crying, we're practically best friends now."

Once our drinks arrived, Maggie took a big gulp, crossed her endlessly long legs capped off in heels, and turned to me. "So, what's your deal?"

"My deal?"

Still holding her wineglass, she pointed her index finger at me, circling her hand. "Your whole knight-in-shining-armor thing. What's the deal?"

"I wouldn't necessarily call it a *thing.*"

The corner of her mouth curled up. "No? What would you call it?"

I drummed my fingers on my glass. "An early childhood with a single mom and little sister who cried a lot. Is there a clinical name for that?"

She found her cell phone in her purse and pretended to type something out. "Let me Google right quick." After a moment, she lifted her gaze to me, saying somberly, "Adolescent pseudo-superhero syndrome."

I snapped my fingers. "Yes, exactly. What about you? What's your diagnosis?"

She absently dragged the tips of her fingers over her kneecap as she stared off in contemplation. "Post-matrimonial neurosis with a hint of premenopausal phobia."

I sucked air through my teeth. "Premenopausal phobia. A little early for that, no?"

"I'm thirty-eight and was stood up even after we had been talking for a few weeks."

"Maybe there was an emergency," I said, hoping to God that was the truth, because I really did feel bad for her. But she shook her head and handed her phone over to me so I could see the message on her dating app.

"Sorry, Maggie," I read out loud, "but I won't be coming

tonight. I recently ran into one of my exes, and I honestly wouldn't feel right going on a date with you after she and I started to rekindle things. I'm really sorry." I winced. "At least he was honest."

"Yeah, he was *the* one good one I've found." She took another sip of her wine. "I can't keep doing this." She pressed her hand to her chest, and my *real* superpower was not acknowledging how her breasts were attempting to escape her dress. "I was married for six years. We dated for two years before we even got married, so basically all of my thirties were with Brian. If I had known I was going to be here, I wouldn't have wasted my twenties."

"What do you mean, here?"

"Here." She waved down the length of her body. "Thirty-eight and single."

"Well, I don't think—"

"You know how hard it is to find a good guy?" She carried on right on over me, her words tumbling out so fast I almost couldn't understand them all. "They're all taken or young and gross. I could go for an older guy, which I wouldn't have a problem with except none of them want to get married and have kids. So that means I need to keep slogging through this trash heap they call the dating pool for a suitable candidate I can marry and make the father of my children."

"You could—"

"Do you know what they call people as old as I am who are pregnant? *Geriatric*," she said with a dramatic whisper. "I'll have a geriatric pregnancy. I might as well give up and stay home. Work on my knitting. Spend my last days decaying into dust while watching *Price is Right* or whatever it is people do in an old folks home."

She finally paused, so I tossed out a casual, "My grandmother got an STI at her nursing home."

"She *what*?"

I took a slow sip of my drink, reveling in her amusement. "Apparently it's a problem. These older folks have a lot of time on their hands and not a whole lot of sex education, so..."

"Your grandmother?" she squeaked.

"They caught her with a man named Ronald."

She covered her mouth. "I'm sorry. I shouldn't be laughing."

"No, it's funny. I mean, *now* it's funny. When my mom found out, she was pissed." I shrugged. "What can I say? Nana might be old, but she's not dead, and she likes to enjoy herself."

"Go Nana."

I pointed at her with my drink. "So, don't let the bastards get you down. You're not geriatric. You're still young. You've got lots of time."

"Tell that to my shriveling eggs."

I leaned over, providing her stomach a pep talk. "Hey, buck up in there. Eat some protein. You got this." When she batted me away, laughing, I regarded her seriously. "I think you might be overthinking this whole thing."

"Yeah?" She shifted closer to me, propping her elbow on the arm of her chair, inadvertently offering me a good peek at her cleavage.

I gripped my glass harder, my fingers itching to touch her, any part of her. Even her shin, which shone like she'd put on some kind of oil. I'd bet anything she was silky smooth and smelled delicious. "Maybe instead of jumping right back into a relationship, you need to have a few one-night stands. Explore a little bit."

She tilted her head. "Is that advice or an invitation?"

"That's awfully forward, Margaret. I'd never suggest such a

thing to a woman who was crying into her wine mere minutes ago."

She eyed me, but her serious air eventually faded with a curl of her lips. "Okay, so you know my sob story. You can't leave me hanging. Tell me yours."

I coasted my gaze around the bar before landing back on Maggie's expectant face, as if she *needed* to hear my secret. Maybe to know she wasn't alone. So, with a deep breath, I told her. "My biological father walked out on us when I was four, and I grew up with this...notion I had to take care of my mom and sister. I had to be the man of the house, but I was in preschool and didn't know how to tie my shoes."

She sighed. "That's both sad and cute."

I placed my drink on the table, slanting my chair to face her, the toe of her shoe brushing my pant leg. "We lived in this little apartment complex, and, as soon as I could manage it, I made a deal with the landlord for him to pay me to mow the grass. I saved up all the money to give to my mom. She never took it, so then I started buying things at the convenience store, candy, magazines, anything I thought might make my mom and sister happy. I had to take care of them. I wanted to take care of them."

"Oh my god." Maggie touched her collarbone, clearly charmed. "That might be the sweetest thing I've ever heard."

"No. It was adolescent pseudo-superhero syndrome." I offered her a smile, which she returned. "But then my mom met this really great guy. We moved in to a house, they got married, and he was the dad I always wanted."

"How old were you?"

I scratched at my chin, thinking. "Uh, fifth grade when they got married. He adopted me and my sister, and life has been pretty great since."

She dropped her head back to her chair. "Ugh, like I said, your story is so much sweeter than mine."

"I'm pretty lucky in that regard. Thirty-seven years old, and no major life setbacks."

"Rub it in, go ahead."

I snagged her wrist when she flicked at my leg. "It can't be all bad."

She let out a tiny sound of disgust. "Oh, what do you know? You don't have geriatric eggs to worry about, and with your clothes and eyes and—" she withdrew her hand from my light hold to flail it around in my direction "—your whole thing, I'm sure you have hordes of people throwing themselves at you."

"Not really."

"Because you're too busy tending to crying women in bars?"

"Yep." If only she knew she was my kryptonite. When she smothered a growing smile, I said, "I split my time between here and LA. I've been out there since college and..."

"You've had a lot of one-night stands, then? Meaningless flings?"

I tipped my head back and forth. "Yeah, sure, I've had those, but I've always wanted to find *the one*, like my mom and dad. Settle down and start a family. I just haven't found her yet."

"Well..." Maggie lifted her glass. "Here's to you and me finding the one."

I clinked my drink against hers. "To us."

CHAPTER TWO

After we finished our drinks, Wes ordered another round. "Okay, so tell me about this ex-husband of yours."

I found an elastic band in my clutch and pulled my hair back in a ponytail, under no illusions of impressing anyone anymore. Not after Wes had already seen me, not at my worst, but not far off from *drunk girl haggling with the guy behind the dollar pizza counter for extra garlic knots* if he hadn't introduced himself and stopped the train wreck waiting to happen.

I had painstakingly styled my hair into big curls and bought a new dress. With this being my first step out into life post-divorce, I thought it called for something special. Then I'd arrived only to get the message from Holton, and I couldn't help the tears that had gathered in my eyes. Holton was sweet and funny, and we had bonded over the demise of past relationships. Although his past relationship was apparently not quite past. And what a blow to the ovaries that was.

I could almost feel the burn on the roof of my mouth from the pizza I wouldn't have allowed to cool before I bit into it.

Until Wes showed up, with his charm and unassuming hunch to his shoulders. He was confident in a quiet way and clearly a family man. I had learned a lot about his mom,

Abigail, who had worked as a nurse until she retired to Florida with her husband, Jeff, and his sister was Danielle, or Dani as he called her, who lived in Delaware with her family. After hearing about their dinners and the raucous neighbors he grew up next to, I felt like I'd grown up on their block too.

But he had succeeded in taking my mind off being stood up, and maybe that was his whole goal to begin with. Whatever the reason he was still here, I appreciated it, and I figured now it was my turn.

"I met Brian through my friend Amber. She and I both went to Pratt Institute and met at a party. We hit it off right away, and after we graduated, we moved in together, doing the whole single girls in the city thing for a long time. She comes from a rich family, her dad is some real estate mogul, and they have houses everywhere, but their home base was a penthouse on Fifth Avenue."

At Wes's wide eyes, I nodded. "Amber knew the best places to go. We were partying every night." I grimaced at the memories. "There were so many nights... Sometimes, I don't even know how I'm still alive. Like, doing a line of coke with some random Brazilian guy in the bathroom of a condo in the West Village. Who does that?"

Wes didn't move to speak, so I kept going, "After one long weekend of partying, Amber's brother showed up. I was in the shower, and I heard them yelling at each other. I ran out, not knowing who he was or what he was doing there. With a towel around me, dripping wet, I threw my bottle of shampoo at him. Hit him square in the jaw."

"The old hit your roommate's brother in the head trope, huh?" Wes clucked his tongue. "Classic meet-cute storyline."

"What do you know about meet-cutes?"

His slow-growing smile was so endearing, I wondered if he

practiced it. "I'm in the film business. Everyone knows a movie's got to have a good hook. That's film school 101."

Film school, that sounded interesting, and I wanted to know more about his background, but before I could ask him, he rolled his finger for me to continue.

"Brian was a few years older, working his way through med school. I was instantly in love, but he thought I was Amber's wild child friend."

I absently swirled my wine, recalling how I'd convinced Amber to bring me along on family vacations and get-togethers on the Cape to have some time with Brian. "He was everything I hadn't found at the bars and seedy apartments Amber had trotted me around to, and once I gathered the courage to confess how I felt, he told me he wasn't interested in a party girl." I dragged my eyes back to Wes, who gazed at me with dark blue eyes that reminded me of the ocean, deep and still. "I wasn't a party girl," I explained, "not really. But I was wrapped up in Amber and how easily she floated around life. Everything had been handed to her on a silver platter, and I wanted that too. After growing up with hand-me-downs until there were holes in the clothes, I wanted to know what it felt like to have money and the freedom to do whatever I wanted."

"I get it," he said quietly. "With only my mom taking care of us, it was hard. She worked a lot, picked up extra shifts, and we were still nickel-and-diming until my stepdad came around. So, I know what you mean when you say you wanted money and freedom."

I dropped my hand off the side of the armchair, my fingers dangling close to his. "It took a long time for Brian to say yes to me. I think he secretly believed he reformed me or something." I rolled my eyes. "People talk about god complexes? Hang out with a cardiothoracic surgeon for a while."

"Yeah?"

When I reflected on it, I couldn't believe I ever loved him. But once again, I had been searching for validation in all the wrong places. "He came from money with a silver spoon in his mouth, *and* he literally saved people's lives? He believed he was God's gift."

Wes's brow pinched. "Sounds like an asshole."

"By the time my blinders came off, I'd already signed the prenup and we were married. There was nothing left for me to do but try to fix it, although it never got better. Especially when we started trying for a baby."

I curled my lips between my teeth to keep from saying any more. Wes probably assumed I was some hysterical woman with how I basically forced him to be my therapist. Too bad I already paid one top dollar.

"What happened then?" he asked, and it was truly amazing he wanted to know more. How he sat there listening like he had nothing better to do.

I cleared my throat, aiming to keep all emotion out of it. "I couldn't get pregnant, so I went to the doctor about it." Residual resentment flared in my joints, and I had to remind myself to unclench my jaw. "I was completely healthy, and they could find no reason why I wasn't able to conceive. They suggested he get tested, but when I brought it up, he flat-out refused. Told me I was overreacting and being overly emotional. Said it was probably psychological why I couldn't get pregnant."

Wes sat forward, his chin jutted out in a pretty good impression of a person pissed off. "He was gaslighting you?"

When I nodded, he rounded his fingers into a fist on top of his thigh.

It was comforting to witness his physical reaction. Finally, someone understood my anger, stood with me in indignation.

"When I tried to talk to Amber about him, she didn't want to hear it," I said, shrugging like I hadn't spent years trying to move past losing not only my marriage but my supposed best friend too. "He was her brother. Obviously, she wasn't going to listen to me bitch about him or take my side. When we divorced, I was pretty much left with nothing and no one. My friends were all his friends or Amber's friends, so…"

"Man." Wes inhaled audibly and sat up, taking a moment to rearrange his features back into the placid expression he'd worn all night. Then he placed a reassuring hand on my knee. "You really had a rough time of it. I'm sorry, Maggie."

I liked the way he said my name, and I closed my eyes at his warm touch. When his fingertips brushed along my skin, it pebbled in goose bumps, and I opened my eyelids to find him studying me with a curious glint. He motioned toward my empty wineglass. "Did you want another?"

I considered it. I'd already drunk three, which was two more than I usually had when I was out, and with a quick glance to the thin watch I wore, I shook my head. "It's after eleven. I'd better not."

"You're right. Gotta get you back to the old folks home."

"Hey. I thought we were friends." I pouted, and his attention dropped to my mouth.

"You're right," he said after a moment as his eyes drifted back up to mine. "I was raised to respect my elders."

I refused to laugh, but when he grinned at me and offered his hand, I took it and stood up. My breasts brushed against his chest, and he cleared his throat, stepping away from me, murmuring a soft apology. Little did he know, the last thing I wanted was an apology.

It had been a long time since a man had regarded me with heat in his eyes, and it had been even longer since my own blood had pumped with excitement. I hadn't flirted and had fun like this since...well, since before I was married.

Maybe Wes was right when he suggested I needed to explore a little bit before I settled down again. My chances of having a baby were dwindling, but they weren't completely extinct. Science was incredible, and I was sure—if I saved up enough money—I'd be able to freeze a few eggs for later. I wasn't an old maid quite yet.

I still had time to have fun.

And there was no better opportunity than the one in front of me.

Outside of the bar, Wes stuck his hands in his pockets. "So, are you taking a cab or...?"

I pointed behind my shoulder with my clutch. "Walking."

"Mind if I walk with you?"

"Not at all."

Even though we hadn't talked about anything of significance—besides, of course, me spilling my guts about my divorce—I couldn't help but feel safe in his presence. I didn't even know exactly what he did for work or where he lived, but it didn't matter. Not when his eyes roamed over my face, the hint of a smile pulling at the corner of his lips.

"I'm a few blocks away," I said, starting off toward my place. While I wasn't short by any means, Wes still stood a head taller, even with my heels on.

"You like living down here?" he asked, slowing his pace to match mine.

"I don't have much of a choice. I'm subletting from a friend of a friend until I find something more permanent."

He dodged out of the path of a trio of laughing twentysomethings. "I'm in Brooklyn. Williamsburg."

It was a trek to come all the way to the Lower East Side for a drink. "Are there no bars in Brooklyn?"

"I met some friends. They're here for a few days, staying at a hotel up the street." He tipped his head back in the direction of the bar.

"And you left them?" I gripped my purse a little tighter, the implication dangling between us.

He left them for me.

"I'm their third wheel." He dipped his head toward mine. "I told you about my best friend growing up, Fitz? It's his sister and my friend slash business partner." He held my elbow as he swerved away from a couple of drunk guys. But instead of moving back away from me, he slipped his hand to my lower back, settling his fingers against my hip.

Slick move.

"My dad worked in finance and taught me a lot about making good decisions and investments with what I had. So, once I had the money, I got into investment properties, and when my parents moved to Florida, I bought them out of their house and started renting it out. A couple years ago, my friend Chris needed a place to stay, and I gave him the keys to the house. He got real close to the Hollingers, one thing led to another with him and Bronte, and now they're happily married."

I smiled up at him. "You played Cupid?"

"Not on purpose, but yeah. They're perfect for each other."

I melted even more. "That's adorable. You're adorable."

"What can I say? I'm a hopeless romantic," he admitted without a hint of irony.

Nudging my shoulder into his side, I steered us to the left, down Mulberry Street. "I'm right here," I said, snagging my keys from my purse. When he moved to step back, I grabbed his forearm, blurting out, "You wouldn't want to come up, would you?"

Under the dim light of the streetlamp above us, Wes's eyes

toggled between my own, as if he really needed to think about the answer, and I wilted. Maybe I'd imagined the connection between us. I had been out of the game a long time and could've misinterpreted his kindness for attraction.

God, maybe I needed to take a class on dating for this decade.

"It's okay." I shook my head. "Thank you for the drinks and for letting me cry on your shoulder. You're one of the good ones, Wes." Then I spun on my heel.

"Wait, Maggie." He caught my hand before I could put the key in the lock and pressed his chest to my back, sweeping the ends of my ponytail away from my neck. "I would really like to come up, please."

Without turning toward him, I nodded, and he placed one chaste kiss on the side of my neck.

"Recent renovation?" he asked once we were inside the building, probably noting the clean white paint on the lobby walls.

"Within the last few years," I said, and he followed me into the elevator, his hand finding my lower back again as I hit the button for the fifth floor. "Like I said, I'm subletting from a friend of a friend. They're in Paris for the year."

Wes's eyebrows shot up. "Nice."

"He needed some inspiration so..."

"So he jaunted off to Paris?"

"Yeah. Anton Sterchi, he's a semi-famous artist around here. We went to art school together, although he was a few years behind me."

"You went to art school?" His fingers found their way to my shoulder when the elevator signaled our arrival, and he stayed glued to my side as we strolled down the hall to my door.

"Yeah. My parents thought it was a waste of money. And maybe it was, but I made a lot of connections from it." I unlocked my door and gestured to the whole of the apartment as evidence of my connections coming in handy while Wes trailed me inside. "Someone could argue an art degree is meaningless, but without my going to school for it, I wouldn't have had any idea how to market myself or have the knowledge of the industry." I huffed. "I also wouldn't have met Brian, so…"

"You win some, you lose some." Wes tossed a wry smirk in my direction, and I laughed.

"Exactly."

"I get what you're saying, though." He leaned against the wall, next to a framed abstract painting. With his hands in his pockets and his feet crossed at the ankles, he seemed utterly at ease, even in this little studio apartment. "I went to college for business with a minor in film studies, knowing I wanted to make movies, but any kind of art is weird to study. It's not an objective subject. You can learn about technique, you can take theory and history classes, but people either like what you create or they don't. Making a career out of it is a whole other process, and I don't think those outside art communities understand that."

Setting my purse down on the kitchen counter, I flicked my fingers between us. "See? You get me." I grabbed two glasses to fill with water. "That's what I like about you."

He accepted one of the drinks and examined the apartment. "It's nice." He crossed the few steps to the windows, reflections of the streetlights coloring the white comforter on the bed just a few feet behind him. "Nice view."

"It is," I agreed, taking in the sight of Wes's back as he stared out the floor-to-ceiling windows. Now that he was in full light, I noticed his hair, which I previously assumed was sandy blond, was actually tinged red. "You're a ginger."

He glanced over his shoulder at me. "Hey now. Don't make fun of me. I'm insecure about it."

I brushed my hand up his spine then combed my fingers into the hair trimmed neatly at the nape of his neck. "I'm not teasing. I like it." I tugged on the strands. "Although, you did make fun of me for being old."

A low sound rumbled from the back of his throat, his eyes closing for a second, as if he enjoyed me tugging on his hair, and I leaned into him, letting my hand lazily drift to learn the curve of his shoulder and hardness of his chest. He opened his eyes to me, his gaze molten hot, and took the glass out of my hand to put it down along with his own on the coffee table.

"*Me* make fun of *you*? I'd never." Then he wrapped one hand around the back of my head and kissed me. At first, his lips moved slowly, like he was warming me up, but then he adjusted his hold to the angle he wanted and slipped his tongue inside my mouth. He tasted faintly of gin and tonic, and he felt like a dream. With his hands holding me to him and his lips pulling at my own, inviting me to open up, I gave in to the fantasy.

CHAPTER THREE

"Maggie," Wes murmured, smoothing his hands down my back, inching away from me, "you don't have to do anything—"

I cut him off with another kiss. But this time, I was in charge, looping my arms around his neck, nibbling at his lower lip before sucking on it. This man, so sweet and funny, was about to inform me I didn't have to do anything I didn't want to.

Well.

I wanted to.

I wanted him.

"Come on." I nudged him back to sit on the edge of the bed and stood between his open knees, kicking off my heels. I dropped down a few inches so his head was level with my chest.

"Can I?"

At my nod, he curved his palms around the outsides of my breasts, appearing hypnotized as he shook his head infinitesimally, and I snorted a laugh. "You like them?"

He squeezed and pushed them together then bent to drag his tongue along the valley he created. "It was hard not to stare at these tits all night." He brushed his thumbs along my nipples until they hardened, and he tipped his head back. "You know how good you look in this dress?"

"I did buy it for my date, so I was hoping..."

"Mission accomplished." He was back to gaping at my breasts. "Christ." He licked his lips, a man starving. "Love these," he mumbled, sucking at the skin of my collarbone.

I gasped as pleasure shot straight between my legs, and I leaned down, kissing him, all teeth and tongue. He let out a gravelly sound, and I climbed on his lap, eager to earn another.

Brian had been silent whenever we were intimate, almost to the point I assumed he hadn't enjoyed being with me. But with Wes? I could bask in his sounds. Bathe in them. Let them soak into my skin.

I was doing this to him, making him hot and hard, releasing groans and pants. And *this*, this desperation was what I needed, what I'd been searching for tonight. I needed to know I was still desirable, still wanted.

When I sat up to arrange my knees on either side of his hips, my dress rode up my thighs. As if he could read my mind, he asked, "Am I a rebound from your divorce?"

"Is that okay?"

His eyes sparkled with boyish enthusiasm. "Very okay." Then he glided his hands up my legs, squeezing my hips, his fingers toying with the strap of my thong. "Though it does put a lot of pressure on me."

"Pressure on *you*?" I laughed into a kiss, feeling braver than I had in a long time. "It's a lot of pressure on *me*."

He snuck his hands under my dress so the soft crepe fabric bunched at my waist, and he trailed his fingertip between my thighs until I rocked my hips into him. "Why on you? I'm the one who has to make it good enough so you forget your ex-husband."

"That won't be hard," I said with a derisive huff that was cut short by a soft moan when he slid his finger up my center. I let my head fall back as he tugged my underwear to the side. "It's been a long time. That's why..." My breath caught when he found my clit. "That's why it's a lot of pressure on me. I think I've forgotten how to do it."

"Well, so far, so good, sweetheart. Now come here." He wrapped one hand around my neck, drawing my mouth back to his, as his other hand tormented me until I was breathing hard against his lips. "You doing okay?"

I couldn't answer, my brain fuzzy, body buzzing. He circled two fingers, teasing at the tight bundle of nerves before slipping inside. He followed that same route over and over, and my jaw went slack as heat crackled low in my belly.

"Tell me how it feels." He placed an openmouthed kiss on my shoulder. "I want to make this good for you." When I hesitated, he tightened the hand around my neck ever-so-slightly, sending sparks of need through me. "Tell me, Maggie. I need to hear you say it."

"A little faster," I breathed, rocking my hips against his hand.

"That's it," he crooned, kissing across my collarbone to nip at the tops of my breasts, his fingers working faster. He dragged his other hand along my spine, finding the zipper at the back of my dress and yanking it down. The thick straps dropped off my shoulders, lowering the neckline enough that he easily pushed my bra out of the way to cup my right breast. "Look at you." He stroked his tongue over my aching nipple. "So gorgeous."

Between his words, fingers, and tongue, I walked a tightrope of pleasure, and I dug my fingertips into his solid shoulders. "Wes, I'm gonna..."

His lips brushed my nipple a moment before he bit down on it. "You like that?"

Nearly delirious with desire pulsing through me, I couldn't answer.

"Maggie," he warned, his tone sharp, while the fingers buried inside me barely changed their rhythm, but it was enough to walk me back from the edge of orgasm. I whimpered at the clear reprimand.

"Please," I whined.

He took hold of my ponytail. "Please what?"

"Please bite me."

He ground out a satisfied-sounding groan then he bit my nipple again as his fingers resumed their sweet torture. I shuddered. "Oh my god, Wes."

He licked my throat, keeping a tight hold on my hair, forcing my back to arch, and he sucked on my pulse point. I was so close, my hips grinding down on his hand, and I swore I could feel him smile against my skin. "Come for me, sweetheart."

And I did.

Like a rocket into space, I trembled as tension coiled to a tiny pinpoint deep inside me then exploded through every part of me.

"That's it," he said, releasing his hold on my hair. "You're such a good girl for me."

I slumped down, my forehead falling to his shoulder as his hand soothed along my spine, the other teasing my wetness up and down my slit. "My god," I mumbled. "That was…"

"Better than anyone else you've ever had?"

"I don't remember. I've forgotten about anyone else."

"Good. That was the point." He shifted so our gazes met. "Still okay?"

I kissed my answer into his lips. "Yes," I said, faltering

when he moved to get up. "W-wait." I placed my hands on his chest to push away from him. "I want to…"

Keeping eye contact so he'd understand my meaning, I knelt on the floor between his knees. His erection strained visibly behind the zipper of his pants, and I wanted to make him feel as good as he did me. Yet now that I was down here, I lost some of my bravado.

"You don't have to," he told me, as if he could feel my hesitation.

"No." I placed my hands on his thighs. "I want to. It's just…"

He dragged his fingertip across my brow until I relaxed the worry I'd been holding there, and he followed the line of my nose down to my lips. "When you looked up at me tonight from your table, the first thing I noticed was your eyes, how big and dark they were, like drops of melted chocolate. The second thing I noticed was your mouth." He tapped the middle of my bottom lip. "This pout and how you had your teeth biting into it."

I nestled into his palm when he caressed my cheek. "I thought you stopped because you can't stand women crying."

"And I stayed because of this mouth," he said, and I licked my lips. A rumble sounded from his chest. "Tease."

His words reminded me of what I wanted, to be brave and put myself out there again. If this was a hurdle I had to overcome into my new, post-divorce life, Wes was practically paving the way in how easy he made it. I reached for his belt, unbuckling it, and we worked together to tug his light gray pants and underwear down enough to release his cock—long, slightly pink, and intimidating.

I swallowed thickly, lifting my eyes up to his. "I need…"

"What?" He traced his fingertip along my jaw. "What do you need?"

"I need you to tell me what to do."

After a moment, when his gaze roamed all over my face as if searching for something, he nodded toward the mattress. "Come up here, next to me. On your knees."

I did as instructed because following his direction made this whole experience easier. His praise didn't hurt either.

He grabbed hold of my ponytail again, this time bunching it in his fist. "Your lips were made for this. See?" He curled his other hand around the base of his length, drawing my attention to the tip, where a bead of liquid formed. "It's practically begging for your mouth."

I reflexively traced my lips with my tongue, and he fidgeted as if that action made him uncomfortable. "Maggie," he rasped. "Put your lips on me."

I bent over, taking him into my mouth, and he wrapped my hair around his fist while he slid his other hand back under my dress, his fingers digging into the flesh of my backside. "Hold on tight to it and lick the head," he told me as his fingers traveled down between my cheeks. I had trouble concentrating when he swiped at my pussy. "Come on, sweetheart, let me see you take me all the way in your mouth."

He gently guided my head down until my eyes watered at the sensation of him hitting the back of my throat. "Look at you doing so well." He massaged my neck, and I started to move on my own, without the control of his fingers or words. I dragged my tongue up from root to tip before sucking again, and he responded by curling what felt like three fingers into me. "You're taking me so well."

I practically purred at his words and felt more than heard his laugh.

"You like this, huh? You like being a good girl for me?" He tugged on my ponytail. "Then sit up."

I swiped my palm over my mouth as I sat back on my heels,

waiting for the next instruction, but for the first time all night, he was the one to hesitate.

"I didn't expect this tonight," he said. "I don't have a condom, but we can keep going like this, if that's what you want."

"No." I hopped up from the bed. "I think I saw some in the closet."

I honestly hadn't considered birth control in a long time. First, because I had wanted to have a child with Brian, and second, because when our relationship soured, we didn't require it anymore. Fortunately, I moved in to this completely furnished apartment with a lot of Anton's belongings still here. Including a few condoms mixed in with an array of toiletries in a small plastic bin in the bathroom closet.

I hustled back out, brandishing the foil packet. "Got one."

"Resourceful." Wes stood to toe off his shoes before removing his button-down. He folded it over the back of a chair in the corner, followed by his pants and underwear then stalked over to me. He was tall and thin, trimmed with muscle, the physique of a runner. All pale skin and a smattering of amber hair on his chest, he stood in front of me with a cheeky grin. "Your turn to strip."

I handed him the condom and shimmied out of my dress so it pooled at my feet. My bra landed on the floor next, but his hands were immediately on my breasts, weighing them in his palms. My panties were already soaked, but with how he alternated sucking on each nipple, they might as well have been nonexistent.

"Wes." I tugged on his hair, and he gave in, straightening to his full height, which had to be well over six feet, given how he towered over my own five foot nine. In one swift motion, he had my underwear off and me bent over, his hands pressing mine into the mattress.

"Keep them there," he said then ripped the foil packet.

Mere moments later, he squatted down, licking up my slit. "Jesus, you're so wet." He swirled his tongue around me, teasing my swollen and tender flesh. "You taste so good. I could stay down here for hours."

I pushed back against him. "No, please don't. I need you in me."

He stood up and wound my hair around his fist, turning my head to kiss me, his tongue plunging into my mouth, and I could taste myself on him. He nipped at my lips, saying, "You've been such a good girl, I guess I'll give you what you want."

And without another word, he lined himself up and pushed inside me with one thrust, wrenching all the air from my lungs. He murmured a few more words of praise as he set a steady pace, and the wet sounds coming from where we connected might have embarrassed me if I were with someone else, but with Wes, I relished it. I loved the way he kept me in the moment, secure and cared for, and especially loved how he checked in.

"Tell me how it feels, Maggie. I need to know."

"I don't want it to stop," I bit out, and he wrapped one hand around my torso, kneading and plucking at my breast. "Harder. I need it harder."

He exhaled a gruff sound and pulled on my shoulder until my back was against his chest. "I know I was joking about you being an elder earlier, but now it's your turn to make fun of me," he said a little breathlessly. "I've lost a lot of stamina in my old age."

I would've laughed if I were able to do anything other than suck in short breaths when his clever fingers found my clit again. I was already taut as a bowstring, prickly pleasure curling my fingers and toes, nearly too painful to bear.

"I need you to come again." His teeth scraped over my ear and down my jaw. "You smell so good, and your skin is so soft." He bit my shoulder before he bent me over again, this time keeping his body molded to mine. "I could stay inside you forever." His rhythm began to stutter, and he grunted as his hands fell to the mattress on either side of my hips. "Maggie, sweetheart," he said, his voice like sandpaper. "Touch yourself. I'm about to lose it, but I want you to come with me."

I angled my head to the side, meeting his gaze. "The heart is willing but the flesh is weak, huh?"

He smacked the side of my thigh as he huffed out a laugh. "Fucking get there."

After a few circles of my fingers and thrusts from him, a thousand tiny fireworks set off from my nerve endings, and I gave in to the rush of tingles and flood of heat.

Behind me, Wes growled out something incoherent and fell on top of me, rolling us both to our sides. He skimmed a hand over my waist, patting my hip with an exhausted, "Good girl."

I giggled drunkenly into the comforter, which had become rumpled and twisted during our romp, and when I turned to face him, he sent me a playful glare. "You laughing at me?"

I wiped my face clear of all amusement. "I'd never."

With one hand wrapped around my middle, he stared down at me. There was something about the way he regarded me with his calming ocean eyes that had me wanting to show him parts of myself I'd closed off.

"Thank you," I said after a few moments, and he caressed my belly with the tips of his fingers.

"Truly, the pleasure was all mine." He kissed me once more and stretched back as if to get out of bed.

I clutched his wrist. "Are you leaving?"

"Do you want me to?"

I bit into my bottom lip, wondering how to play this. Then again, I didn't want to *play* anything. I was almost forty; I had to be honest with myself and with him. So far, he'd been accepting. There was no reason to stop now.

"No," I said. "I want you to stay."

He smiled. "Then I'm staying. Bathroom?"

I pointed him down the hall, and he stepped into his underwear before walking away, granting me a few minutes to slip an oversized T-shirt over my head. I was in the middle of grabbing a few snacks from the kitchen when he came back out, heading for the living room area, where he'd found some of my work.

"You did all this?" He gestured to the piles of stickers, postcards, pop art, and other miscellaneous items I needed to send out to my Etsy shoppers.

I nodded and held up the off-brand pop-tarts I had loved since I was a kid. My parents were never able to afford name-brand food, and I had grown to love the overly sweet flavor of the cheap stuff. Though, really, all the cheap stuff was sweet. Too sweet. "Would you like the strawberry or blueberry flavor?"

"Blueberry, please."

"Perfect. Strawberry's my favorite."

"So, tell me more about your work," he said, sitting down on the couch as he tore open the package I handed him.

And that was how we started, or rather, continued talking until after four in the morning.

CHAPTER FOUR

Wes

I jolted from sleep when something nailed me in the calf. I rolled to my side, finding the culprit frowning at me.

"I'm sorry." Maggie's hair was all disheveled, her cheek pink from where it rested on the pillow.

"You okay?"

"Just a dream. I was falling down a hill."

"Hate dreams like that." I sat back against the headboard so my feet didn't hang off the end of her mattress anymore.

"I didn't realize how small this bed was until there was a second person in it." She yawned. "Especially a giant-sized one."

My laugh was broken up by her contagious yawn. "What time is it?"

She grabbed glasses from the bedside table before checking her phone. "Barely eight o'clock." Then she flopped back to her pillow. "Sorry I woke you up."

"It's fine. I should probably head out anyway." I scrubbed my hand over the side of my hair and jaw, my eyes sluggishly roving over her next to me. "You're cute in the morning."

She threw her arm over her face. "If you like dragon breath and dried-up makeup."

"As it happens, I do." I tugged on her wrist. "I like your glasses too." I tapped the thick red frames before scooting down to the mattress, propping my head up on one hand while the other wandered over her stomach, soft and slightly rounded. "You usually wear them?"

"When I'm home, which is most of the time."

Even though I was barely awake, energy crackled between us as I studied her face. The shine of her hair, her slightly elfin-like ears, her narrow nose, that mouth. Good god, that mouth. I scrutinized her like I was going to be tested on her skeletal structure later.

"I know I told you last night that you should spend some time getting your ex out of your system, have some one-night stands, but..." I hoped she wouldn't think I was an asshole for misleading her, although I doubted this attraction was one-sided. We had stayed up almost all night talking. Most people didn't do that with someone they only planned on spending one night with. "I would really like to see you again."

"You would?"

"Yeah." My brow ticked up. "Why do you sound so surprised?"

"Therapy has worked wonders for me, but it hasn't brought about any miracles." Then she slapped her hand over her mouth, squeezing her eyes shut. "Oh my god. I'm delirious from so little sleep."

I laughed, towing her to my chest. This was exactly why I knew what we had was special. We'd been so honest with each other. Not that I had ever been afraid to open up to a woman before, but I'd never felt compelled to. Not like I was with Maggie. I wanted to know her inside and out, and for her to know me that way too. "What are you in therapy for?"

"Failed marriage, being my parents' perpetual disappointment—you know, the usual."

"Sure, sure." I twirled a lock of her hair around my fingers. "So, you up for a date?"

"Definitely." She traced the thin blue line of my vein along my bicep, and I bent to nuzzle her neck.

"We can grab dinner and a movie. I promise I won't talk through it." I'd told her how everyone always got so annoyed with me because I couldn't seem to keep my mouth shut during movies, yakking about details no one else cared about like the audio mix or why the director went with a two-shot instead of a close-up.

She indulged me with a smile. "I won't mind if you do."

It was the perfect answer. She was perfect. And I growled into her throat. "I knew I liked you."

She wrapped her arms around my neck. "But I can't speak for the other people in the movie theater."

"I don't care about them." I nipped her ear. "Only you." As soon as I shifted over her, planting trailing kisses down her chest, my phone vibrated from its spot on the coffee table, momentarily stilling me. Normally, I would've let it go to voice mail, but since our meeting yesterday, I had to answer it on the off chance it was *the* call. "I should get that."

I carefully lifted off her, my boxer-briefs doing nothing to hide my burgeoning erection as I reached for my cell, but once I checked the screen, I groaned. "It's my mom."

Maggie bit back a laugh. "Well, don't leave her hanging."

I raked my gaze over her, her breasts tormenting me from where they were half hidden beneath the taupe sheet. "I don't have to."

"I'm going to use the bathroom anyway. Go ahead."

I slouched back on the bed with a sigh and answered the call. "Hey. It's a little early for you to be calling, isn't it?"

Maggie smiled at me over her shoulder, the bottom of her ass peeking out from the hem of her T-shirt. "Mama's boy," she mouthed, and I had to rub the heel of my hand against my hardening dick. I couldn't talk to my mother like this.

"Hey, hon, I know it's early, but your father and I are meeting Cheryl and Joe for breakfast, and I thought I'd quickly call to remind you it's Nana's birthday tomorrow."

"I know. I have it in my calendar. I'm sending her flowers."

"Great. Hey, how'd the meeting go? I was expecting a text from you."

Maggie wasn't wrong when she accused me of being a mama's boy. I absolutely was.

"It went well, I think." I heard the toilet flush in the bathroom and the water run in the sink. "At least, I hope."

A moment later, Maggie poked her head out of the doorway, her toothbrush in her mouth, offering me a sudsy smile.

"What are you up to today?" my mom asked, and I stood, making my way to Maggie.

"I've got a few errands to run."

"Okay. Well, I'll talk to you later. Love you."

"Love you too," I said and hung up, crowding Maggie back into her bathroom, forcing her ass right up against me when she bent to the sink. I gave it a good squeeze. "She wanted to remind me it was Nana's birthday tomorrow. She'll be ninety."

"Wow. Your Nana is amazing."

I nodded and handed her my phone. "Add your contact."

She plugged it in, her bottom lip between her teeth, and I tugged it out before taking my phone back. "What do you have planned for today?"

She shrugged. "Work. Take a nap, probably."

I curled my finger around the collar of her shirt, tugging her to me. "I gotta grab my dry cleaning and some groceries, but I'll text you later."

"Don't stand me up."

Her words didn't quite sound like a joke, and I pressed my

forehead to hers, hoping she understood I definitely wasn't joking. "I won't."

After a kiss goodbye, officially ending our whirlwind of a night, I headed toward the subway station, exhausted and exhilarated. As I waited for the train, I flipped my cell phone between my hands, unable to contain my nervous energy. I didn't want to jump the gun on this, but the hopeless romantic in me was ready to leap out and pirouette around a light pole like Gene Kelly.

I had always been a sucker for a happy ending. After a tough few years as a young kid, the world had flipped right side up when Jeff came into my mom's life. He was the husband she deserved and the dad Dani and I had always wanted. Jeff Isaacson was our happy ending.

And god help me, I was ready to turn right back around and go back to Maggie and her perfect mouth and her obviously gentle yet beat-up heart. She put up a good front in the set of her shoulders and her long strides when she walked, like no one in the world could touch her, but I had seen through it. If not in her literal tears at being stood up but in how her eyes drooped with melancholy when I had asked about her family. She'd made some flippant comments, but I knew she'd been hurt in the past, by a lot of people, and the instinct to shield her from any more pain was what had me imagining a future with her.

A future where she would laugh like she did last night, where she didn't feel the need to pretend she was okay. Because she would be, I would make sure of it.

I smothered a smile as I stepped onto the train car and found an open orange plastic seat, thinking of how she'd knelt on the floor in front of me.

I need you to tell me what to do.

I had practically expired on the spot when she'd said those words.

For all Maggie had been through, all of her experiences running around with that Amber chick and her marriage to Brian, there was still something so innocent about her. Fragile.

She bared that wounded part of herself to me last night, and though it had been a mere few hours, I understood it was precious. *She* was precious.

With the image of us curled around each other last night, or really, early this morning, I let my head fall back and my eyes close. The warmth of Maggie's memory was enough to let me drift off to sleep on the ride back to Williamsburg.

The tinny voice announcing "Prospect Park" woke me, and I hopped up, following a gray-haired woman out to the platform, where I jogged up the steps into the sunshine. I was an efficient guy, made a mental, if not written, to-do list every day, so I always stayed on task and on time.

I swung by the dry cleaners then grabbed a few groceries, enough to get me through the next few days. When I had been in the market to buy something in the city, I knew I wanted room, more than Manhattan offered, so I searched in Queens and Brooklyn before settling on the small two-story in Williamsburg. With the help of a contractor, I added on to the little deck in the back, fixed up the yard, and renovated the kitchen. Being three blocks from the park, when I decided to resell or rent, I'd make a pretty good profit.

After putting away the groceries and hanging up my clothes in the closet, I stripped down to my underwear and fell face first into bed for a nap, waking three hours later, ready to get back into the day. First thing I did was reach for my cell phone to check my email, but it wasn't in the usual spot on my dresser. I swiped my pants from the laundry, making sure I didn't leave it in the pockets, my brow furrowing in confusion.

Hightailing it downstairs, I scoured the kitchen. When I didn't find it, I placed my hands on the counter, mentally retracing my steps through the day. A moment later, it dawned on me. "Shit."

I hadn't had my cell phone since the subway ride. I fell asleep holding it but didn't recall having it in my hand as I completed my errands, because I *never* held it in my hand. It was always tucked safely away in my pocket until I got home, where I set it on the charger.

"Shit," I said again, tugging on my hair. I locked my hands behind my head and spun in a tight circle, taking a deep breath to hold my panic at bay. This was a problem but fixable and exactly why I backed up my phone on a monthly basis. For some unforeseen occasion exactly like this.

I kept a ton of information in my phone, basically my entire life, passwords, bank information, and contacts for a number of movers and shakers in Hollywood. I needed to protect all of it and jogged up the steps two at a time to get back to my bedroom, where I opened my laptop. The chances of locating my phone remotely were probably slim to none, but I attempted anyway, and when it didn't pop up on the tracker, I wiped the data and hopped into the shower. I now had one more errand to run.

Hours later, I was back home with my new phone and a headache. I grabbed a beer from the refrigerator and flopped down on the couch in the living room, swiping my thumb over the screen to scroll through the contacts, intent on messaging Maggie. It was almost five and I was already beat, but I promised I would text. She'd probably find humor in the wild ride my day had been, but I couldn't find her name.

And that was when I realized, like a slap to the back of the head, in my haste to solve my lost phone issue, I hadn't backed up my data before wiping it. It normally wouldn't have been an issue, except any new contact was lost.

My new contact being Maggie.

"Oh my god." I threw my head back on the cushion. "You fucking idiot."

I pressed the cold beer to my forehead as if that might jump-start my brain into working order. First losing my phone and now losing her goddamn number? It had to be because I had my head in the clouds over her. Letting out another curse, I opened the internet browser on my phone.

I knew her name, so it wasn't all lost. I'd find her.

I started typing Margaret Levan... I stared into blank space. "Levansky?" I frowned. That wasn't right. "Levan... Levanduski." When nothing populated for that name, I recalled her website with the faded purple, green, and cream background. I closed my eyes, picturing the swirling letters in her logo but couldn't remember her godforsaken name. "Levandecky... Levandecki... Levandecker... Levandower..."

Googling any and every combination of names and phrases I could think of to find her, no Maggie or Margaret Levan... anything who was an illustrator was found. With a grumble, I got up from the couch to pace. I could go see her. I hadn't paid much attention to her address, my eyes glued to the curves filling out her red dress as opposed to the street signs and numbers, but I knew the neighborhood. I could...walk around, see if anything was familiar, maybe yell her name out like Marlon Brando. The thought actually drew a pitiful guffaw from me. Until my phone buzzed in my hand.

It was my mom again.

"Twice in one day," I said by way of greeting, but instead of her usual hello, she sobbed.

And my bad day was about to get a whole lot worse.

CHAPTER FIVE

Maggie

When Wes didn't text or call, I spent the night attempting to come up with excuses. There had to be a reason, maybe a business emergency. He was a busy guy as far as I could tell. Or maybe a stomach bug. Or maybe he had simply fallen asleep. I did end up sleeping most of the day after we'd been up all night. It was perfectly rational.

I couldn't imagine he'd break his promise to text me. Not after we cuddled for hours on the couch talking about everything from our work to the irregular subway schedules. He kissed me with gentleness and passion, like he couldn't get enough of me, yet he wanted to be careful not to break me. And someone who took such care in their kisses wouldn't purposely dismiss me.

But then I didn't hear from him the next day.

Or the day after that.

And that was when I opened a bottle of wine and got drunk while watching *Schitt's Creek* for the hundredth time.

I had convinced myself I had some connection with Wes, a white knight who'd come in to sweep me off my feet. When really, he was a guy with a kink for crying women. He'd gotten what he wanted and left.

Add him to the list of people I couldn't convince of my worth.

On day five post-Wes, I laced up my sneakers and took a walk to Tompkins Square Park, clearing my head in the fresh summer air. I'd sulked long enough and had to get back to the work I had ignored while pretending I wasn't heartbroken.

Which was so stupid. I'd known him for all of twelve hours. It was ridiculous to be so upset over a one-night stand.

Relaxed on a bench, I watched two kids who appeared to be of high school age lay on the grass next to each other, laughing about something on their phones. I tugged my iPad out and sketched the rough outline of teenagers spending a lazy day under the sun, turning them into cartoon images before uploading it to my social media.

While I was at school, I had pictured a life and career much different from the one I had. I had dreamed of being a sought-after artist, spending my days creating "serious" work and my nights at parties with interesting people who smoked clove cigarettes, poured wine into decanters, and spoke multiple languages. But the reality of a struggling artist wasn't so romantic, and I quickly learned if I wanted to make money, I had to take any job I could get, which sometimes meant spending months working on a commission for an awful children's book author who couldn't make up her mind or selling illustrated shirts, magnets, and wallpaper designs. It wasn't the high-brow art found in a gallery I assumed I'd be creating, but my Etsy shop paid the bills and the upkeep of my social media presence provided more eyes on my work.

While on Instagram, I scrolled through posts, idly wondering if I'd be able to find Wes. But if I did, what would I do or say?

Hi, remember me? The girl you fucked into a false sense of security and then pulled the rug out from underneath?

Clearly, he didn't want to find me. It was pointless to even search his name. I'd only be met with heartache on the other end.

After another hour of playing around with different images, refilling my well of inspiration, I put my iPad away, and opened up my notes app with the grocery list. Maybe it was time for a cleanse, a green juice diet to reenergize me before I got back out in the godforsaken dating pool. I added spinach, apples, and turmeric, and with a quick check on my calendar, I also typed in tampons. I was supposed to get my period next week.

Maybe that was why I was so emotional over Wes, early PMS.

Yes, that's what I'd blame it on.

Biology.

CHAPTER SIX

With a bone-weary exhalation, I collapsed on my couch, handing Chris a bottle of water. "You didn't have to come here."

"I did. I had to come see for myself that you're all right."

I extended my legs out to the coffee table and took a big gulp of water. "I'm fine."

He eyed me.

"I am."

"I know how close you were to your grandmother. I'm sure it was really tough."

I dragged my hand over my hair with a sigh. "Yeah. It was really hard on my mom." I had stayed in Florida for two weeks while my mother grieved the loss of *her* mother. "She was hours away from turning ninety. Crazy, right?"

"We should all be so blessed to live so long."

I tossed him a dubious brow. "Bronte say that?"

He grinned. "Of course."

"Thank her for the flowers and the food. I know you weren't the one who specifically got the nut-free cookies for my sister."

"My wife never misses a thing, including allergies of a

woman she hasn't seen in years." Chris gave my shoulder a squeeze. "How's everything else? How's Jeff?"

"He's good. We got in a round of golf while I was down there. Dani, Colin, and the kids came down for the funeral but had to get back to go to some camp. I stayed as long as I could, but…" I trailed off with a shrug.

"You're still going to LA?" He leaned his elbows on his knees, examining me a little too close for comfort, and I rubbed my fingers along my forehead, hoping he didn't see how tired I was.

"Yeah. I gotta keep my ear to the ground, see what meetings I can drudge up."

And since it seemed the universe wanted to kick me while I was down, I had gotten the official pass from Columbia. They'd said *Turning Leaves* was "too quiet" of a concept, and even though Chris had tongues wagging about the short film he directed and premiered at the Toronto Film Festival last September, they didn't trust him to "get a feature over the finish line."

I had left all that out when I delivered the bad news. Because they were wrong.

Now, Chris remained silent though his knee bounced.

"Hey," I said. "I got it covered, okay? We're going to get this movie made, rip, shit or bust."

Chris scratched at his beard. "I could come with you."

The offer was halfhearted at best. While he was great in front of a camera, he didn't do well in business meetings. "It's fine. Until I have something set in stone, don't worry about it. Besides, I'm going to a conference." When he furrowed his brow, I flicked my hand out, explaining, "It's a scriptwriting thing with a pitch event, so I figured I'd see if there were any worth a read."

"You know they have people for things like that. They're called assistants."

"The day I hire someone to do my own job, I want you to punch me in the face." Some people legitimately needed assistants. People with families and jobs that required them to be away from home. But I was single, had no pets, and thrived on my work. I had no reason to have an assistant to keep my calendar and read scripts before I did.

"Could be arranged," Chris said with an elbow to my side. "I always thought your face was too pretty."

I snorted. "Thanks, man."

He tipped his chin to my hand as I methodically flipped my cell phone over end to end. "What's with that?"

"Huh?"

"The fidgeting."

I set my phone down next to my hip, only to pick it back up a moment later, swiping the screen on as if a text message would magically appear. "Remember the woman from the bar?"

"Your kryptonite?"

"I went back to her place that night, and it was..." I licked my lips, trying to come up with the words to describe those hours. "It was special. *She* is special. But I lost her number. I've tried searching for her, but everything with Nana happened and..."

"And you got your own Cinderella?"

"Without a slipper," I told him, and Chris hummed pensively. "I have a vague recollection of where she lives, but I can't remember her last name to save my life."

"You really like this girl?"

I uselessly typed another version of her name into the search bar, like I'd done every day since I left her apartment. Even as I sat at my grandmother's wake, I had snuck away to a corner, wanting —needing—to talk to Maggie. While my mother had Jeff, and my sister had her husband and kids to lean on, I was there by myself.

"I haven't been able to stop thinking about her, even after just a couple hours together."

"Okay." Chris stood up, crossing the few feet to the kitchen, where he dug through my junk drawer for a pen and paper. "Let's make a list of all the stuff you do remember about her. Maybe we can come up with a way to find her."

I barked out a laugh because Bronte had so obviously rubbed off on him. "You're kidding?"

He shook his head, scribbling something down on the paper. "What time's your flight tomorrow?"

"Flying out of JFK at 1:45."

"Well, let's go, Prince Charming. Stop wasting time."

I started to chuckle again, but at my friend's determined face, I scrubbed my hands down my jeans. "Yeah, okay. All right. Let's make a list."

"What do you remember about her?" he asked, ready with his pen.

What did I remember? The divots of her spine, the thick, dark strands of her hair in my fist, the flush of her skin and how she warmed under my palm, the heat of her tongue, and the taste of her lips.

But none of that would help to find her.

CHAPTER SEVEN

Maggie

"Signs of early menopause," I mumbled to myself, clicking on the link. When I missed my period, which was supposed to come at the end of June, I tried not to freak out. My cycle had always been like clockwork, and I hoped it was a simple fluke. But the other night, I had gotten such a hot flash, I'd stood in front of the open freezer door for five minutes, and when that didn't help, I took a cold shower to cool down. And for the last two days, I'd had a headache that just wouldn't go away. Those things by themselves didn't seem abnormal, but combined with my missed period, I dreaded my worst fear was coming true.

My childbearing years were coming to an early end.

With a deep breath, I read the first line of the medical website. "In the United States, the average age of menopause is fifty-one, although the onset for some women may be as early as forty."

I slapped my palm to my forehead, whimpering, "Oh my god."

I scrolled down, skimming the article for symptoms of premature menopause. Words like *hot flash, mood swings, missed period* standing out.

"Dry skin," I read, my fingers dragging along my legs, bare under my sleep shorts. They didn't feel very dry. I used coconut oil every day. "Sleeplessness." That had my head tipping in consideration. I didn't have sleepless nights; in fact, lately I'd been sleeping like the dead. "Decreased sex drive." I let out an agitated sniff. The last person I'd had sex with, I was wild for. But he'd pretty much stolen my sex drive, so I couldn't necessarily attribute that to menopause.

A bit farther down, I read, "If you think you are going through premature menopause, contact your doctor. A physical exam and blood sample will rule out any other possible conditions for the symptoms listed above, such as pregnancy or thyroid disease." I froze, silently rereading that last sentence... *possible conditions such as pregnancy.*

"No way." I opened another tab to search signs of pregnancy.

"Missed period," I read aloud, because, yes, that was what led me here to begin with. "Tender, swollen breasts." I palmed one breast and then the other. They didn't hurt, although they did feel kind of heavy. I had DDDs. They'd always been large, but now that I was thinking about it, my bras did feel unusually tight lately. "Nausea...not really," I muttered, my mind reeling. "Increased urination, no. Fatigue, yes. Spotting or cramping..." I winced at that one, recalling how I felt around the time I should have gotten my period. I had a few weird pains but assumed it was something I'd eaten that didn't sit right. The juice cleanse, maybe. "Bloating..." I stared down at my stomach. I was a solid midsize chick, but my belly appeared no bigger than normal.

I scoured three more sites, all of them listing the same information, and slumped back in my chair. First, I assumed I'd run out of time to get pregnant. Now, I worried I *was* pregnant.

A hysterical laugh bubbled up my throat. "I can never get my timing right."

I closed out my browser and grabbed my purse, hurrying down to the closest pharmacy, a little place in the middle of Chinatown. I purchased a gigantic bottle of water and a pregnancy test, but I didn't even wait until I got home, chugging the water while I stood in line to pay. In front of me, a man spoke in soft Cantonese to the woman behind the counter. They laughed about something, and my anxiety ratcheted up another notch. I didn't have time for their friendly chitchat, and I leaned around him. "Hi, I'm so sorry, but I'm in a bit of a rush. I'm so sorry," I said again, raising a trembling hand with the pregnancy test. "I'd normally never do this, but please... Can I pay and use your bathroom?"

The short, gray-haired woman at the register inspected me up and down, as if deciding what to do with this rude, interrupting white woman. She murmured something to the man then waved me around.

He offered a cheery, "Good luck!" in a thick accent.

Clumsily ripping open the cardboard box, I tossed the shards at the sink and quickly read the directions. It was pretty self-explanatory—pee on the stick, wait three minutes—but I still wanted to make sure I had all the information before I got down to business.

It was after I washed my hands and set the timer on my phone that I realized I was still wearing my glasses, along with two different colored socks and a pair of black leather slides. They were the closest shoes in my closet, and the socks... Well, I wore socks around the apartment tand didn't think to take them off when I ran out. Hell, I still had on my pink sleep shorts and oversized T-shirt with Andy Warhol's Marilyn Monroe printed on it.

My embarrassed laugh morphed into panicked breaths as I

dropped against the tiled wall, my gaze drifting up to the ceiling, taking in the cracks in the vinyl, like threads of a spider web. Like the threads of my sanity.

I closed my eyes, inhaling through my nose and exhaling through my mouth a few times, wondering what was worse: losing the ability to have children or getting pregnant by a man I'd never see again.

The timer went off, and my eyes popped open to the answer.

The stick displayed two little pink lines. I was pregnant.

Pregnant.

Holy shit.

I picked the test up with one hand and held the other over my mouth as tears stung my eyes, vacillating between ecstasy and disbelief.

After divorcing the man who I'd assumed would be the father of my children and having a one-night stand, *now* I was pregnant.

This wasn't my dream scenario, but a baby, that was what I wanted. At thirty-eight years old, I didn't have much time left, and after the divorce, I'd presumed the chances of having my own kids were slim to none. I never expected to find someone else, fall in love, and get married all before my biological time stamp expired.

Except I didn't need love and marriage to have a baby. It wasn't a necessity, simply a hope.

I hadn't grown up with a lot of emotional support and tended to seek it in all the wrong places. Love was an elusive thing, a shadow on a wall, here and then gone again. While a baby certainly wouldn't make me whole or complete as a person, it would give me someone to love and cherish as I wished to be loved and cherished. And after everything with

Brian, I wasn't about to give up my chance to become a mother.

Without another thought, I shoved the test into my purse and unlocked the bathroom door, where the man and woman waited for me. They raised their brows expectantly.

"I'm pregnant," I said, and the two strangers threw their hands up in excitement, congratulating me in both English and Cantonese.

When I took my wallet out to pay, the woman shook her head. "My gift to you. You do not need to pay. Go and take care of the baby, okay? Drink lots of water."

"Take care!" the man said, and I backed out of the store with a chagrined wave.

At home, I lay on the bed, my hands on my stomach, attention turned to the window as the summer sun drifted over the sky until it dipped toward the horizon, sending beams of hazy orange light into the apartment.

I had wanted a baby for so long, I didn't have to decide what I was going to do, only *how* I was going to do it. With the father not in the picture, I was going to be a single mom, and I couldn't imagine a scenario to make it work in the city without any support. Unfortunately.

That left me with one option.

I brought my gaze down to my abdomen, tapping two fingers over my belly button. "You're probably not even the size of a seed, and already, you're causing me problems, huh?" I sniffled through a smile. "It's me and you now, kid. I need you to give me some strength for what I'm about to do."

After a big exhale, I cleared my throat and reached for my cell phone.

My mother answered with her typical rushed "Hello" like she was in the middle of something.

"Hey, Mom."

"I'm doing laundry, Margaret. What do you need?"

I had long ago gotten used to her curt tone, though it still stung. Especially now. "I have to talk to you about something."

She responded with a distracted "Mm-hmm."

"It's, uh...um..."

"What is it, Maggie? I'm busy."

"I'm pregnant," I blurted before I could think better of it. Silence met me on the other end. After a moment, I tried again, "I just took a test and—"

"With Brian?"

"Oh. Uh, no. It's—"

"*Margaret*," she said with an exaggerated sigh, and I could imagine my mother rubbing her hand along her forehead, eyes closed. It was what she always did whenever I had any news. Because, according to her, I never had good news. "Are you serious?"

"Yeah." I picked at my comforter. "I wanted to talk to you about—"

"Whose baby is it?"

"This guy I met a few weeks ago," I said quietly because I knew how she would react. Sandy Levendoski was nothing if not predictable.

"Are you kidding me, Margaret?"

Even if I did have an answer to the hypothetical question, she didn't let me get it out. She kept going like a Mack truck through a crystal department.

"This really, *really* takes the cake. What are you going to do now? Having a baby with a man you met a few weeks ago? This is crazy. What does he have to say about it?"

"He...well..." I wrinkled my nose. "He doesn't know."

"Oh, dear god." Something thumped on her end of the call, and I supposed it might have been her hand pounding on a wall or chair or maybe her chest. I would be the one to give my mother a heart attack. She'd threatened it enough times.

"I wanted to talk to you because I'm keeping this baby and—"

She huffed. "Of course you're keeping the baby. The one thing worse than having it would be aborting it. Good god, Margret. What are you even thinking?"

My mother worked as a secretary for the Catholic school my parents had sent my sister and me to growing up—it was the only way they would have ever been able to afford it—and Mom still sang in the choir every Sunday. Her strident Catholic beliefs were the reason why she was still married to my father. They should have been divorced long ago, long before they ever had children, yet remained unhappily married all these years. She blamed their money problems on him and his drinking problem, while he blamed her for their miserable life. Their home was a spectrum, either silent or screaming.

"I'm thinking that this baby is what I want," I said, trying and failing to keep my voice from wavering. I had always been the black sheep, the problem child, the one who wanted too much, asked for more than my parents could give, and I supposed this was my pièce de résistance, becoming a single, unwed mother.

The ultimate shame for my mom.

"How are you going to pay for this baby?"

"With my money." I could practically hear my mother's sneer on the other end of the line. "But I won't be able to afford to live here anymore. I'll need to move."

"You expect to move back in here? With your father and me?"

Her enthusiasm matched my own, but with so few options, it was either staying with my parents or my sister. Like choosing between my favorite form of medieval torture.

"Not for the long-term," I said. "Just for a few weeks, months at the most. Until I find a place of my own."

"I can't believe this," she went on as if she didn't hear me. "Of all the crazy stuff you've done, this is the worst. So irresponsible. What goes on in that head of yours? You flounce around there in the city, doing whatever you want. See where it got you? You've made your bed, now you've got to sleep in it. You think it was tough growing up in this house? Your father and I each worked, and we still lived on scraps. You're going to be raising this baby on your own. Do you even have insurance?"

I rubbed at my eyes, thinking about the two people at the pharmacy who were happier for me than my own mother. "Yes, I have insurance. I have a good following, people love my stuff, and I'll focus on putting out a lot more designs until the baby comes."

"Yeah, right. Do you know how much diapers cost? Formula? Why do you think stores keep it locked up? You'll need to sell a lot more than some drawings to feed this baby."

The way she said *drawings,* like I was selling heroin on the street corner, never failed to make me feel like shit.

"I'm going to figure it out. I wanted to let you know you'll have another grandchild."

In the silence, I hoped maybe my mother was coming around, until she said, "Your sister had the good sense to go to college to get a real job and marry a good man. Her kids are well taken care of. I pray this finally makes you see the light. You can't live in a fantasy world all the time. This is reality."

"Yeah." I sniffed. "I gotta go. I'll let you know when I have plans set." I hung up before the first hot tear fell down my cheek. I sank down to the floor and curled my arms around my knees, hiding how I cried even in the empty apartment.

CHAPTER EIGHT

Maggie

July lapsed into August in a blur of prenatal vitamins, panic-selling clothes on Poshmark, and lots of phone calls about apartments in my hometown, which wasn't exactly a bustling city, but it still wasn't a great time to be in the housing market, even in Vineland, New Jersey. After I made arrangements with Anton to move out of the sublet, my mother finally caved and agreed to let me stay for a few weeks. Though the definition of a "few weeks" was up for debate. If I couldn't find a suitable apartment, it might be a few months, and the idea of bringing my baby home to my parents' house rendered me nauseous. So, I redoubled my efforts to scrimp and save as much money as possible. Which was why I was heading to the post office for yet another drop-off. This one of Etsy shop items as well as the pair of black slides I'd come to think of as my pregnancy shoes. They were Italian leather, purchased on my honeymoon with Brian. They were barely worn, practically brand-new, and snagged a good resale price.

The August heat was unbearable in the city. It visibly simmered, the sidewalks a sizzling grill, people ping-ponging in sweat-soaked clothes. While pregnancy so far had been relatively easy, I was feeling it on days like this, when I had to carry multiple bags while hotfooting it between hordes of cars and tourists.

Stopped at a corner, I dragged the back of my hand across my upper lip to wipe away beads of moisture there and, in the process, accidentally knocked my elbow into the head of an elderly woman next to me.

"Oh my gosh, I'm so sorry." I reached both hands out, bags swinging, and the woman curled her lip in disgust, letting out a string of what had to be curse words in some Eastern European language. "Are you okay? I didn't mean to hit you."

The wrinkled woman raised her fist and voice, drawing a few curious eyes from bystanders at the crosswalk as she tore into me. She lifted her crooked index finger, her crepe-paper skin going blotchy, and I legitimately worried she would have a stroke. And it would be my fault. All because of a rogue elbow.

"I'm really sorry," I said. "It was an accident."

The woman continued yelling in her native tongue, and I shifted my gaze around, hoping help would arrive. But, of course, it wouldn't. This was the middle of the day in down-town Manhattan; no one batted an eye at a verbal confronta-tion. If only the traffic signal would change, I could make my escape from the crowd.

As the coronary waiting to happen poked me in the shoulder with her dagger of a nail, the light changed, and the human stampede started off across the street. Thank god. I darted around a man and power-walked as fast as my feet would carry me, sparing occasional glances behind to make sure I wasn't being followed. I never spotted the wall of navy cotton headed right for me.

I smacked into it with an audible *oof* as hands circled my shoulders, and I grimaced. Not again. It had to be some record. Knocking into two different people in the span of a few minutes.

"I thought that was you."

I shot my head up, and my jaw dropped. "Wes?"

His eyes lit up as he tugged me into the shadow of an awning, out of the way. "Maggie, Jesus, I can't believe it's you."

"What are you doing here?" I asked at the same time he said, "I've been looking for you."

I stepped away from him. Between the humidity and my adrenaline, I couldn't make sense of anything. "I don't..." I shook my head. "You've been looking for me? But it's been weeks."

He blew out an audible breath and shoved his hand through his hair, his navy polo shirt revealing his biceps and forearms, tanned and freckled like he'd been in the sun recently. "I know, I know. I can't believe you're standing in front of me now." His gaze swept over the length of me, and his tongue darted out, wetting his lips. I hated myself for even noticing his mouth. It was the least important thing I should have been thinking, and yet images from our night bombarded me. How he kissed my throat and breasts with that mouth.

"Where are you headed? Can we talk?"

"Don't you have somewhere to go or something to do?" I swiveled my head back and forth, double-checking I was in Lower Manhattan and not some fifth dimension. "Why are you here?"

"I'm meeting a friend for lunch."

"Chris? Your friend from..." I was afraid to finish the sentence. Articulating any detail from that night would be proving exactly how often I remembered it.

"No." He had his phone out, texting somebody. "Just an old buddy of mine. It's fine. I can reschedule with him. I need to talk to you."

I blinked, at a total loss for what to do. It had been over two months since I'd seen him. What could he possibly have to say to me now?

When I was about to move home to have a baby.

Our baby.

And it was for that reason I agreed. "Yeah, okay. We should talk, but I need to get these to the post office first."

"Can I carry them for you?" He reached for the bags. "Are you feeling all right?"

I laughed. I was overheated, and the father of my child suddenly appeared out of nowhere. No, I was not feeling all right. "I could use some water."

He held my bags in one of his hands, steering me back to the sidewalk, and there was that fissure of electricity again. Even with the slight touch of his palm at the base of my spine.

We walked in relative silence for the two blocks to the post office, where Wes helped me go through the packages to send. He shook the shoe box. "This doesn't sound like illustrations."

"They're not. I've sold some of my clothes and shoes."

"Why?"

The clerk called me forward, saving me from answering, and I quickly got everything paid for and shipped off.

He held the exit door open for me. "So, business has been good?"

I nodded, terrified to speak. All my concentration had to be centered on simply putting one foot in front of the other when he was next to me. I hadn't imagined ever running into him again, let alone *wanting* to be in his presence. I had buried the feeling of rightness along with my hope at the bottom of a bottle of wine before I found out I was pregnant. Now I was focused on being the best mom I could be.

Without him.

"Are you sure you're feeling all right? You're so quiet."

"I'm in shock." I caught his eyes. "I never expected to see you again."

His hand inched over, as if he wanted to hold mine, but he didn't. Instead, his pinkie merely brushed the side of my palm. "I'm so sorry about that, Maggie. You can't know how crazy that day was. I wanted to tell you. God, I even had Chris helping me search for you." He let out a chuckle that sounded amazed, if slightly manic. "I can't believe I ran into you today. Like finding a needle in a haystack."

Then his fingers did find mine, pulling me into a Starbucks. "Is this all right?"

I nodded and followed him to an open table near the bathrooms. Which was good because I'd probably have to pee soon.

"What would you like? One of the specials?"

"Oh no, I can't have any—" I stopped myself. That night, I'd told him how I loved coffee, especially trying all the secret menu items or whatever the seasonal drink was. The sweeter, the better. But since I'd visited the doctor and was told to lay off the caffeine, I hadn't had any. It had changed my morning routine of taking a walk to grab one before getting to work, but it also saved me some money, so...

"I'll have an iced green tea."

"All right. Don't move," he said in a cute warning. "You can't disappear on me again."

As he stood in line, I wiped my hands down my shorts. They were denim overalls, and I'd spent a few minutes this morning in front of the mirror turning side to side to see if they made me appear pregnant or not. I certainly noted changes in my figure and wondered if Wes did too.

I had to figure out what I was going to say. Something along the lines of *I'm having a baby, and you're the father. I've already made plans to move home. You don't need to be involved, unless you want to be.* That seemed reasonable enough.

Until he sat down across from me and asked, "What's your last name?"

My brain waves scattered. "I'm... What?"

"Your last name. I tried Googling you but haven't been able to find your shop or website."

"You've...been Googling me?"

"Yeah." He leaned his forearms on the table. "I wasn't lying when I said I've been looking for you. I even went to your neighborhood, but I couldn't remember which building was yours. I was in a Maggie fog that night," he added with a sheepish tilt of his lips, "and didn't pay much attention. I was two steps away from taping pictures up on poles, *Have you seen this woman?*"

I swiped loose hair away from my face and retied my bun. "I...I'm having an out-of-body experience right now. I assumed..."

He curled his hand around his iced coffee, swirling it a few times. "That morning, I couldn't think about anything but you while I was on the train home. I normally keep my phone in my pocket, but for some reason, I held it that day. Maybe because I was desperate to talk to you again, I don't know." He shrugged, and my heart flip-flopped. I didn't know if I should be excited or terrified at the prospect of him looking for me this whole time. I had already made up my mind about my future, but I couldn't see it clearly anymore.

"I ran a few errands and then pretty much fell dead asleep. When I woke up, I immediately wanted to call you, and that's when I realized I'd lost my phone somewhere on the subway. I was a little panicked, and I deleted my data without backing it up, so I lost your number."

It sounded like the rational explanation I was hoping for. And yet, "It's been over two months."

He wiped at the condensation on the table with his hand,

his laser-like attention dropping away from mine for what felt like the first time since I'd run into him on the street. "It sounds like I'm making this up, I know, but I'm not. It was only, like, an hour after I bought my new phone that my mom called to tell me my grandmother had passed away."

I covered my gasp with my hand, and Wes lifted his head, his eyes wide and a little sad.

"I'm so sorry. I know you said how close you were." I instinctively reached for him, curling my fingers around his. He tightened his grip, and I recalled how he'd combed his fingers through my hair that night as he reminisced about staying at his grandmother's house, watching old films. "Dani and I were latchkey kids," he'd said. "But we stayed with Nana a lot too. I got my love of movies from her."

In front of me now, he explained, "I was in Florida for two weeks."

"How's your mom?"

"She's okay. I think we were all in disbelief because Nana was so lively, you know?"

I nodded because, yes, I did know. Not because I'd ever met Nana but because Wes talked so lovingly about her.

God, that night, we'd talked about so much. I could remember almost every detail about those few hours as if it were last night.

"I wanted to tell you," Wes went on. "I was at the funeral, and my sister was there with my brother-in-law, my mom had my dad, but I was there by myself. I..." He blinked a few times, and when he stared at me again, his eyes were bloodshot. "I swear, Maggie, I wanted to find you. I tried. But then I had to go to LA, and life got in the way, and by the time I got back here, it was already the end of July. I assumed you might've lost interest in me. Or wouldn't care."

I let go of his hand to press my palms to my heated cheeks.

"This is insane, Wes. I thought *you* didn't care about *me*."

He held up his cell phone. "No, really. I searched Etsy, Instagram. I tried to find your website... What is it?"

"MaggieMayL.com," I said and watched as he typed it into his browser.

"Maggie May and the letter L?"

"Yeah."

When the website popped up, he pointed to it. "See? I knew what it looked like. I even remembered the little swirly things, but I couldn't remember the name." He pinned me with a curious stare. "Why May?"

"It's my middle name."

"What's your last name?"

"Levendoski."

"Spell it."

I snorted. "You want me to spell my last name?"

With his thumbs perched above the contact page in his phone, he pinched his brow into a completely serious expression. "I'm not losing you again. I'm putting all your information in here. Maybe even zodiac sign and blood type."

I cleared my throat and spelled my last name then added, "My zodiac is Pisces, and my blood type is O positive."

I grinned as he finished inputting the information with a definitive tap of his thumb before turning his phone over on the table between us. "You know your blood type? How? I have no clue what mine is."

I swiped my palms down my shorts again. I wasn't sure if it was the hormones or being so nervous about delivering this news that had me sweating so badly. "Well, I've had to have my blood drawn lately."

He sat forward in his seat. "Why? Are you okay?"

"Yeah. I'm fine, just..." I swallowed down the watermelon in my throat and ripped off the Band-Aid. "I'm pregnant."

CHAPTER NINE

Wes

"I'm pregnant."

I chuckled, but when Maggie didn't give any indication she was joking, my smile dropped. "What?"

"I'm pregnant."

My heart lurched to a stop as her words sank in. She was pregnant. "With a baby?"

"With a baby," she confirmed, a reluctant curve tugging at her lips. Lips which had haunted me for weeks on end.

Christ.

I blew out a breath, rubbing the pad of my hand into my chest, where pain emanated from underneath my rib cage.

Maggie had wanted a baby for a long time. That was her whole thing. Why she'd been crying the night we'd met. Or, partly the reason. She'd been stood up, already brokenhearted over her divorce, and needed to push her life plans back. But now she finally had what she wanted.

And it wasn't until this moment that I realized *exactly* how much I wanted her. Sure, I had daydreamed about being with her and became borderline obsessed with locating her. And, yeah, I had imagined a future with her in the way a person who is attracted to anyone else does, in the planning dates and dreaming of good sex. But now that the chance of a possible long-term relationship and future with Maggie had been ripped away, I couldn't *not* envision what I was losing.

Waking up next to her every morning.

Movie nights and cuddling with her hair tickling my chin.

Vacations and holidays with her laughing and smiling.

A ring on her third finger and a bunch of little girls who were tiny replicas of her, but maybe with my red hair.

Growing old and gray together.

It was foolish to see it all after literally knowing her all of twelve hours, and yet I didn't mind being a fool. Up until this moment.

I licked my suddenly dry lips. "Wow. This is…" I backed away with a resolute nod and moved to stand. "I'm happy for you. Thanks for hearing me out." I pocketed my phone, allowing myself one last glimpse of her. "Congratulations. I hope whoever the father is…" Her dark eyes teared up, and my heart crumbled. I would have loved to reach for her, but she wasn't mine to comfort and hold, so I curled my fingers into fists at my side and forced my words out. "I hope he's everything you want."

Then I turned.

"It's you." Her hand clasped my wrist. "It's you, Wes."

I froze midstep, stomach bottoming out. I didn't know if my life would flash before my eyes before I died, but it sure as hell flashed in the second my life changed forever.

Relief washed over me, immediately followed by soul-spasming fear. Maggie was having *my* baby.

Glancing over my shoulder, I saw her face beginning to fall, and I spun around, stooping down. "Don't cry."

"I swear I'm not crying to make you feel guilty. I had it all planned out." She wiped at her cheeks. "I never expected to see you again, so if you still want to leave, that's fine. I'm figuring it out on my own."

I curved my hands around her knees, thumbs rubbing the insides of her thighs, her words punching a hole clear through my chest. "Figuring it out on your own?"

She blinked a few times until her eyes cleared. "I'm moving back home to have the baby. I don't expect you to help with—"

"Help?" I nearly shouted, and she wrenched back. Out of the corner of my eye, I spied people turning their attention to the man losing his mind, but I didn't give a shit. "Maggie, no. Don't say that." I took my seat again, trying not to scare her off after my outburst. "I know what it's like to grow up without a father." I didn't have to think twice about it when I said, "I'm not doing that to this baby or to you."

She opened and closed her mouth a few times, at an obvious loss for words, but I wasn't going to change my mind. "Seeing you like this, so shocked anyone would want to be there for you, makes me want to murder people."

That earned me a watery laugh.

"Maggie, you're not doing this alone."

She swiped at her nose with a napkin before meeting my gaze once again. "Okay."

"Okay," I repeated, not bothering to consider what a silly, insignificant word it was to make a verbal promise to have and raise a child together.

Although it was all I could come up with at the moment.

I pounded my iced coffee, hoping the caffeine would afford me some clarity or at least kick-start my brain. "How, uh, how did this happen?" Then I backtracked with a stiff shake of my head. The coffee wasn't helping. "I mean, I *know* how this happened. I understand biology... But how...?"

Maggie lifted her shoulder, somehow remaining patient through my ramblings, and the hole in my chest was shrinking every second I was in her presence. The idea of raising a human was frightening. But doing it alongside Maggie? That was right. Perfectly, heart-achingly right. Exactly the way it was supposed to be.

"I blame the condom," she said. "It wasn't mine. It was with Anton's leftover stuff, and I don't know how old it was or where it came from."

"Ah. Right, well..." I sifted through the millions of questions flying around my head to find the most important ones. "How far along are you?"

"About nine weeks. I went to my OB-GYN to be sure. The due date is March 20th. First day of spring."

I smiled at that. "How are you feeling? Are you doing okay?"

"Relatively, yeah. Mostly really tired."

I pushed her iced tea toward her with a fingertip. "And you can't have your fancy coffees anymore?"

She flashed me a cheeky grin, and it was the first glimpse of the Maggie I knew. She'd been so obviously rattled about what I was going to say in response to our little surprise, but her smile let me know she was all right. We would be all right.

"Since this is a *geriatric* pregnancy, I've been advised to get some tests done to make sure everything is okay, but I was going to wait until I found a new doctor at home."

"Wait." I held up my hand. "You're moving home?"

"That's what I was going to do, yeah. I didn't— You weren't—" She closed her eyes on a wince, and I couldn't stand the idea of her living somewhere else.

The words were out before I could stop them. I didn't want to stop them. "You can't move."

She opened her eyes, her pupils huge. "I don't have anywhere to live as of next week. My parents are letting me stay at their house until—"

"Stay with me." I had a house. She could stay there, live there.

She practically choked on her next breath. "Wes, I couldn't do that. We barely know each other."

I gestured to her middle. "We're having a baby, and I think I know you well enough to say with confidence you don't actually *want* to move in with your parents."

"But—"

"I'm about to make a deal with another studio to back my movie. I'll be in Los Angeles a lot. You can have the whole place to yourself." The explanation was an avalanche, and even as the voice at the back of my head told me to slow down, I couldn't. "I have a house and an extra room."

When I expected an argument against it, she didn't. Instead, she asked, "You'll be in Los Angeles a lot?"

My brain screeched to a halt.

I'd never considered maintaining a film schedule *and* having a baby. I'd never had to, but now I did. An array of problems and possible solutions to my sudden lifestyle change rotated like a carousel in my mind, and I grabbed hold of Maggie's hands, hoping to anchor myself and my floating thoughts before they flew away. "If you think we don't know each other, then let's use this time to learn." I nodded to myself. This could work. It had to. "While I get everything situated in California, you can move in and get comfortable."

"I don't know. It feels like I'm going from one sublet to another. I need something permanent. I need stability." She slipped her hands out of mine to press them to her stomach. "The baby needs stability."

"I'm stable," I told her, trying not to sound too miffed. But what the hell? Everything she and the baby needed, I could provide.

"You're going to be on the other side of the country."

"No, I won't."

"Wes." She huffed. "You just said you had to go LA. For how long?"

I bit the inside of my cheek. She had me there. I'd planned on going out there for the rest of the year, and when I didn't answer, she frowned. She knew.

No one in the industry had to live in Los Angeles, but it did make everything easier. The deals, contracts, meetings, they were all built from connections, which formed *there*. Maggie understood that; we'd discussed how she'd made her connections through art school. It was all about who you knew. "I will make this work."

Her eyes drifted past me, brow crimping, and I lifted my hand to her chin, calling her attention back to me, determined to convince her. "I can't imagine how scared or worried, or-or-or... Fuck, Mags, I don't know what has been going through your mind for the last few weeks. But, please, don't make your decisions because you think you're alone. You're not. I'm here for you, one hundred percent." I was on the edge of my seat yet still not close enough. If I could, I would haul her across the table into my lap except, with how she stared at me like a deer in headlights, I didn't think it would help my argument. "If you want to move home, okay. I'll be there when you need me. I'll make as many trips as I have to from wherever I am, but moving in with your parents is not your only option."

I am an option, I didn't say.

She bent her head, mumbling soft words.

"What?" I slid my chair around the table so it was next to hers and wrapped my hand around her neck. "I didn't quite catch that."

"I don't want to," she said, lifting her gaze, and it hit me like a slap in the face. Like that night at the bar. Maggie wasn't merely my kryptonite; she held my whole world in those sad eyes, grew it deep down in her belly. I would protect her, no matter the cost.

"You don't want to do what, sweetheart?"

"Move home."

I took her in my arms, kissing her hair. "Then don't."

She tucked her face into my neck for a few moments. "You smell exactly like I remember."

I backed away enough to take her cheeks in my hands. "You're better than I remember."

She smiled, even though her teeth sank into her lower lip, and I slid my thumb under her mouth until she released it. Her lips were wet and too tempting not to kiss. That was, until she anchored her hands around my wrists. "My mom is utterly disappointed in me. Again," she told me with a little shrug. "She said I should have more sense at almost forty years old."

"More sense than what?"

"More sense than getting knocked up by a one-night stand, not having a steady place to live, being an unwed, single mom... Take your pick."

I knew close to nothing about her family, except how they constantly made her feel like crap, so I bit my tongue for now and, instead, set the record straight. "You know it was never supposed to be a one-night stand, right? That's not what I wanted."

She nodded silently.

"And you have a steady place to live, with me. If you want it."

She sucked her lip between her teeth again.

"And you can't convince me you're near forty. You don't look a day over thirty-five."

She thumped my shoulder, and I laughed, towing her into me with a hand on the back of her head. I kissed her forehead. "I got you."

CHAPTER TEN

Maggie

Wes was *good*. There was no other word to describe him. He was one of the good ones. As he ushered me up the tree-lined street and the four steps to his front porch, my fear had all but disappeared for the moment. He couldn't solve each of my problems, but he did solve a lot of them.

"I got a new door," he said, jangling his keys. "The old one was solid yellow from the '70s. I know this one looks a little old-fashioned, but I like it."

I loved the stained glass, although it wasn't as if I had any say one way or the other. I was a guest in his house.

"And this awning can come down." He pointed up to the green canopy rolled back against the brick so the small porch was in full sunlight then unlocked the door, allowing me inside first. I stepped into the living room, filled with light from the huge bay window, and spun in a slow circle, taking in the burnt sienna wainscoting and dark wood floors.

I pointed to the marble fireplace. "That's original?"

"Yeah." He squished a decorative green pillow, fluffing it a few times before tossing it back down to the couch, and I detected some nervous energy. Funny, this was his house; he had no reason to be nervous. I was the one invading. "It was built in nineteen twenty...something. My mom helped me decorate."

The room was filled with rich hues of green, orange, and brown, masculine while still keeping the style period of the house, which carried through the dining room with the long chestnut table and matching chairs, and into the kitchen that had been clearly remodeled.

"This is gorgeous." I ran my hand along the art deco backsplash.

"You like it?" he asked with a hitch in his voice.

I tapped my index finger on one of the glass panes of the white cabinets. "I do."

He tugged me out the sliding back door to the little deck, nodding to the postage-stamp yard below with a bistro table and chairs. "I know it's not very big, but it's enough for when I'm staying on this coast. It's—"

"It's more grass than I've ever had living in New York."

"Come on, let me show you upstairs." We strolled back through the kitchen to the staircase off the little alcove between the dining room and living room. The ceiling of the second floor had a skylight at the top of the steps, inviting even more sun into the house, and I poked my head into the room in front of me with a desk and lamp in the corner.

"I never use this room. It's yours if you want it."

"How many rooms are there?"

"Three bedrooms." He opened the door to a guest room, painted light green with a few unobtrusive pieces of art hanging across from the bed. "And the bathroom's right here."

It was small but had another skylight, highlighting the bright-white subway tile and porcelain sink. I pointed down to the other end of the hall. "And that's your room?"

He waved for me to follow him. The walls were cocoa, while the cream comforter matched the quilted headboard. I smiled at the bed. It was huge, maybe special-ordered so his feet wouldn't hang off, and I was instantly back to that night again. To his long legs not fitting on my mattress. I blinked away the memory and focused on the large black-and-white photo of the Brooklyn Bridge, but what really caught my attention were all the closets.

"Four?" I opened one of them. "You have four closets?"

He offered me a hopeful smile. "Nice, right?"

"Yeah."

"So..." He stepped closer to me. "What do you think?"

"There are four closets in here but only one in the guest room."

"I can move my stuff. Is that your sole complaint?"

I nodded. "It's very cozy."

"Cozy enough to move in?"

Before I could nibble on my lip, Wes curled his hand around my jaw, angling his head for a kiss.

"Wait."

He stopped, his lips hovering above mine, his breath smelling like his iced coffee. "What?"

From the moment those two pink lines had appeared in my life, I hadn't had to think twice about what I wanted. Until now. "I don't think we should..."

He backed away, rubbing his palm over his mouth. After a moment of his eyes trailing over my body that did absolutely nothing to quell my second-guessing, he tugged on my wrist, urging me to sit next to him on the bed. Under my hand, the bedspread was soft and warm from the sun filtering through his open curtains.

"I think we should press pause," I said.

"Press pause?"

I stared at the lamp on his bedside table. "If we're going to do this, really do this, don't you think we should focus on how to become parents?" When I finally met his gaze, he merely raised a brow for me to continue, and I placed my hand on my belly. "This is...a lot. You found out about the pregnancy two hours ago. And I'm..." I blew out an exhausted breath. "I can barely keep my eyes open most days. I want to do what's best for the baby. I *need* to do what's best."

"You—"

I shook my head, expecting him to talk some sense into me or my feelings, but we would have to psychoanalyze my need to prove value not only to myself, but also to my family, to Wes, and especially to this baby, later.

"You're going to be away a lot, and that's fine," I said, hoping it sounded like the truth. "You need to do what you have to for work, but what we had before..." My hand fluttered to the past. "It was different, the possibility of what we had was different from what we have now. We can't pick up where we left off. It's not that simple."

"Why not?"

His honest confusion had me laughing incredulously. "Because, Wes. Our lives are going to change. I've had weeks to come to terms with that, but you just found out."

"Yeah." He shrugged. "So?"

"So." I straightened my shoulders because I'd been talking through this in therapy. "I'm going to provide the best life I can for the baby. That means I need to be the best version of myself and not settle. So, I'll move in here for the time being until we can figure out what we're going to do and I find another place to live, but—" I pressed my fingers against his mouth to keep him from arguing "—I am not going to go backward and fall into a relationship with you. I will not settle for something casual, and if you're going to be living part time in California, that's all you'll be able to offer me."

His nostrils flared and eyes narrowed, though I was not backing down on this point.

"Fine," he murmured after a few moments, and I ignored how his lips grazed the soft skin of my fingertips, sending a spark of friction up my arm. And I definitely ignored the feel of his chest when I accidentally brushed up against him when I stood.

Then he gently clasped my bicep with an even gentler smile, his eyes alight with excitement and something that looked a lot like a promise. "I've got a lot of lists to make. Come on."

CHAPTER ELEVEN

Wes

Maggie and I had spent the entire previous day at my place, talking logistics. I had always pictured how romantic it would be when the woman of my dreams told me I was going to be a father. Like some tear-inducing bank commercial, where she'd hand me a box with tiny baby socks in it and a voice-over saying something like, "The most important moments in life should be celebrated. Let us take care of you so you can take care of them."

When I had bumped into Maggie, it was as if a fairy godmother had placed her in the middle of the street. I'd finally found my Cinderella, and then I'd gone from elation to despair in seconds after she told me the news she was pregnant. After getting over the first initial shock and sudden fit of jealousy I'd had when I had assumed Maggie had been with another man, I understood the reality. And it was not at all like a commercial.

However, I knew immediately what I had to do. What I *wanted* to do.

The man who had donated his sperm and then walked out of his family's life without a backward glance was no father to me. But the man who later took me in as his own was. I still remembered the Hanukkah when Jeff had handed Dani and me envelopes filled with adoption papers, making it official.

Jeff Isaacson was everything a father should be, kind and patient, always there to listen and give advice, and he gave the best hugs. Like my dad, I would never allow my child to wonder if they were loved or have to worry about their mother or siblings. I would never leave, never let them go a day without knowing one of my hugs. There would be no doubt.

Maggie, on the other hand, was one giant question mark.

She had stiff-armed me when I had tried to kiss her. She wasn't necessarily wrong on her point of our lives being irrevocably changed, though having to stay away from each other because of it felt like a bit of an overreaction.

Maggie made me happy—at least when we were together. She'd driven me nuts for those two months when I'd lost track of her. And if I could make her happy, then I didn't see any problem with picking up where we'd left off. It seemed logical that happy parents were good parents.

Then again, I wasn't in Maggie's shoes, and I didn't want to force her into anything she wasn't ready for, especially when she was the one growing our kid. Besides, I still needed to figure out how the hell I was going to get *Turning Leaves* into production while not missing out on anything with Maggie and the baby. It was nerve-racking, to say the least.

So, I'd sat Maggie down at the table, handed her a glass of water and some chips, and made my lists, much to her amusement. She forwarded me all of her doctor's appointments, while I searched for information on insurance and savings accounts. We hadn't exchanged bank information or anything, but I knew how hard Maggie worked to keep her head above water when it came to bills, and I was more than happy to make sure our little one was well taken care of. I had also made a note to call my lawyer to write up a will.

"You know this doesn't all have to be done today," she'd said as I fiddled with her phone, naming myself as her emergency contact.

"The first thing you should know about me, besides everything else you already do—" I'd raised my brow at her, because she acted as if we were strangers, when we had spent an entire night spilling our guts to each other, and that *had* to account for something "—is that I love a good list. I like crossing things off. Makes me feel accomplished."

"At least one of us is organized."

I'd shut my computer down when she had yawned and walked her to the subway. Although when she had insisted—became indignant, really—she could make it back to her place safe and sound, with a promise to text me, I had let her go home by herself.

I hadn't slept much during the night and was up at the crack of dawn, sipping on a mug of coffee on the front stoop, which I suddenly supposed needed to be spruced up. I had done work to the house, but now that Maggie was moving in, I wanted it to be perfect.

What would she like? An enclosed front porch? Outdoor furniture? A little welcome mat?

I added it all to a list of possible fixes to make.

At seven o'clock, I fired up my laptop. I assumed my mom might not be awake yet, but Dad had always been an early riser. A few moments later, he appeared on the screen, though not quite steady.

"Hold on a sec," he said before I heard the familiar click of their sliding door moving into place on their deck. Then he was there, futzing with the newspaper. "Hey, kid."

The first time my mom had introduced Jeff to Dani and me, he'd sunk down to my ten-year-old eye level, lifted my chin, and said, "Hey, kid. What's up?"

With his wavy dark hair, suit jacket, and shiny shoes, I had thought he was like someone out of the movies, handsome and charismatic.

Now his hair was more gray than black, but his smile was exactly the same, if not a little worn.

"Hey, Dad. How's the weather?"

"You called me at seven in the morning to ask me about the weather?" He tilted his head to the side, a far too knowing smile crossing his features as he leaned back into the white wicker chair. "But it's good. Might try to hit the links before it gets too hot."

My parents had retired to Tampa and bought a place right behind the seventh fairway of a golf course. On-screen, Dad steepled his fingers. "Okay, so tell me what's going on."

I shifted. Then shifted again.

I never had a problem talking to either of my parents, even when Fitz, my best friend from my teenage years, and I were constantly finding trouble. But all of a sudden, my words caught in my throat. This wasn't an *I scraped the paint on the new car* or *I got caught skipping school* conversation.

This was important. Life-changing.

I scratched at the back of my head. "Remember when I told you about the girl I couldn't find?"

He slipped off his reading glasses, tucking his newspapers away. "Yeah."

"Well, I found her."

He sat up. "You're kidding."

I shook my head. "I ran into her yesterday, believe it or not. In a city of eight million people."

"That's wild. So, what happened? Did you get to explain everything about why you couldn't contact her?"

"Uh-huh." I cleared my throat. "I did."

"What did she say?" When I didn't answer, he sighed. "This suspense is killing me, kid. Is it bad?"

"No, not bad, just... It's, um... Well, I'm going to have a baby."

His face dropped as he went silent, and I propped my elbows on my knees. I didn't need my parents' approval, because I had it, no matter what. They had always supported me, but it was still stressful, waiting for his response.

"When she didn't hear from me, she figured— Hey, where're you going?"

He held up his index finger and walked offscreen. I drummed my fingers on my coffee cup, afraid of what was about to go down. A minute later, Mom appeared, her blond bob in disarray. She was still tugging on her robe. "What is going on? I'm being dragged out of bed. Wes?" She peered at the screen, blinking fully awake. "Are you okay? Your father ran in and shook me awake like the house was on fire."

"I was telling—"

"He found her," my dad announced. "The girl whose number he lost."

Mom's face lit up, and she clapped once, clearly not tired anymore. "Oh, I'm so glad." Her blue eyes widened in interest. "What happened? What did she say? Do you still love her?"

I whined with all the dignity of a thirty-seven-year-old man. "Mom."

"What? It sounded like you did from the way you talked about her."

I blew out a breath, but my mom went right on.

"When you know, you know. Like me with your father." She smiled over at my dad, who nodded in agreement. "When I met him, it was this feeling I had." She turned back to me on the screen. "I knew he was something special, what we had was really good, you know? And I'm sorry, but the way your face changed when you told us about this girl? I've never seen you like that. So, excuse me for jumping to conclusions, but I thi—"

"She's pregnant. With my baby. We're having a baby together."

Her jaw went slack as Dad beamed next to her.

"I told you it was good," he said. "Had to get you up."

"You're...having a baby?"

At my nod, she broke down in tears

"Mom, I'm—"

"Wesley, honey, I'm so ha-happy," she got out between blubbering breaths. "You're having a baby!"

"Congratulations," Dad said, dropping his arm around Mom. "I can't wait to meet this new grandbaby."

When my mother finally pulled it together, she folded her hands. "This is such wonderful news after your grandmother passing. Life always goes on." She sniffled. "So amazing. You're bringing us such joy."

I rubbed at the tightening in my chest. Nana would have loved to meet another one of her great-grandchildren. Thinking of her had my eyes stinging, but I blinked away the evidence of my emotions before Mom could see. It would set her off again.

As it was, she flapped her hands at the screen before darting away for a moment, returning with a box of tissues. "When's the due date?"

"March 20th."

"And you found out yesterday?"

I relaxed in my chair. "Yeah. I was stunned but also..." I set my mug down. "I'm really happy."

"What are you going to do now?" Dad asked.

"We talked all day yesterday, and she's moving in with me. When she found out she was pregnant, she assumed I had ghosted her, so she made plans to move in with her parents in New Jersey. But since she doesn't get along really well with them, I told her to move in with me."

My parents both nodded like that made absolute sense.

"She also said she wasn't going to settle for a casual relationship with me."

"What's that supposed to mean?" my mom asked, all defensive.

"I was planning on going back to LA for a while and... We're about to sign contracts for this movie, and I can't not be there."

"Well..." Mom started, tipping her head back and forth, unable to be offended on my behalf anymore. My parents were supportive but fair.

"I didn't think about it when I told her to move in with me. I saw her and freaked out, and then she told me she was pregnant, and it was like I lost all intelligent thought. All I knew was I couldn't let her move away. I couldn't let her go."

Mom pressed her hand to her collarbone like it was the sweetest thing she'd ever heard, completely ignoring my problem.

"And now that we're going to do this, I don't know how. I can't be in two places at once." I rubbed at my forehead. "It's really bad timing."

"Sounds like it," Dad agreed.

When he had no words of advice, I lifted my hands. "That's it?"

"Yeah." He grinned. "Sounds like you have a lot to map out."

I dropped my chin toward my chest. "Not helpful."

"I can't tell you what you need to do because I don't know, but I do know how overwhelming it is. My whole life changed when I started dating your mom, and she introduced me to two fully formed humans who needed homework help, school lunch money, and love. One day you're a guy going about his business, and the next you're a dad. It's not easy."

I picked my head back up and frowned at my dad. He shrugged. "But you have to do it. If you want to have a family, if you want to make it work with her, you have to. You be there for her, support her, show her she can trust you."

When Mom dabbed at her eyes with a tissue, he kissed the top of her head before staring at the screen. "Life doesn't always go in the order you want it to. You can only adjust and do the best you can."

"I love you so much, honey," Mom added. "You're going to be a great dad."

I tipped my chin to my laptop. "I had a great example."

He winked. "Love you, kid."

"Call us later. Let us know how everything is going." Mom smiled and waved. "We'd love to meet her soon."

"I will. Love you, guys. Talk later." With that, I closed my laptop and grabbed my cell phone, typing out a text to Maggie.

> I told my parents. They're really excited. When you're feeling up to it, I'd love to find a time that we could both call them.

I didn't expect her to answer because she had been so tired yesterday and I hoped she was sleeping in, but I wrote one more text before pocketing my phone.

> I'm going upstairs to clean out my closets for you. I'm going to the grocery store later. Let me know if you want anything special.

Surprisingly, she replied.

MAGGIE

Pretzels and Nutella.

MAGGIE

I'm craving salty things.

I was in the middle of typing up a message about how I had something salty for her to suck on, when she texted again.

MAGGIE

And I don't want to hear any jokes about your
nuts.

Give me some more credit than that.

It was going to be about my dick.

MAGGIE

Maybe I should move in with my parents.

Then who would make you laugh with terrible
innuendos?

MAGGIE

I am not laughing.

Don't lie to me.

MAGGIE

How do you know I'm lying?

Because we know each other. As much as
you'd like to deny it.

I'll take your silence as agreement.

MAGGIE

I'm buying a bus ticket to Jersey.

Nope.

Let me know if you need help packing. I have
the spot for your toothbrush all prepared.

CHAPTER TWELVE

After a week of shuffling and arranging boxes to move, I was finally settled in Wes's house. Or, more accurately, I had my stuff in Wes's house. I was completely unsettled.

I'd been living on my own since the divorce and had gotten used to my tiny studio sublet, but now I was in this two-story Williamsburg house with an attic. An attic!

Obviously, I'd been accustomed to Manhattan far too long because the concept of storing things in an attic and having a yard and a parking space was mind-boggling. If I'd moved in with my parents, I would have had all that too. However, their house would have been missing a man in black mesh shorts, wiping sweat off his forehead with the bottom of his T-shirt.

Wes had me parked in the kitchen while he zipped back and forth between the house and car, moving all of the bags and boxes inside. When I attempted to bring them upstairs, he shook his head and sat me at the table with water and chips. "You don't have to do everything yourself. My arms work too."

He hefted another two boxes up for yet another trip to my room. "You're not supposed to be doing heavy lifting."

"That's not true." I flicked my hand to the pile of books he had purchased and stacked on the counter, all of them about pregnancy and babies. "I'm sure these books say I should be staying active and—"

"And continuing the same workout regimen you were doing before you were pregnant, yes, I know. So, unless you were making multiple trips up flights of stairs with heavy boxes, you can't carry this."

I rolled my eyes when he handed me a caddy with my toiletries, but I followed after him anyway. I realized, seconds too late, what a poor decision I'd made as my eyes drifted down to Wes's ass, directly in front of me.

Thank god he was leaving tomorrow for a short trip to Los Angeles. It would give me time to get used to living in this house—and maybe stop fantasizing about him.

Him and his hands that had caressed my neck and memorized every one of my curves.

And his deep voice and sweetly murmured praise.

And how he would be sleeping mere feet from me.

"Ugh!"

Wes glanced over his shoulder. "What happened?"

"Nothing." I reared back, not having meant to verbalize my frustration, but now that I had, I dove for the first excuse I could think of. "I'm really hot."

"You are?" He hurried up the last three steps, set the box in my room then turned on the window unit. "Old house, no central air. Sorry." He pivoted around, his hands on his hips. "It should cool down pretty quick, but if you're still hot, I can get a fan."

"Oh no, that's okay."

His gaze tracked down my body. I wore spandex shorts and a loose T-shirt, but for how he took his time admiring me, I might as well have been naked. And it was a real problem.

Since all I could think about were our text messages from the other day and his joke about his salty nuts and dick. Because, yes, I was highly interested in relearning his flavor, but it wouldn't do anything to help our situation. We had to be pragmatic about this and keep our attraction in check. I wasn't going to end up with another failed relationship, especially now that another person was involved. I couldn't fail my baby because I couldn't keep my pants on.

When Wes finally brought his attention back up to my face, he said, "There's one last box. Your shoes, I think."

"You could bring that right to your room."

"You really want me to?" he asked with earnest eyes.

"No, I'm kidding."

"Well, whatever you need room for, I have." He pointed in the direction of his bedroom. "I cleared out the one right by the door when you walk in."

I sank down to the floor, grabbing scissors to open the box next to me. He watched me for a minute, maybe to make sure I wasn't overextending my delicate constitution. It was both adorable and infuriating how worried he was about me. Then he quietly padded back downstairs and returned with the last box, which was, indeed, full of my shoes.

"All right. You good?" he asked, bending to meet my eyes.

"Yes. Thank you."

"You don't need to thank me."

I set my few art books and supplies on the bed and broke down the cardboard before he took it from my hands, sinking down to his haunches, his stare drilling into me.

"This isn't some favor, Maggie. I'm not doing this out of the kindness of my heart." He briefly closed his eyes, and when he opened them again, they were blazing with a mixture of emotions I couldn't quite interpret. Maybe exasperation or anxiety or...lust. "If I didn't lose those weeks with you, if you weren't pregnant, I'd still be here, doing this. Do you understand?"

I opened my mouth to speak, but the words crumbled to ash on my tongue and I swallowed them down as the threads of my heart unraveled beneath my chest.

"I would still have wanted you here...with me." He lifted his gaze to the wall behind me, saying, "I spent my life knowing what I wanted, but lately I've felt like I was floating around. I couldn't quite put my finger on it. I was happy. I love what I do. But..."

I slanted toward him, waiting with bated breath for him to continue.

"There was something special about that night."

He didn't have to elaborate. I felt it too. Those few hours at the bar and then even more at my apartment. They were special. Incredible.

"So, don't thank me, okay?" He swiped his hand through his hair, mumbling something I didn't catch then stood up to leave my room. "Let me know if you need anything. I'm going to clean up the kitchen and take a shower."

Still a bit dazed from his confession, I stared at the blank space where he'd been moments ago.

I would still have wanted you here.

There was something special about that night.

I collapsed back against the bed. In the weeks after our night together, I had convinced myself that it didn't mean anything, that I had imagined how good it had been between us or blown it out of proportion. But now I knew, for certain, he had never wanted it to be a one-time thing, and he had thought about me for all those weeks.

Like I had thought about him.

And yet...

I placed my hands on my stomach. This little peanut had changed everything.

No matter how charming and considerate Wes was, no matter how many times he reminded me he was one of the good ones, I couldn't give in to him. I couldn't jump back into bed with the sweet-tongued man down the hall, particularly because I wasn't even sure when he would *be* in his bed.

I peeled off my clothes and stepped into the tub, the cool spray of the shower on my chest exactly what I needed to unwind my muscles. Scrubbing my hands over my hair, I pivoted so the water hit my back, and my shoulders curled over with fatigue. I could have paid the movers to bring Maggie's stuff from Manhattan to Brooklyn, but it wouldn't have been worth the money when I was able to fit all of the boxes in my car. Even though I couldn't see out of my review mirror and I was so close to the steering wheel my ribs were practically indented, we'd made it in one trip.

I was surprised she had so little. Then again, she didn't have any furniture of her own and had sold some of her belongings for money. That was her grand plan, to sell most of her stuff to pay for the baby, and it still would have been virtually impossible to go it alone with almost no savings to her name.

The other day, she had informed me she didn't receive any alimony, and I was appalled. Maggie was brilliant, but not when it came to finances or fine-print details. Good thing I was.

"That's what I get for never reading through contracts,"

she'd said with an embarrassed wince.

"Mags," I'd grumbled. "We gotta work on that, sweetheart."

Then she had tipped her head to the side, a small smile flickering at the corner of her lips.

"What?"

"I like when you call me that," she'd said quietly.

"What? Sweetheart?"

"Yeah, that too." She'd laughed. "Mags. No one else calls me that. It feels…" Her words had trailed off, and my chest swelled with something I couldn't quite name: pride or possessiveness.

I liked being the only one to call her Mags. Like she was *mine*.

And now she was living in my house. She was going to be walking around in her two-sizes-too-big T-shirts with her cherry-red glasses and kissable lips, not realizing how fucking gorgeous she was. Especially with the tiny bump growing in her midsection that I put there.

Some primal impulse had me smiling in self-satisfaction as I grabbed shower gel to soap up. I hadn't been lying when I said I'd felt like I'd been floating through life. I was a fastidious guy, organized and driven, and I considered my romantic relationships the same way. I didn't want to waste my time and energy on something I didn't see going anywhere. I'd had a couple of short relationships here and there, but when I knew what I wanted, I *knew*.

And I had wanted Maggie since the moment she gazed up at me at the bar.

As I envisioned her in that burgundy dress, my blood warmed, even under the cool water. I brought familiar memories to the forefront of my mind—the same ones I had fantasized about almost daily since that night—of Maggie on her knees, her mouth on my cock, and before I was even conscious of it, my hand was there, stroking up and down as I closed my eyes, recalling her quiet words. "I need you to tell me what to do."

I propped an arm against the wall, remembering how it felt to wrap myself around her and sink into her soft, wet heat. I loved her fevered sounds when she climaxed and the way she drunkenly giggled afterward, when I'd all but pinned her to the bed in a heap of exhaustion. Picturing my hands around her, my fingers pressing into her hips and ass, my tongue on her breasts, I came with a grunt and stepped back under the shower, washing away the evidence of my orgasm along with the notion of having her any time soon.

This was my new normal. Cold showers with the memories of our one night together.

But it would have to do.

After shutting off the water, I patted dry then wrapped the towel around my waist and grabbed my clothes from the floor. I stepped out of the bathroom at the same time Maggie was striding down the hall, and we nearly collided.

"Whoa, sorry, sorry," she said as I steadied her with a hand on her elbow.

"You all right?"

"Yeah, sorry. I wasn't watching where I was..." She stopped, her gaze drifting from my face down to my chest and abdomen before blinking away, shaking her head slightly. "I was going to hang this up in your closet."

I ignored how she refused to meet my eyes and instead focused on the well-known dress in her hand. "You kept it? I thought you got rid of most of your dresses."

"I did." She caressed what I knew to be soft material between her fingers. "I have no place to go, no fancy parties. I don't need so many cocktail dresses, but I like this one, so..."

"I like it too. Red's your color."

She fixed her glasses more firmly on her nose, her cheeks blushing, and motioned to my room. "Well, uh, can I?"

"Oh, yeah. Sorry." I gestured for her to walk ahead of me to my bedroom, where she opened the closet, hung up the dress then set a box of shoes on the floor. "I think I— Oh my god!"

I tugged my underwear up, letting the elastic snap against my waist before I turned around. "What?"

"You can't... You were..." She threw her arm out toward me. "I just saw your butt." At my chuckle, she flapped her hands around her head. "I think we need to have some ground rules or something."

"Ground rules." I began to close the gap between us, but she held up her palm. "You stay right there. And put on a T-shirt and pants, for god's sake."

"You've seen me naked already. Nothing new."

"Yeah." She bunched her hands on her hips, pointedly glaring at the floor. "I know, and that's why we need to set some ground rules."

"Am I making you nervous?"

"I can hear you getting closer. Please, Wes," she whined sweetly. "I'm being serious."

I gave in and threw on a shirt and shorts. "Okay. I'm dressed."

She waited a few seconds before lifting her head. "Thank you."

"Now," I said, already hating the words about to come out of my mouth. "Your rules?"

She held up one finger. "No walking around in towels."

I crossed my arms, working on keeping my smile at bay. She was adorable when she was flustered. "Afraid to raise your blood pressure?"

She rolled her eyes and listed off another rule with a

second finger. "No acting like I'm a Victorian lady about to faint. I'm healthy and pregnant, not sick and dying."

"You think I'm being overprotective?"

"You're constantly hovering."

I huffed. "We've barely been around each other."

"Yeah, and every time we are, you look at me as if I might break at any moment. No more waiting on me. If I want something, I'll get it."

I nodded in acquiescence.

"And," she started, her eyes darting over my shoulder for a moment before moving back to my face but not quite meeting my eyes. "If you're going to go out...with someone, can you not bring them back here? I know this is your house, and that's asking a lot, but..." She fiddled with the bottom of her shirt, and I heaved out a sigh, irritated she would even assume I'd ever go out with another woman. "Or, if you want to have someone over, let me know, and I'll make other plans, okay? I don't want you to think I'm—"

"Maggie."

She stopped her rambling. "Hm?"

"I will not be going out with another woman, let alone bringing one here."

She chewed on her bottom lip. "Why not?"

"Why not?" I dropped my arms. "Why not?" I closed the distance between us, not caring about her protests. "You honestly think I am going to bring another woman to the house where the mother of my child is living?"

"I—"

I silenced her with a hand curled around her neck. "You didn't want to pick up where we left off and—" I forced the next part out "—I'm fine with that, but don't think that means I'm going anywhere in the meantime. I am here for you and only you. I want there to be no misunderstanding between us. Is there?"

She silently shook her head, and I gently squeezed her neck.

"Words, Maggie. I need to hear them."

Her throat worked on a swallow, and it was a struggle not to kiss her there. "No. There is no misunderstanding."

"I will follow your rules. I'll wear flannel from head to toe all day long, I won't bug you or hover or ask if you're feeling okay every hour, but I have one rule of my own. When you do need something, whether it's a food you're craving or an errand you need run or something else," I said, letting my other hand drift over her side meaningfully, "you have to tell me. This time, I need you to tell me what to do. Okay?"

"Okay." Her voice cracked, and she tried again. "Yes, okay."

With one last squeeze of her neck, I let her go and stepped back. "I'm hungry for pizza. Want any?"

"Sure. I need to finish unpacking, though."

I grabbed my laptop. "All right. I'll be downstairs. What do you like on your pizza?"

"Pepperoni."

I followed her out to the hall and trotted downstairs when she ducked back into her room. "I'll order in a bit. Let you know when it's on its way."

"Thanks," I heard her call out, and I flopped on the couch in the living room, confident she did understand what I meant —that the ball was in her court when it came to our relationship—but also a little weary of how concerned she seemed to be about living in such close quarters with me.

Her panic was plain on her face when I got close to her. She hadn't been that way during our night together. In fact, she had been the opposite, open and laughing and wanting more. Now, though, she was clammed up and apprehensive. I just hoped I would be able to prove we could have it all—the baby and our relationship—while still keeping my career on track.

But I couldn't do anything about it right this second, so I streamed *Top Gun*—one of the top ten greatest movies ever made, I would brook no argument—as I read a couple new *Variety* articles. An hour later, when the pizza arrived, I called up to Maggie, who had showered and changed as well. Her hair was wet, and her shirt was fitted enough to show the practically nonexistent bulge of her stomach. No one else would have noticed she was even pregnant.

"Mmm, smells so good." She slid two slices onto her plate before helping herself to iced green tea. "So, you need a ride to the airport tomorrow?"

I shook my head. "I'll take the train."

Once we were both seated at the table, she said, "Seems like a waste to go there for only a couple days."

"Nah, it's fine. Quick meeting about finances."

"Explain to me again why you need another film studio. If you have your own production house, why do you need other people?"

Satisfaction swelled in my chest that she had remembered, a little bit anyway, what I had explained to her about it. "Booksmart is making the movie, we have the script, we'll get the crew, Chris will choose the actors, all that, but like you need Etsy to sell your merchandise, so do we. Even if we'd be able to cover the production costs ourselves, which we can't, we would still need a distributor." I paused to shove a piece of crust into my mouth. "Let's say we go it alone, completely indie, we strip the budget down and get it done, we'd still need to shop it around to festivals, get some momentum going for either a streaming service to want it or sell the rights to another studio for a theatrical release."

She nodded as she chewed and swallowed. "Okay. What's your budget now?"

"Forty million."

"Oh? A forty million. That's it?"

I laughed at her haughty tone. "Yeah. We have name recognition in Chris, but—"

She snorted. "I still can't believe you work with CJ Cunningham and, like, are best friends, and you call him Chris."

"You'll meet him, don't worry."

Her brows shot up. "Ooh la la."

"He's not that cool in real life."

I ignored her frown of mock disappointment. "We need the backing of a bigger studio to cover costs and help guarantee a theatrical release."

"Got it." We ate quietly for a minute before she had another question. "What's your work schedule like?"

I stuffed a piece of pepperoni in my mouth. "Depends. Some weeks are crazy, some weeks I have to travel, but other times, I'm working on my computer."

"In LA?"

I dropped my focus to the table, where I scratched at a tiny dent, aware of what she was really asking. *How can you be there when I'm here?*

"I know you live there the majority of the time. You told me."

I grumbled in frustration but mostly astonishment. "You remember everything I said to you that night, huh?"

She arched her eyebrow over the rim of her cup. Calling me out as if I didn't remember everything she had said too.

"I don't know if I live anywhere," I said after a while. "I spend a lot of time in California, but I also have this house and the rental in Pennsylvania, and that one in Utah."

"Utah? You have a place in Utah?"

"Yeah. It's a little condo I bought a while ago. I go to Sundance every year, so I figured why not? I rent it out the rest of the year to filmmakers in the institute. Plus, Chris is obsessed with Robert Redford. He used to go down there to try to stake him out. You shoulda seen the day he met Redford. I thought he was going to shit himself."

Maggie sat back in her seat as she tossed her second piece of pizza on her plate, half eaten. I was about to open my mouth to ask what was wrong but stopped myself. That was against the rules.

She rubbed at her sides. "I'm full already."

"Are you sure?"

"Yeah. Sometimes it feels like there's no room, which is weird, right?"

I shrugged. The hell if I knew what it felt like to grow a human.

"It's still so little, but it already feels like there is nowhere for it to go. Nowhere for my food to go."

When she grimaced, still rubbing at her sides, I pointed. Technically, I wasn't asking.

"My ribs feel like they're being stretched. Doesn't feel great. Makes me lose my appetite."

"I'll put the rest in the fridge if you want any later."

She stood with her drink in hand. "Thanks. I'm going to go upstairs and take off my bra." And then she froze, as if recognizing what she'd said. "I mean... I'm..." She exhaled through pursed lips and rolled her shoulders back before staring at me head on. "I am. I'm going to go upstairs and take off my bra. It hurts my ribs too much."

"Hey." I grinned. "Don't wear one on my account."

She eyed me. "Rule number four, don't flirt."

Maggie

The next morning, I stood on the front porch next to Wes, my eyes shifting all over the place like being at a middle school dance, unsure what I was supposed to do or say.

He hitched his carry-on bag higher on his shoulder. "If you need anything, call me."

"I will, but I won't need anything. It's two days."

He stuck his hands in his pockets. "Still. Call me."

I spluttered a laugh. "To let you know how my day goes?"

"Yeah. Why not?"

"It won't be very exciting. I'm going to work all day today and go to yoga tomorrow."

He tipped his head to the side in that irritatingly studious way, while his gaze drifted over my face, pausing briefly on my mouth before meeting my eyes. "I want to hear about it."

"Do you?"

"Mm-hmm." He stepped close enough that I could smell the mint of his toothpaste on his breath.

"Okay, well..." I cleared my throat. "Have a good flight." Then, like a complete goober, I held up my hand for a high five.

He stared at it like he'd never witnessed such a gesture before. His eyes, so very light in the morning as if they were still waking up too, toggled between my own for a moment before he very slowly raised his palm to smack mine with a soft chuckle. "All right, Mags, you win this one. I'll talk to you later."

And with a wave, he was off.

I waited until he was almost at the end of the block, heading toward the subway, to go back inside and explore my new abode. I spent some time finding appropriate spots for my art supplies and organizing my toiletries in the bathroom before showering.

Wes had told me to make myself at home, but it was weird to be there alone, without him. This was his house, and I was basically his roommate for the time being, so I was hesitant to touch anything. He had every streaming service known to man, and yet the remote control for the television was something out of a sci-fi movie. There was nothing for me to clean since the place was already immaculate, thanks to the biweekly cleaning service Wes had come in. And while we hadn't discussed rent or bills, I made a mental note to talk to him about that. I had to do *something* to make myself feel like I wasn't mooching off him.

After a few hours of work, I ate the leftover pizza and put on an anti-aging face mask, all while keeping my cell phone within an arm's length. Wes had told me to call him, had said he wanted to hear about my day, but he couldn't have meant it literally.

Or did he?

Knowing him, yes.

So, I found his contact and dialed his number.

"Hey, Maggie," he said after three rings. "I'm glad you called."

"You told me to."

"I know, but I didn't think you would."

Maybe this was some kind of test, getting me to admit how I *did* want to call him. From the night we'd met, I found it so easy to talk to him, about anything and everything. But now, we were having a baby together, and I struggled to tell him the truth. That I feared failing in yet another relationship.

Before, I wouldn't have minded dating Wes. I wouldn't have cared if he had to travel a lot. I wasn't a jealous person and had never been uncomfortable being alone; I could handle long-distance.

But not pregnant.

If we were going to have a relationship, it needed to be one hundred percent committed and together. And I couldn't see that happening right now.

"How did the meeting go?" I asked.

"I have good news and bad news. Good news, it went great. Bad news, I'm going to have to stay here for another day or two."

"Oh." I nodded to myself. "Okay." When I agreed to move in here, I understood what I was getting myself into. He had things to do, a career which mostly required him to be in another state. This wasn't a surprise, yet disappointment hit me like a sudden snowstorm, making me cold and crabby. "I'm happy it's all working out for you," I said, because it was true. Mostly.

It was also proof of why I'd made the right decision in telling Wes we wouldn't pick up where we'd left off.

"I'm sorry," he said.

"No, no, don't be. It's fine. I knew this was your job. It's—"

"But I want to be there for you."

I got up to walk the length of my room. "Maybe... I don't know..."

"What?"

I pivoted in front of the wall and made my way back across the room to the door. "Maybe we rushed into this."

"Rushed into this," he said deliberately, as if trying to translate the words.

"I know you want to be a part of the baby's life, and I'm so happy about that, but I had a plan of my own. I don't—"

"No," he bit out. "Don't say it. Yes, we rushed into this, we're having a baby after one night together, but I told you, I want this."

I wanted to believe him, and yet three thousand miles was too far of a gap to bridge. "I don't understand how it can work."

Three seconds passed—I knew because I took three steps out into the hall, staring at his open bedroom door—before he spoke again. "To be honest, Mags, I'm not sure either, but I'm figuring it out. You and the baby and the movie, I didn't expect it to happen all at once, but I promise you, we will make it work."

By the time he finished speaking, I stood at his doorframe. After flicking the light on, I swept my gaze around the room, his bed made, nothing out of place. Like he was never even here to begin with.

"Okay," I said after a while, and he seemed satisfied with my answer because he changed the subject.

"How was your day?"

"Fine." I leaned my forehead against the doorjamb. "I didn't do much, but I'm so tired."

He clucked his tongue. "Baby's kicking your ass, huh?"

I yawned. "Mm-hmm."

Long seconds passed, an echo of the awkward high five this morning. But this time, it was Wes who mumbled a disjointed, "Well, I'll let you go, then."

At least I wasn't the only one who wasn't sure what to do in this in-between space.

"Call me tomorrow," he told me, and I picked my head up and shut off his bedroom light.

"I will."

CHAPTER FIFTEEN

"Honey, I'm home," I called, closing the front door. After four days away, I was anxious to get home and see Maggie again.

She stood from where she had been perched at the dining room table, a plate of grapes, her iPad, a magazine, a water bottle, and a few notebooks and markers scattered around her. "Hey. How was your flight?"

I kicked off my shoes, tossed my bag to the floor, and strode toward her, though when she was within reach, I hesitated. This was the part when I was supposed to take her in my arms, bend her back, and kiss the shit out of her. Throw her over my shoulder and take her upstairs to bed. But none of that was allowed.

"It was good." I held up a bag of groceries. "I got stuff to make dinner."

She shifted her gaze between the bag and the industrial wall clock in the living room. "Oh yeah. I'm starving."

"You're one of those people who gets so into their work they forget to eat, aren't you?"

Her forced laugh was answer enough, and I rubbed at my tired eyes, mumbling a frustrated, "Maggie..."

She offered me a wide, fake grin and pointedly snatched the plate of grapes, which had undoubtedly sat untouched next to her on the table. She shoved three into her mouth.

I sighed and nudged her to the kitchen. "I got the ingredients for lemon mushroom chicken."

As I got everything out, she leaned her elbows on the counter. "Are you sure you're up for cooking? You look drained."

"Jet lag."

"We could order takeout."

"No, you need something good to eat." I pulled a cutting board and knife from the drawer. "I'm sorry I wasn't here for your first couple of days to help you settle in."

"It's fine. I'm used to being on my own."

"I know, but it's still not what I want...for either of us." I opened up the package of chicken breasts and cut them into strips.

"I wanted to talk to you about..." She flicked her index finger between the chicken and herself.

"About dinner?"

"No." She laughed. "About how we're going to do this. Paying for food and groceries. I figure we can buy our own and, maybe, have shelves in the fridge. You know, yours and mine."

I slapped my hand down on the counter. "You want us to label our food?" When she nodded, completely serious, I reared back. "No. That sounds..." *Awful,* was what I wanted to say. "Like we're roommates. Are you going to want to split the utility bill too?"

"We are roommates, and yeah, I don't want you paying for everything."

I opened the fridge for an egg and cracked it into a bowl to coat the chicken before flouring each piece.

"I know you can hear me," she said.

"Can you grab those two lemons?"

"Can you tell me your Venmo?"

I went about my business of cooking as she let out a tiny, adorable growl behind me.

"Wesley."

"Margaret."

"I'm going to stuff cash into your socks."

"And I'm going to force-feed you lunch every day." I glanced over my shoulder. "How 'bout that?"

She folded her arms. "How are you going to do that when you aren't here?"

She had me beat there, and I opened my mouth to once again reassure her, but I stopped. Her tone of voice and her defensive posture told me she was upset I hadn't been home. No matter how often she said it was fine, that she was fine —*fine, fine, fine, fine*—she wasn't fine. I knew in my bones, in my *heart*, she was upset I wasn't here, because she wanted me to be.

She just wasn't ready to admit it yet.

"It won't be like this forever," I said, "only for right now, until I get this movie off the ground." I tilted my head to the side. "But if you miss me that much, you could always come with me, let me feed you lunch every day."

She rolled the two lemons across the counter to me. "I didn't miss you."

I dared to brush the tips of my fingers along her jaw, combing loose pieces of hair behind her ear, and her cheeks warmed with color. I beamed. "Yeah. I didn't miss you either."

She rolled her eyes, not quite hitting her target of indifference. "You're the worst."

"Listen," I said, getting back to the task at hand, "before you came along, I was paying for everything without issue."

"Yeah, and now that I'm here, I'm using more water, eating more food, turning on more lights."

I opened the fridge again for butter and milk, tossing some of each into a pan on the stove, followed up by a tablespoon of flour, whisking it all together.

"Come on, Wes."

"What?" I paused for a moment. "I'm listening, but I gotta pay attention. I'm making a roux. I don't want to burn it."

She huffed and marched up behind me, flicking the stove off. "And I don't want to be a leech."

Forgetting about the roux, I spun around. "You're not a leech. Why would you think that?" When she moved to step back, I clasped my hand around her wrist, keeping her close. "Because of your ex?"

She shot her gaze out the window. "He didn't mind paying for things while we were together, but when we split, I had nothing."

"Hey." I called her attention back to me with a shake of her hand. "I'm not him, and I'm not leaving you with nothing, no matter what happens." Yet even saying those words had a pit forming in my stomach, like she was planning for it not to work out between us. She wasn't merely assuming the worst would happen, but waiting for it.

"Remember I told you I went to Catholic school?" she asked, and I finally let go of her to lean against the sink, ready for her story.

"My mom's the secretary there, so my sister and I went for free, but everyone knew we were the poor kids. It was a well-known fact that my father pissed away his paycheck at the bar, and around the holidays, people would give my mom things, because they knew we didn't have a lot." She pulled the sleeves of her shirt over her hands and crossed her arms. "My mom *hated* it. She never wanted to accept help from anyone, didn't want to rely on other people, but at the same time, she said my hobbies were too expensive, my dreams too high. They didn't have money to buy colored pencils or to send me to art class on the weekends."

I nodded, only now understanding the full picture of her life and the root of her concerns.

"My sister went to community college and worked full time to pay her way through school. Meanwhile, *I* was the one who wasted time and money, even though I received a scholarship and took out loans to pay for my degree on my own."

"I'm sorry," I said, because I didn't know what else to say.

"I know I have a complex about it, about people giving me things." Her gaze dropped to the floor. "But I'm also afraid of being destitute, and I work hard to make sure I have my own money. I don't want people thinking I'm taking advantage of them by accepting anything."

I rubbed my hands up and down her arms until she uncrossed them, then pulled her in for a hug, kissing the top of her head. "If you want to contribute, great, but I'm not going to keep score. If you want to buy groceries, do it. If you want to pay for things here and there, fine. I won't stop you, but I also learned from my dad what it means to share. When you care for someone, you don't worry about what's mine and yours." I tipped her chin up with my knuckle so she'd meet my gaze. "You are *not* taking advantage of me. You're having my child. You really think I give a shit about line items on the grocery bill? Or how much water you're using?"

She bit into her lip for a moment. "No."

"No," I repeated. "I don't. Now, can I get back to cooking dinner? I think I ruined the roux."

"Oh no. Not the roux."

I pushed her away to sit at the table. "I can make, like, three dishes really well, and this is one of them. Now, please, let me concentrate. Or else it'll be hot dogs and boxed macaroni and cheese for dinner."

Behind me, she said, "I'm okay at cooking, but I'm a pretty good baker."

"Yeah?" I grinned at her over my shoulder. "In that case, I'll take my payments in cheesecakes, please."

CHAPTER SIXTEEN

Maggie

By my second week living in Wes's house, I had begun to think of it as my house too. Although he was up early every morning for a run, I never heard him leave, but I knew he had gone by the smell of coffee brewing by eight a.m. That was normally when I'd pad downstairs and sit across from him while he poured me a cup of hot tea, still in his sweaty clothes. Then he'd ask what was on my schedule for the day, which was usually some combination of website updating, post office run, yoga, walk to the park, or nap. Always a nap.

For his schedule, he parked himself at his laptop and held his phone like it was a lifeline. The guy had a lot of irons in the fire. Outside of *Turning Leaves*, he also worked with other film-makers. One night, he'd explained that he was a line producer, the guy at the heart of the production, allocating funds and ensuring the film stayed on schedule. Somehow it turned into showing me spreadsheets and budgets for movies he'd worked on, and my eyes rolled to the back of my head. Then he'd smoothed his hand over my hair with a laugh and instructed me to go to bed.

Now, with Wes's blessing—meaning he was offended I even asked—I planted a small flower bed in the backyard.

"What do you think?" I asked after I finished.

"Yeah, looks great." He leaned on the railing of the small deck. "I like the..."

"Black-eyed Susans."

"Yeah. Very sunny." He touched the vine of the hanging plant near his head. "I was thinking we could call my parents tonight. Introduce them to you. Is that all right?"

I brushed off my hands and scraped at the dirt under my fingernails. "Yeah. I guess it's about time."

He raked his perceptive eyes over me. Like he could see right into my brain and pull out every thought before I verbalized it. "They're really excited, Mags. You have nothing to worry about."

"I know, but..."

"But nothing. This isn't a test. This is my mom and dad meeting the mother of their grandchild. Contrary to popular belief, some people don't hold such high moral standards that it makes them assholes."

I flinched, and he immediately held out his hand.

"I'm sorry, but after I heard your phone call—"

"I know." I stopped him, not wanting to rehash how he had glowered the whole time I'd spoken to my mother on the phone yesterday. She interrogated me about Wes, asking for everything short of his social security number, before diving into the disappointment segment of the call. "I'm going to take a shower and clean up, then we can call?"

"Sure," he said, and I ignored how his sharp gaze followed me inside.

I showered, scouring my hands, and took the time to braid my hair away from my face, even put in my contacts before making my way back downstairs. Wes was relaxed on the sofa in the living room with one arm behind his head, his feet bopping along to the song the characters sang on the television.

"*Singin' in the Rain*? Really? I thought you were into David Fincher and Ridley Scott."

"I'm into anyone who makes a good movie." He bent his knees, making more room for me on the sofa. "This is one of my favorites."

"Why?"

"Whenever we stayed with Nana, she always had TCM on. She loved the old movie-musicals." He lifted one shoulder. "I did too. The idea of making a big, sweeping movie like that, with people dancing all over and the camera moving to catch it. I think that's what really got me into filmmaking."

"And yet you make movies about people driving in cars and having conversations around dinner tables."

"Hey." He poked my thigh with his foot. "Find me the next Gene Kelly, and I'll make a musical."

I laughed and unthinkingly wrapped my hand around his ankle. We both noticed at the same time. He didn't seem to mind, but I tore my fingers away like I'd been burned. "So, we should call?"

He was slow to move but eventually paused the movie and got up to grab his laptop, connecting a FaceTime call. "Hey, Mom. I have Maggie here. Is Dad around?"

"Right here," I heard his mother say before Wes sat back down on the couch, positioning the computer so we were both on-screen.

Abigail Isaacson wore her light blond hair in a bob, her eyes almost the same color as Wes's, and as soon as she spotted me, she started crying.

"Pull it together, Mom." Wes chuckled.

"Hi, Mrs. Isaacson."

"Oh, honey, no. Call me Abby, please. Maggie, I..." She

rubbed a tissue over her top lip. "I am so happy to meet you. Wes has told us so much about you."

"He's told me a lot about you as well."

On-screen, Abby shifted over, and Wes's dad took a seat, waving. "Maggie, I'm Jeff. Nice to meet you. I wish we were able to do this in person."

"We will soon," Wes promised, and Abby started throwing out all kinds of dates, offers to fly up or purchase plane tickets for us to visit.

"Mom," Wes said at the same time Jeff folded his hand over his wife's with a quiet, "Slow down, sweetie. We have lots of time."

Abby quieted for a moment then leaned forward with all the excitement of a toddler in front of a birthday cake. "So, do you have names picked out yet?"

Wes and Jeff both burst out in laughter, and I got the sense that Abby was always like this, enthusiastic and uncaring about the reaction from her husband and son. They all got along great, able to playfully poke fun at one another, so unlike my family.

"We won't find out the gender until the end of October," Wes said.

"As soon as you know, tell me. There's this little baby boutique with the cutest stuff down here. You should see it. They can personalize blankets and— I'm sorry." Abby pressed her hand to her heart. "I'm going off the rails again. I'm sorry."

"No, it's okay." I smiled. "Really, it's fine."

"Maggie, Wes mentioned you're an illustrator. How did you get into that?" Jeff asked, and I relaxed into Wes's side as I relayed how I'd found the creative outlet early in life and had known I was never going to be a person with a nine-to-five job.

"It's important to know what your strengths are," Jeff said, his voice laced with pride. "When Wes wanted to go into the arts, I sat him down and told him it wasn't going to be an easy road, but he had to figure out how to make a living doing what he loved."

I slanted my eyes to the man next to me. No wonder he was so even-keeled and encouraging; he had Abby and Jeff as parents.

And it was no wonder I was still in therapy.

"I'd love to take a look at your website," Jeff said. "Could you forward it along?"

I nodded. "Of course."

"Yes!" Abby clapped. "I want to buy something."

"No, you don't need to buy anything. I can make you whatever you want."

Abby sliced her hand through the air. "Absolutely not. We want to support you."

"Well, thank you very much. That's very kind."

She waved her hand like it was nothing. But it wasn't nothing. It was everything. Wes's parents were welcoming me into their life like I was one of their own. And my heart ached in gratitude for them but also disappointment in my own family.

"We don't want to take up any more of your time," Jeff started. "But it was very nice talking with you, Maggie. I hope we'll get to do more of this?"

"I would really like that."

"And take care of yourself." Abby listed directions off on her fingers. "Make sure you're drinking lots of water. Get as much sleep as you can now while you're still feeling good before the baby comes. And if you get heartburn, try honey in some warm milk. I had such bad heartburn with my kids." She touched her fingers to her collarbone, grimacing like she was reliving it.

"Thanks, I'll try that."

"Okay, we'll let you go." Abby waved. "Wes, we sent you your birthday present. It should be arriving Monday."

"Love you," Jeff said.

"Bye, kids! Love you!"

Wes ended the call, and I knocked his shoulder with mine. "Your birthday? Why didn't you tell me?"

"It's not until next Saturday." When I thumped his arm, he grabbed his bicep. "Ow. This baby giving you superpowers or what?"

"It's your birthday, and you didn't tell me."

"We've kinda got a lot going on. It's not really the first thing on my mind."

"But we have to celebrate," I told him, already planning what I could do.

"I don't need a party."

"A cake. You need a cake. I'm going to make you one. You like cheesecake, right?" I grabbed my phone. "Okay, I think I know a good recipe. Are you sure you don't want a party? Don't let me rain on your parade. You should go out, have a few drinks."

"Nah. I don't want to go out. But maybe Chris and Bronte will be able to come up."

"You're going to be thirty-eight?"

He shut his laptop and grabbed the remote. "Yep. Catching up to you, old lady."

I smacked his arm once more for good measure and stood up, intent on getting some work done before going to bed. I'd been falling asleep earlier and earlier lately.

"Hey, where you going?" He pointed to the television. "Don't you want to watch with me?"

I considered him for a moment. "If you'll be quiet."

"I thought you liked all my tidbits of trivia."

I slunk back down to the couch and curled up in the corner,

intending to take up as little room as possible, but Wes huffed out an agitated sound. I turned to him, hiking up my brow in question.

"Come on, spread out." He tapped his lap, and when I didn't move, he grabbed my ankles and yanked me down, resting my feet on his thighs. One big hand bracketed them, as if he knew I'd try to move.

"Comfy?" he asked, and I settled my head on a pillow, humming my answer. With his thumb stroking the arch of my foot, I was more than comfy, I was downright blissful. A bad sign when I couldn't let myself get used to it, this attachment, all snuggled up, watching a movie with the father of my baby. Not when I wasn't guaranteed permanence.

Not even when I sensed my body being lifted, a solid grip on my back and legs. I was barely awake enough to realize I had fallen asleep and Wes was carrying me upstairs. He gently set me down on my bed, covered me up, and brushed his lips along my forehead, murmuring a goodnight.

No, I couldn't get used to that either.

CHAPTER SEVENTEEN

After spending the whole day locked away in my room on the phone or in Zoom meetings, I practically sprinted down the hall. "They're in!" I burst into Maggie's room, where she was wrapped up in a towel, evidently just out of the shower. "Miramax is in!"

I picked her up off her feet and twirled her around as she swatted at me. "I'm soaking wet."

I refused to put her down. "I don't care."

She draped her arms around my neck, her words tickling my ear. "I'm really proud of you."

Her lavender-scented shampoo permeated my already exhilarated brain, so all I could do was curve my hand around the back of her head and brush my mouth along her jaw. I was beyond relieved to have finally made the deal and so goddamn happy, I couldn't think straight. Especially when I had Maggie in my arms. When I let my tongue taste the skin below her ear, she gasped, wiggling in my hold.

"My towel," she rasped, "it's falling."

With one hand still wound in her hair and the other around her waist, I set her feet on the floor, and her hands blazed a trail down my chest to her own, where she secured the beige towel. But I couldn't find it in myself to let her go. Instead, I pressed my forehead to hers, my mind clogged with desire, and I hoped maybe she wanted me too with how her breath shuddered.

"Wes," she whispered, and fuck, I loved the sound of my name coming from her perfect lips.

I cupped her face in my hands, thumbs bracketing her mouth. "Yeah?"

She backed away a few inches. "Does this mean you won't be traveling anymore?"

Her dark, guileless eyes stared up at me, and the crackly, heavy, needy moment between us fell apart when I didn't immediately answer. She stepped out of my grasp, and my hands felt useless without touching her. Like the only thing they were meant to do was touch her. "It'll be a quick trip."

"Quick trip, like two days or five days?"

I wiped away the few drops of water lingering on her collarbone, and her teeth left white marks on her bottom lip. "I'm leaving Wednesday, but I'll be back for the weekend. We can celebrate."

Her gaze drifted past my shoulder for a long moment. "Yeah." Then her mouth twisted into an imitation of delight, but it wasn't her real smile, the one that was slightly lopsided. This one was straight and fake. "Double celebration, for your birthday and movie. Exciting."

I shoved my hands into my pockets, my own excitement knocked down a few pegs. "They still have openings left for the parenting class I found. Did you have a chance to check out the link I sent you?"

"Oh yeah. It looks good."

"Should I sign us up? It starts next Tuesday."

She turned her back, effectively dismissing me. "Yeah. Sounds good."

I waited a few seconds to see if she'd add anything else. She didn't, and I scratched at the back of my head. "All right, well, I'll, uh, let you get dressed."

Then I closed her door behind me and silently cursed. I was supposed to be showing her how I would be there for her, support her, and I was failing. It was one step forward and two steps back as long as I had to keep flying across the country.

But soon, I wouldn't need to. We only had to make it through the next few weeks, and then I was determined to show her I was in this, with her, forever. I wasn't going anywhere, I wasn't putting her second, and I sure as shit wasn't going to let her think anything or anyone was as important as the family we were building.

I shut my computer down before heading to the kitchen to cook something up for dinner. While I chopped vegetables for chicken stir-fry, I heard Maggie make her way downstairs. She settled on the couch with her iPad, the telltale violin music playing to let me know she was working.

Once I had the meal all plated up, I set it on the dining room table and padded over to the sofa. "Dinner's ready."

"Okay," she said but didn't make a move to get up, so I peered over her shoulder.

"What are you working on?"

She shifted to show me the colorful but not suitable for work piece.

"Hey now." I jerked back. "That's... Wow."

"You like it?"

"I..." I bent down next to her, studying the illustrated scene of a man and a woman in a shower. "Is it weird I'm turned on by this?"

She finally gave me her attention and laughed, all signs of her previous discontent gone. "I do character sketches for romance authors."

I dropped my arm along the back of the couch. "You have so many different commissions. Isn't there one—" I searched for the appropriate word "—specialty you could focus on instead of so many different projects?"

She tapped a few buttons on her iPad, saving her work, before setting it and her stylus on the couch. "Not really. Some months, I sell a lot of stickers or sweatshirt designs from my store. Some months, I can get by on bigger projects. It all depends on what people want." She pointed to her own T-shirt depicting a woman wearing sunglasses with her hair in a side ponytail above the words *Girls Just Wanna Have Fundamental Rights* in bold, neon letters. "This always sells well around elections."

"You ever make any men's shirts?"

"All the designs are unisex."

"I'm not a huge Madonna fan." I tipped my chin to her shirt, which was tight around her chest.

"Cyndi Lauper, but fine, what do you want on your shirt?"

I scratched at my jaw, and Maggie's eyes followed the movement. Between her art and what happened upstairs, I was ready to pounce. Did she even know how she was looking at me? Like she wanted my few days' worth of stubble rubbing on her thighs? Because I wanted that more than anything in my life.

"Oh wait, wait, wait." She grabbed her iPad again. "You watched *No Country for Old Men* last night. You love that movie, right?"

"I love anything by the Coens."

On her screen, she pulled up the movie posters, scanning over them until she found one she liked. "See how this one has an old Western feel? The colors and the faded edges?"

"Mm-hmm." Though, my eyes were on her. When she was enthusiastic like this, it was impossible to focus on anything else except her. Or, really, I had trouble focusing on anything else but her. Period.

"I can sort of recreate the background and place a uterus right up front, with *No Country for Old Men* around it in similar block lettering."

"A uterus?"

She narrowed her eyes. "Don't tell me—"

"Everybody with a uterus should be able to do what they want with it," I said. "I've just never worn a shirt with one on it before."

"So, can I also put you down for one of the *Smash the Patriarchy* shirts with the She-Hulk fist on it?"

"Yeah." I laughed as she opened up her Adobe app, already starting to draw, but I flattened my palm over it. "Nope. Come on, time to eat."

I dragged her up and over to the table, where we ate in companionable silence for a while until I cleared my throat. "I was wondering if you've ever considered living anywhere else?"

She speared a carrot. "What do you mean?"

"Have you ever considered living in another city or state?"

She swallowed her bite of food. "Not really. It's always been my dream to live here. This is where I wanted to be, and for a long time, I was able to until..."

"Until you got pregnant and planned on moving back home?" I finished for her, and she nodded. "But what if..." I set down my fork and shoved my plate away. "What if I said I don't want to travel so much? If I wanted to live permanently somewhere else."

"Like LA?"

"Yeah."

A long moment passed before she asked, "Are you asking if I'd be upset? Or if I would move with you?"

I swiped my palm over my mouth, not really sure either. I wanted to know what she might say. If she was interested. "Yeah, both."

She tapped her index finger on the table a few times. "I don't know." She lifted her gaze, and I could see hope and longing in the dark depths of her eyes, but she blinked and it was gone. "This is already such a big change, having this baby. And you and I, we're not..."

We're not together is what she didn't say, but I nodded stiffly anyway. "I'm asking because I want to make this work, and I don't mean just for the baby, but for you and me too."

She played with her fork, scraping the tines along the left-over teriyaki sauce, and when she didn't respond, I leaned forward. "I'm trying to show you this is what I want, and I'm doing my best, but it feels like you have one foot in and one foot out of this. Like you're ready to bolt. You're scared."

Her fork clattered to her plate as she laughed.

"What?"

She lifted her palm as if it should have been obvious to me. "Yeah. I'm scared."

"Of what?"

She shook her head as her giggles subsided.

"What?" I repeated, my fingers inching across the table toward her.

"You love movies so much, so I guess you'll understand when I reference one." At her unexpected answer, I quirked an eyebrow, earning another round of snickers. "You ever see *Dirty Dancing*?"

"Not in a long time, probably since my high school girlfriend made me watch it."

She exhaled a long breath and pushed away from the table, crossing to the staircase. "Well, in this scenario I'm Baby and you're Johnny."

"What's that supposed to mean?"

She paused long enough to toss an exhausted glance in my direction. "I'm scared of a lot of things. Including you."

Then she traipsed upstairs, and I made a note to watch *Dirty Dancing* as soon as possible.

CHAPTER EIGHTEEN

I didn't bother to get up and see Wes off for his trip. He'd been stewing ever since our semi-heated exchange over dinner, but I didn't care. I had known since our first night together that he had a hopeless romantic streak in him, but sometimes it blinded him to the real world. To complications that weren't as simple to solve as saying, *Yes, I want you.*

But I knew better. I'd been manipulated and demoralized by those I loved, so of course I was scared. Like Baby's big confession to Johnny, I was scared of everything. Of having a child, of being a good mom, of my feelings for Wes. I had been heartbroken too many times in my life, and I wasn't sure I'd be able to survive it with him.

So, instead of watching him walk away again, I stayed in bed until I was sure he was gone. Then I got dressed for my yoga class and strolled downstairs for breakfast. As I bit into my toast, my phone chimed with a text alert.

> WES
>
> Don't forget to eat lunch and call me tonight. I want to hear about your day. I'll be home Friday. I promise.

Ignoring how my stomach flip-flopped, I polished off my tea and toast then slipped into my shoes. I loved my yoga studio in Manhattan and refused to find another, so every week I made the trek to South Street Seaport, where I was able to stretch into my sun salutations while staring out at the water.

At the end of the class, I rolled to all fours before standing up, while the woman next to me struggled to do the same.

"You need a hand?" I asked with a laugh, and my neighbor grasped my outstretched palm.

"Thanks. I assumed it would be easier the second time around, but I'm bigger and more exhausted with this pregnancy," she said in a slight French accent.

"When are you due?"

"Middle of February."

"We're not too far apart." I gestured between our stomachs. "I'm middle of March." I rolled up my mat, realizing I'd been doing hip opening stretches and deep belly breaths next to this woman for the last few weeks, yet it was the first time we'd ever said anything more than hello and goodbye to each other. "I'm Maggie, by the way."

"Vivienne." She pulled a long-sleeved T-shirt over her head to cover up her pink tank top and swung her long box braids over her shoulder. "Is this your first?"

"Yeah."

"How has it been so far?" Vivienne asked as we walked out of the yoga studio together.

"Good. I'm thirty-eight, though, so when I have aches and pains, I'm not sure if it's because of the baby or because I'm old."

She flicked her hand in the air. "Tell me about it. I had my first when I was thirty-six. Now, I'm thirty-nine. Practically middle-aged."

I pushed my glasses up my nose. "What moisturizer do you use because you don't look anywhere close to thirty-nine?"

She skimmed her fingers over the creamy dark brown skin of her cheek, not a wrinkle in sight. "All of my skincare comes from France."

"That's where you're from?"

She shook her head as we started off in the same direction. "Quebec. I came here for a study abroad program during university and met a man." She slanted her gaze to me, one thin, dark brow raised in amusement. "Of course."

I laughed, knowing exactly how a man could throw a life off course. "He didn't want to move to Canada?"

"We did long-distance for a few years, but his job was here, so..." She lifted one shoulder. "What about you? Are you married or...?"

"I...have a situation."

She grinned as she pointed to a frozen yogurt spot. "I always treat myself after class. Would you like to join me? I'd love to hear about this situation."

For the first time in a long time, I felt genuinely optimistic about meeting a new friend. "I'd love that."

We bought our yogurt and settled into our chairs before I explained my "situation" with Wes. Vivienne nodded along, smiling or frowning in the right places, and soon we were chatting about how she used to be a French teacher but now stayed at home while in grad school.

"Cute, eh?" She showed me a picture on her cell phone of her husband, a tall Black man with a beard, their adorable son on his shoulders. "David and Henry," she said. "Henry speaks fluent French."

"That's amazing. I wish I were multilingual so I could teach my kid something besides English."

"We can do it together since we both have flexible schedules. Yours can learn from mine."

"That's perfect."

After exchanging cell phone numbers with a promise to make this a weekly practice of frozen yogurt together after yoga, we parted ways. At home, I showered and spent the rest of the day working, but I made sure to eat a sandwich for lunch and cooked up a pot of spaghetti for dinner.

Once leftovers were put away, I sat down to watch TV, but nothing caught my interest. I suspected, without Wes to watch it with me, nothing would, which was endlessly irritating. So, I marched upstairs, but instead of turning into my room, I headed straight for his. I flicked on the light and sat on his bed, dialing his number.

"Hey!"

I wrinkled my nose. "You always sound so surprised when I call."

"I am, pleasantly surprised." When I grumbled, his voice rose in amusement. "Can you blame me? After how we left our conversation?"

Afraid I'd give something else away, I stayed quiet.

"How was your day?"

"Good. I made a friend at yoga."

"Aww, sweetheart," he crooned, and I growled back at him. "Tell me about your new friend."

I gave him the low-down on Vivienne and how happy I was to not simply have a new friend, but a *mom* friend.

"That's really great," he said, "I was reading about postpartum depression the other day and why it's so important for mothers to have people to talk to about it."

"You have to stop reading books."

"I want to be prepared."

Although, he might have been a little too overprepared. I was once again hit with a wave of melancholy. I laid my hand on his comforter. "You get all the contracts signed or whatever it is you needed to do?"

"Yep. I'll need to take one more trip out here, and then that should be it."

"Mm-hmm."

"And you always sound so skeptical when we talk."

"I am, carefully skeptical."

"Well, I've got plans for you," he said, all low and flirty, so my skin broke out in goose bumps from the visceral memory of his rasp in my ear and his hand between my legs. "I've started putting a schedule together for us. Parenting class and dinners and dates."

"Dates?" I asked through a yawn.

"Yeah. That's assuming you can stay awake. Double feature at the movies, pumpkin picking—"

"Oh, there's this farm on Long Island my friend and I went to a few times that has the best apple cider doughnuts," I said before I thought better of it. I had always loved the fall, though I hadn't gotten to experience much of it lately.

"Yeah? Let's go there too."

I smiled, but it dropped when he said, "I watched *Dirty Dancing* on the plane ride over here, so I finally get your reference. You're afraid of everything, huh? Including 'walking out of this room and never feeling the rest of my whole life the way I feel when I'm with you.'"

He quoted it with such accuracy, I huffed in annoyance.

"So, you miss me?" he asked.

"Not at all."

"Liar."

I snorted. "I'm tired. I'm going to bed."

"Okay. Sleep tight."

"Night, Wes."

"Night, sweetheart."

Then I got up from his bed, shut off the light, and trudged back to my bedroom. It was a long time before I fell asleep.

CHAPTER NINETEEN

Wes

By the time I had returned home from LA, it was almost eleven, and I'd found Maggie asleep on the couch in the living room. When I had shaken her awake, her eyelashes fluttered open, revealing those chocolate-drop eyes, a sluggish smile crawling across her face.

"Hey." Her voice had been sandy with sleep.

"Hey." I'd slipped my arms under her to carry her upstairs.

She'd weakly batted me away to stand on her own. "I want to hear about your trip."

"Tomorrow," I'd told her, steering her to bed.

"Happy early birthday," she had rasped, curling the covers up to her chin, and I kissed her forehead, desperate to slide in next to her. That was the only present I wanted.

Instead, I closed her door and slunk down the hall to my room.

In the morning, Maggie made toast and scrambled eggs for breakfast. We didn't discuss anything important, mostly the really good shrimp tacos I had eaten for lunch one day and the new design idea she had from all the taco talk.

It was weird and wonderful how comfortable it felt to do those normal routines, like loading the dishwasher and putting snacks on a tray for our friends. That was until we parted ways, heading to opposite rooms to get changed for the day.

I especially hated that part.

But I couldn't sulk about it too long because Chris and Bronte arrived. I walked with him to the kitchen. "Hey, man, I want to make sure you guys are okay."

He straightened from grabbing two beers at the bottom of the fridge. "Okay?"

I tossed a pointed glance back toward the living room where Bronte and Maggie chatted. "I know how hard it's been for you two..." I swiped my hand over my mouth. "I don't want you to feel bad about the baby."

He furrowed his brow. "Oh, come on, you really think we'd be upset?" He set the beers down on the counter before pulling me in for a hug. "We're so happy for you."

"But—"

"No." With his hands on my shoulders, he backed away a few inches. "I love you. Bronte loves you. We would never begrudge you happiness."

I had come to think of Chris as a brother over the years, a younger, troublemaking brother, and would certainly never do anything to hurt him. But pregnancy and children were sometimes sensitive subjects for people, particularly for those who were having trouble conceiving. Chris and Bronte had struggled for a while now, and here were Maggie and I having a kid by accident. A happy accident, but an accident nonetheless, and I expected it might sting for them.

"I don't want Bronte to feel bad or anything."

He waved the notion away then passed a beer to me, clinking the bottles together. "No way."

Satisfied I wasn't inadvertently hurting my friends, I took a sip. "You're the only other people who know besides our families. We haven't told a lot of people yet."

"Aww. You really do love me. C'mere, big guy."

I chuckled as he towed me in for another hug. We had a bit of a height difference between us, as Chris came in at around 5'9" to my 6'5", so we were quite literally big brother, little brother.

I smacked his back twice before letting go and grabbing the bowl of sourdough pretzels along with the spicy mustard—Maggie's choice of snack for the past few days—while Chris carried the plate of cheese and crackers.

In the living room, Maggie and Bronte had their heads bowed over a cell phone.

"I don't know," Bronte said. "I can't decide what to do."

"How many windows did you say are in the room?"

Bronte lifted her head, pantomiming with her hands. "Two really big ones, floor-to-ceiling."

Maggie pursed her lips, her eyes squinting as if she was mentally picturing these windows. "If you go with a glossy color, remember it'll reflect all that light. You also have to think about what color the bookcases and furniture are going to be. That'll affect how bright or dark the shades appear."

Chris sank down next to Bronte on the couch. There was barely enough room for him, but he still wiggled his way in as if he couldn't stand not being in close contact with his wife. "What're you talking about?"

"The library. I was telling her how I can't make up my mind about the paint."

Dropping down into the leather chair in the corner with a few pieces of cheese, I sent Bronte a wry smirk. "Can't make up your mind? No, not you."

Chris scrubbed his hand over his beard. "You showing her all your paint samples? All eight of them?"

"Yes." Bronte raised her hands as if it were perfectly standard to take a photo of eight different colors painted on a wall. "I need opinions."

"She's been asking everyone," Chris told me. "Even the clerk at the grocery store."

"She loves me. I go to her checkout aisle all the time. We're basically friends at this point." Bronte turned back to Maggie, explaining, "We're living about fifteen minutes from where we were, so I had to find a new grocery store, and you know how it is when you aren't used to a new store layout? It's a nightmare finding anything."

"Travesty," Chris mumbled, and Bronte backhanded him.

"It is!"

"No, I get it," Maggie agreed. "I'm still going to my yoga studio in Manhattan because I didn't want to go through the process of finding one I felt comfortable in, and it's taken me a while to get used to living in this borough. I get it." She pointed to Bronte's phone. "And I don't have any opinions on color. Pick whichever calls out to you."

"Maggie," Bronte groaned pitifully. "You're the artist. I hoped you'd tell me."

"Okay, well, what do you imagine when you think of the room? What do you want the vibe to be?"

"*Beauty and the Beast*. A wall of built-in bookcases with a rolling ladder."

Maggie leaned over for the pretzels, squirting a bit of mustard on a paper plate. "Yes, love it."

Chris put a slice of cheese on a cracker and handed it to Bronte. "It took us forever to find land to build on because she didn't know where she wanted to live, what school district, yadda, yadda. Settling on the design took another six months, and I don't even want to bring up the carpet or wood floor fiasco, but what was the one thing she knew she wanted? Library from *Beauty and the Beast*."

"Obviously." Maggie sniffed. "Beast is top-tier prince material."

Chris froze with a piece of cheese halfway to his mouth. "An anthropomorphic *beast* is prince material?"

Maggie and Bronte exchanged a look then both regarded Chris with completely serious expressions. "Yes."

"*What*?"

Bronte listed Beast's traits on her fingers. "He rescued her from wolves, can dance, has a gigantic library—"

"But he can't read," Chris said.

Bronte ignored him. "He hates everyone but her."

Maggie dropped her head back with a familiar moan. "Ugh, the best."

"Let me get this straight." Chris raised his hand. "You think an animal, like, with horns, who can't read and hates everyone else but her is top-tier prince material?"

"Pretty much." Bronte nodded.

"Yeah, and…" Maggie shrugged. "You know he can fuck."

Bronte spluttered a laugh while Chris clapped his hands, bent over in hysterics. But I only stared at Maggie. She tamped down a grin, sucking the corner of her thumb into her mouth to lick off a smear of mustard. "It's true."

Chris snarled at Bronte, probably hoping to put himself in the same bracket as Beast, but I couldn't stop gawking at Maggie and her teasing pink tongue sliding along her lips. The lips that had, mere moments ago, uttered the phrase, "You know he can fuck."

And flashbacks of *our* fucking played like a movie in my brain.

She said something to Bronte about considering wallpaper, but I couldn't concentrate as I shifted in my seat, my jeans suddenly tight. Her eyes sparkled when she laughed, her lips pouting out each of her words, and goddamn. I thought she was beautiful the night we'd met, but I loved seeing her like this, in jeans and a T-shirt, her hair piled on top of her head with her big red glasses on. She looked so relaxed in my home.

I wanted to make it *our* home.

I wanted her in my bed. *Our* bed.

I wanted to relearn the taste of her tongue and discover all her new curves. Each day with her was the best and worst day, to spend so many hours with her but say goodbye or good-night with nothing more than a smile. Like we were buddies.

"Wes?"

I yanked my attention from out the windows to Maggie, who inclined her head in question.

"Hm?"

"I said are you ready for cake?"

"Oh." I set down my now-warm beer on the table, evidence my mind had taken a long walk. "Yeah, sorry. Cake. Let's do it."

Maggie got up from the couch, fixing her shirt over her baby bump, scuttling ahead into the kitchen, and Chris whacked my shoulder as we followed behind Bronte. "You making big career plans or what?"

I shook my head. "All the talk of paint…"

"You're telling me," he said, although with the way his dark eyes pinched, I knew I wasn't getting away with it. "What is it, really?"

I shoved my hands in my pockets, shoulders up by my ears, gaze trailing over Maggie as she opened and closed drawers, retrieving plates, utensils, and birthday candles she'd hidden away.

"You got that punch-drunk twinkle in your eyes." When I slanted my head to my friend, he elbowed me. "You really like her, huh?"

"I remember how you told me about meeting Bronte, how you were instantly calm, like nothing else felt right before then."

Chris dragged a hand over his hair. "Yeah."

"That's how it feels with me."

"You think you love her?"

I shrugged as Maggie pulled her cake out of the refrigerator. It was a colorful monster of a cake that she'd refused to let me see, hiding it behind a paper bag. "I'm honestly not sure. I thought I knew what it felt like to love someone, but..."

Maggie lit the chunky numbers on the cake.

"This feels bigger. But maybe it's because she's pregnant."

"Maybe," Chris said as Maggie picked up the cake, carrying it toward me, her grin practically glowing behind the small flames of the candles. "Or maybe you should trust the hopeless romantic in you and go with it." Then he broke into song, hitting all the high notes of "Happy Birthday," while Bronte snagged a few pictures on her cell phone.

"Make a wish," Maggie told me, and I closed my eyes for a moment, wishing for lots of things, not the least of which was to spend all of my birthdays with the woman in front of me.

I opened my eyes and blew out the candles to Maggie's cheers. The cake was delicious, three layers with a cheesecake in the middle, and after we sat around the dining room shooting the shit for a while, Chris and Bronte took their leave, two wrapped-up pieces of cake in hand.

Not even twenty minutes later, I received a text from Bronte.

BRONTE

Thanks again for having us over! We love Maggie and hope you have a great birthday!

She attached a few photos, including two of Maggie and

me together, my arm around her waist, her head on my shoulder, both of our hands on her belly.

This was how it was supposed to be.

This was my happy ending.

I turned to Maggie, who was in the middle of smashing garbage down into the can, and I knocked her hands out of the way. I handed her my phone so she could see the text while I took the bag out, grumbling about how she insisted on stretching garbage bags to their absolute limits. It was one of her infuriating and endearing quirks, and she was never allowed to touch the garbage again.

"Aww, that's so nice. They're both really sweet and fun. It's weird how Chris is, like, not at all famous. He's a regular dude."

I put a new bag in the garbage can. "Almost as if movie stars are people."

"How about that?" She reached for the tied-off bag, but I beat her to it and hauled it outside.

When I returned to the kitchen, I watched her wipe down the counter. "Thanks for baking the cake, it was delicious."

"Part of our deal, right? Payment in desserts."

I hid my eye roll, ready to tell her I didn't care about our fucking deal. Then again, if I did, she'd get defensive. She was like a cat in that way. She had to come around on her own terms, or else she'd skitter away. There was no rush, except for the blood in my ears when she wrapped her arms around my waist in a hug.

"Did you have fun?"

I settled my hands at her back, drawing her protruding belly against my torso, and spoke my words into her hair. "Of course."

We stood there like that, her nestled against me, and couldn't she see? Couldn't she feel how right this was?

As if she was answering my internal questions, she stepped away from me. I loathed to let her go.

"I hate to be a party pooper, but this dragon baby is ripping through my ribs again."

I glided my hands up and down her arms. "Need anything?"

"No. I'm gonna soak in the tub."

I dropped my chin toward my chest, the image of a naked and wet Maggie invading my mind. "Okay, let me know."

I kept my gaze lowered until she'd gone upstairs then waited another few minutes while my blood cooled and dick settled down. Which was absurd. All she did was hug me, and yet my body responded to her warm scent and hair tickling my chin like she'd propositioned me.

After an unsuccessful attempt at finding a movie to watch, I hoped I'd be able to take my mind off Maggie in the bathtub by rereading the script for *Turning Leaves,* and I jogged upstairs, only to find Maggie's bedroom door open.

She caught my reflection in her mirror and gasped, covering herself with her T-shirt. But those two seconds were long enough for me to get a glimpse of her.

Her full breasts and hard, dark nipples.

Her round belly and wide hips.

Her naked ass that called to me.

"Oh my god!" she shrieked, and I hightailed it down the hall.

"Sorry! I didn't know!" I sat on my bed as I heard her shuffling around in her room.

A minute later, she appeared in my doorway. "Sorry about that."

"My fault," I said. "I didn't mean to scare you."

Her cheeks bloomed red.

"You're embarrassed." When she nodded, I frowned. "Why?"

"I don't want you to see me like that."

"Like what? Naked?"

She didn't answer, the corner of her lip disappearing under her teeth. She had her hair up in a bun, while a few strands hung loose and wet from her bath. Her skin was clear and dewy, and she had nothing to be embarrassed about.

"You're beautiful, Maggie. You were before. Still are now."

When she dropped her eyes to the floor, I assumed she'd leave, so I scooted back toward the headboard and grabbed my laptop from the side table, surprised to find her tiptoeing farther into my room.

"Thank you," she murmured, and when she was right at the edge of the mattress, she dropped her fingertips to it. "What did you wish for when you blew out your candles?"

"I can't tell you that. It won't come true."

She hummed thoughtfully, and she wouldn't be winning any acting awards for pretending she didn't know *exactly* what I wished for. "I didn't celebrate my last birthday," she told me. "I stayed in by myself and watched *Schitt's Creek.*"

"So, you didn't make a wish?"

"No, I did. I wished to have someone to watch *Schitt's Creek* with me on my next birthday."

"What about someone right now?" I set down my laptop and opened my arm to her. "Come on."

She hopped in bed and snuggled down next to me, and this time, her hum was one of contentment. It wasn't my whole wish but at least part of it.

CHAPTER TWENTY

Maggie

Over the last two weeks, Wes and I had settled into a good routine. Every morning, he'd go for his run then we would eat breakfast together. Usually I walked in the mornings to clear my mind before sitting down at the dining room table or on the living room couch to work while Wes was on his laptop or out for meetings. He always made sure I ate lunch, whether he was home or not, and in the evenings, we talked over dinner. Parenting class was on Tuesdays, and afterward, we'd grab dinner somewhere and stroll around in the cool October air with his arm around my shoulders. Fridays, we ordered pizza, and almost every night, I fell asleep against him while we watched a show or movie.

Like Wes had promised, we'd gone on two dates, one to a pumpkin patch and another to a street fair, where I purchased a couple pieces of art from a vendor. And though I'd gotten comfortable holding hands and cuddling with him, we hadn't come close to another kiss like the one we'd had on the day he'd settled his deal with Miramax.

Which was good.

Because I still didn't trust myself not to fall completely in love with him.

I couldn't be too careful, waiting for another letdown.

Which was exactly what happened when I trotted down the stairs to find Wes at the dining room table. It was a lazy Saturday, and I'd spent the morning in bed, buried under the covers, scrolling social media.

"Hey, you got me nervous," he said, his eyes on his laptop screen as he clicked on something. "I was about ready to come check on you."

"I was up late working," I told him, and he finished whatever he was doing to glare at me. "Don't side-eye me. I can't help that I'm a night owl and your kid is trying to break my ribs open."

He pushed up from the table. "Again?"

"Every time I lie down, it feels like it's prying my bones apart with its tiny little fingers."

He drifted his hands over my shoulders and down to my sides. With his palms on either side of my waist, he rubbed soft circles that felt so good, I closed my eyes and leaned into him.

"I'm sorry. What can I do?"

"Don't stop." I dropped my forehead to the bottom of his throat. "Oh god, feels so good."

He smoothed the heels of his palms from my stomach to my back in a repetitive motion. "Haven't heard a moan like that in a while."

"Don't make sex jokes right now. I might have an orgasm on the spot from you massaging me."

His laugh was rough, and it didn't help my case in not orgasming. It had been months since I'd been with Wes, and it wasn't like it hadn't been on my mind.

It was.

Every day.

But all those memories of his mouth by my ear, ordering

me to touch myself, flew right out of my mind when he said, "I'm going to LA next week."

"Oh." I forced myself to let go of him, backing up two steps so he had to drop his hands back down to his sides. "Okay."

"Chris and I have some production meetings for the movie."

I tucked my hands into the pockets of my sweatshirt. "How long are you going for?"

"I'm leaving Tuesday and coming home Sunday night on the red-eye. But this should be the last one. All the rest is up to Chris and..." When I refused to meet his gaze, he stopped and bent his knees so we were eye to eye. "Is that okay?"

Is that okay? Yeah, of course, it was okay. It was his job. I'd just gotten used to him being home, and it felt like the rug was being pulled out from under me. But that was my fault for getting too comfortable. And now he was going to be gone for five days.

"Do you want to come with me?" he asked, and I flailed my hands.

"No. No, no, no, you need to work, and so do I."

"You can, though, if you want. Stay in my house out there, work in the sunshine."

"No, it's good for us to spend some time apart," I said, making my way to the kitchen.

Wes was hot on my heels. "What's that supposed to mean?"

"Bronte and I have been texting a lot. She finally decided to go with Seaworthy, by the way. It's kind of like a bright navy, and she's going to do gold accents and velvety furniture so it's luxurious but also homey, you know?"

He gave me a bland look.

"So, anyway." I put the kettle on to boil. "I feel like I'm reverting to my old patterns, exactly what I was afraid of."

He stalked closer to me, and I had to hold my ground, even when he stared at me with those soft ocean eyes and his fingers curled around my hip. "I don't understand."

"I'm relying on you too much."

"You're supposed to rely on me."

"Well, yeah, I know, but that's not what I mean. I told you my life has always been about someone else, and I don't want to be like that anymore." When the kettle whistled with steam, I poured the water over the tea bag, my back to Wes. "I can feel you staring at me," I said after a while.

"Because I don't understand what you're saying."

Growing up, I had wanted to prove to my parents I could make it as an artist without their help. Being friends with Amber, I wanted to prove I could hang with the beautiful, rich, party people. In marrying Brian, I was trying to prove I could be the perfect, patient wife. All those years, of changing myself, of trying and failing to be what others wanted, never worked out, and now I needed to figure out who I was, on my own, before I could be anyone's mother.

With my mug in hand, I turned, ripping off the stream-of-consciousness Band-Aid. "I'm living with you and talking to your friends, and now you're going across the country, and I'm sad about it. I can't keep getting so wrapped up in other people's lives. I have to do things for myself. I have to have my own life outside of you and—"

"Wait." He grabbed my free hand, tugging me closer. "Did you say you're sad about me leaving?"

"Did I?" I rolled my eyes up to the ceiling. "I don't think I did."

"You did."

"I think you misheard me."

He chuffed my chin. "Nope."

"So, anyway." I stepped around him, careful not to touch

him or I was liable to give in to the truth. "As I was saying. You know how much I appreciate you, and I love your friends, but if we're going to be doing this co-parenting thing, I need to focus on me and my life, instead of intruding on yours."

Wes held up his hands, blinking a few times, as I sat at the small kitchen table. "I don't even know where to begin with that."

"You don't need to. This is about me."

He sank down in the chair opposite me. "Mags, you're not intruding on my life. We're having a kid. Our lives are forever intertwined. That's not an intrusion. We went over this before, with you and your rules and your ridiculous idea about splitting bills."

I thumped my fist on the table. "It's not ridiculous."

He huffed.

"Don't huff at me."

"Don't keep acting as if you're some stranger I picked up off the street to live as my roommate. You're not."

"I'm trying to—"

"I want you in my life. You *are* in my life," he said with a jab toward my stomach.

"I've already explained how it was with Brian and—"

"Here we go again with that fucking guy." He crossed his arms.

I wiggled my hands up by my ears. "Oh, sorry if my emotional baggage from my six-year marriage is too much for you to handle. I've been open with you from the beginning about it, and you didn't have a problem with it before. You're the one who practically begged me to move in with you."

He bent forward, his voice low. "You're goddamn right I did. I don't give a shit about your emotional baggage. You work through it however you need to, but stop acting as if you're some burden to me." He poked his index finger into the table as he spoke, his jaw tight, his words barely above an angry whisper. I'd never seen him like this before. "I get that a lot of people in your life have given you some warped sense of self and made you feel as if you weren't worth it, but you are, Maggie. You're worth it."

He settled back against his chair, brows narrowed, gaze laser–focused, and I didn't know how to respond. No one had ever said that before. *You're worth it.*

Wes was always so blatantly honest with his feelings, as if he wasn't afraid to be hurt, and I wanted to be like that, fearless. But it'd been too many years of people I loved squashing my confidence to lay it all out on the line like him.

Instead of admitting how every day with him felt so perfect, I worried it was too perfect. It felt like going down a slide with no bumps or jagged edges to slow down, and I feared hitting the bottom. So, I clung to something easier. I scowled at him. "You know, I really don't like your tone right now."

He tipped his head. "You sound like a mom right now."

After a moment of glowering at each other, I gave up with a shake of my head. "Was that our first fight?"

He exhaled harshly. "I think so."

"Wasn't too bad."

"No," he agreed.

"I didn't expect you to be so...ruffled."

He laughed my favorite easygoing laugh. "Ruffled?"

"Yeah, usually nothing ruffles your feathers."

"You do," he said and stood, opening the fridge as if he didn't wrap his fist around my heart and yank it out of my chest. "You want something to eat?"

"That's it?"

"Unless you want to go another round?" His challenging eyebrow shot straight to my core.

"No, I'm good."

"But don't think you got away easy. We'll be coming back to that co-parenting comment you made."

I sipped my now-cool tea. We weren't together, so we had to co-parent. It was our only option. Unless...

I coughed and pressed my hand to my chest, hacking a few times.

He slanted a worried gaze at me, but I held up my palm. "Went down the wrong pipe."

When, really, it was the seriousness of Wes's voice and the truth behind his words that had me breathing funny. He didn't want to be single and co-parent with me.

He wanted to *be* with me.

Even though he'd never hidden that fact, it'd been easy enough to ignore with so much on my plate, namely a person growing inside my body. But now that I could see how our life together would be, it was increasingly difficult to overlook the innate rightness I felt with him.

"Maggie."

"Hmm?" I tore my gaze away from where I'd been staring out the window.

"Pancakes?"

"Oh yeah. Pancakes sound good."

From my seat at the kitchen table, I watched Wes whisk batter together. He concentrated so hard, like he did with everything in his life, and I had to admit, it was amazing to be the center of his attention.

"You want blueberries, chocolate chips, or bananas?" he asked without taking his eyes off his task. "Or all of the above?"

"Ooh. All of the above, please."

He glanced at me, and I could have sworn his attention

dropped to my mouth before it was back on the bowl. "You got it."

With his pale skin sprinkled with freckles, he had a child-like quality about him. Except, he hadn't shaved in a few days, and when he lifted the hem of his T-shirt to wipe off a bit of batter that somehow landed on his chin, the muscles along his abdomen tightened. There was nothing immature about the line of amber hair that trailed down from his belly button below his jeans. This *man* was making me breakfast.

"You want some tunes?" he asked, and I dragged my gaze up from the hole in his distressed denim. A hole I knew was there by accident because Wes would never waste money on clothes people put holes in on purpose.

I tucked my fist under my chin. "Sure."

"Alexa, play Rod Stewart." He brushed his hands off on the sides of his shirt and grabbed two dishes to serve up the pancakes as the first notes of "Maggie May" sounded from the speaker in the corner.

"You think you're cute."

"A little." He set the first plate down in front of me with a fork and maple syrup. "Two for you and one for the baby," he said, pointing to the regular-sized pancakes and then the third, tiny one.

If my ovaries hadn't already done their job, they'd be working overtime for Wes. I practically whimpered at his feet. "Okay, but that was really cute."

He sat across from me with his own pancakes and grinned. "Back to the part about you missing me while I'm away."

I sliced my fork in the air. "Arrogance is a turn-off."

"You were the one who said it."

"No, I didn't," I countered.

"You did."

"I'm hormonal."

"Well..." He took his time drawing a circle with his syrup before capping it. He cut a piece of his pancake and put it in his mouth, chewing slowly. Like he had all the time in the world. Like I wasn't on the edge of my seat waiting. He finally swallowed and licked his lips.

I gaped unabashedly.

"Any time you want me to, I could help you out with those hormones."

His lips curled sinfully, and I darted my eyes up to his.

"I'm sure it's not easy being pregnant. I know how tired you are, how bad your ribs hurt." He shrugged and might as well have been informing me the sky was blue. "But I could make you feel good."

I reached for the syrup as a life preserver so I wouldn't drown in his eyes. "Let's put a pin in that."

"You're killing me, Mags." He sucked air through his teeth. "Killing me."

CHAPTER TWENTY-ONE

Maggie

Tuesday night, I paced my room, having tried and failed to get work done before deciding I'd put on a face mask, aiming for some self-care and relaxation. Except it didn't make me feel very relaxed.

Wes had left for Los Angeles this morning, after slinging his arm around my shoulders to pull me against his chest. "Make sure you take notes at class for me tonight," he'd said then kissed my forehead. "And don't forget to eat lunch."

"Yeah, yeah." I'd waved him off but waited on the front porch until he was out of sight.

And damn it all, if his being gone wasn't the reason I couldn't settle down.

I knew I would miss him, and this restlessness was the exact reason I was supposed to be working on myself. So I didn't *need* him.

Yet with another lap around my bedroom, my hand digging into my sore side, wishing Wes were here to massage it, I grabbed my cell phone. Two rings later, he picked up. "Hey, Mags."

"Hi."

He let out a soft grunt like he'd sunk down into a chair. "Okay, so fill me in. How was your day?"

"I updated my Etsy shop and sent off a couple orders. And you'll be happy to know I had a big salad for lunch."

"Good girl," he said, and my temperature rose at the praise. He might as well have had his fingers in my hair and his mouth at my ear for how my nipples tightened and skin pebbled. Even underneath the pajamas and hoodie I wore.

"What about class?" he asked.

"All about breastfeeding."

"Ah, well. Guess I wasn't really needed for that one, then."

"It was mostly about the benefits of it, where to go for help, stuff like that."

He hummed, and I exhaled a long breath, the mere sound of his voice calming me. "How was your day?"

"Fine. Chris and I are going out to dinner with a few people tonight."

"But it's so late."

"Not here."

"That's right. You're three hours behind." I rubbed my temple. "Pregnancy brain."

He breathed out a laugh. "What are you doing? Watching *Schitt's Creek*?"

"No, but I will now."

"You want to watch it together?"

"How?"

"Tell me what episode you're watching, and I'll put it on here too."

I booted up my laptop and curled on my side, placing my phone on speaker. "Season five, episode nine. One of my favorites. David plays baseball."

"Okay, I'm ready," Wes said on his end, and we both pressed play.

And that was how I fell asleep, with Wes's voice in my ear.

Wednesday, I spent the afternoon with Vivienne after yoga as I fielded texts from Wes, each one a photo documenting his day, including a selfie of him lounging on what appeared to be his deck, sunglasses on.

WES

This could've been you right now.

That night when I called him, he greeted me with, "Hey, sweetheart," and then, "Chris says hi."

I tried not to warm to the fact that Wes clearly called me sweetheart in front of his friend, which meant—if I wasn't so behind in dating etiquette—he was staking a claim.

"What are you up to?" he asked.

"Getting ready for bed." I turned the light on in his bedroom. "How was your day?"

"A long meeting, hashing out timelines and funding and blah, blah."

I rummaged through his closet, all of his clothes pressed and hung up. "Sounds boring."

"You gotta get through that stuff to get to the good part, all the creative meetings."

"Does that happen soon?" I asked, finding a dark hoodie. I brought it to my nose. It smelled like him.

"A couple weeks. We gotta get a casting director on board, start scouting locations."

I slipped the hoodie over my head. "When does shooting start?"

"Early next spring, but don't worry, I'm not needed for that. My focus will be on you and the baby when it comes."

"I'm not worried." And that was, surprisingly, the truth.

When I yawned, he told me, "You're tired. Why don't you go to sleep?"

"You don't want to watch *Schitt's Creek*?"

"I can't tonight. We're going out for a drink with Chris's agent."

I tried not to sound too disappointed. "You've got a packed schedule."

"I've got to get as much in as I can since it's a short trip. I'm sorry. We can talk more tomorrow."

"Yeah," I agreed with a tired mumble. After we hung up, I burrowed down in his sweatshirt, fired up *Schitt's Creek*, and snapped a selfie to send to him.

This could've been you right now.

WES

Are you wearing my sweatshirt?

No.

WES

Liar.

WES

You look cute in it.

Thursday, I took a walk in the park and worked at a Starbucks for a while before returning home to tend to the garden. Later, I reheated leftover chicken and texted Vivienne about where she bought her maternity clothes, which led into a long conversation about underwear and down a rabbit hole of lingerie, which I doubted I'd ever feel comfortable in again after this baby came out of me.

That night, when Wes called, I answered before the first ring ended. "Hi."

"Hey," he said in an amused tone, as if he knew I'd been waiting to talk to him. "What are you up to?"

"Nothing. Lying in bed."

"In my sweatshirt?"

"No comment," I said because I wasn't about to tell him it wasn't only his sweatshirt I had commandeered but also his bed.

"It's okay. I like you wearing my sweatshirt. Means you're not so afraid to let me take care of you after all."

I fluffed the pillow beneath my head, inhaling the lingering scent of him still on it. "Can you watch *Schitt's Creek* with me or not?"

"Yeah." He laughed. "What episode?"

That was how I found myself realizing I was, maybe, possibly, doing the thing I didn't want to do.

Falling in love with the father of my baby.

CHAPTER TWENTY-TWO

Wes

It was about three in the afternoon when Maggie called. Right on time.

"You didn't have to do this," she said without preamble when I answered.

"I didn't want to miss Pizza Friday. It's our thing."

"Yeah, but—"

"I got some too." Even though Maggie and I had talked every day through phone calls and texts, when I realized what day it was, I knew I had to order her dinner so we could eat together. "Hold on. I'm gonna FaceTime you."

I propped up my phone and smiled when she appeared on my screen, glasses on and hair up in a messy knot. She wore my hoodie again. "Hi."

Her face softened like she really did miss me. "Hi."

And when my rib cage hurt, I assumed it was sympathy pains. "Tell me about your day."

She pulled a piece of pizza from her box. "I went shopping with Viv today."

"You guys hung out every day this week. Am I being replaced?"

She blew over her steaming slice. "I love her so much. She's staying home with her kids *and* working on her PhD. She's such a cool mom."

I opened my own box. "You're a cool mom."

"I will be." She grinned.

There was that pain again. Like my bones were cracking. Like they couldn't contain my heart.

"What else did you do?"

She quieted down at the question, suddenly very interested in her pizza.

"Uh-oh. That bad?"

"No, but I, um... I had my therapy appointment this afternoon. We talked about you."

I put my slice down and wiped my hands off on a napkin. "Yeah?"

She picked off a small piece of crust to eat. "We talked about how it's okay to want and need the same thing. It's been hard for me to reconcile that. In the past, I've confused my emotional needs with physical needs and..."

She blinked away from her screen, and I waited, albeit impatiently, for her to continue.

"I've always looked for emotional reassurance but settled for material possessions instead, and since those relationships never lasted, I ended up resenting the things given to me. If I couldn't have their love, then I didn't want their money or gifts or whatever either. None of it meant anything. So, in the last few years, I've become suspicious of anyone actually caring for my emotional *and* material needs."

When she dropped her gaze, I hated being three thousand miles away from her. I needed to hold her, touch her, be there for her, but all I could do was stare at my screen uselessly.

After a moment, she picked her head back up, and the hurt in her eyes broke my heart. "You were right when you said I'm afraid. I've been pushing you away because I'd decided I was going to do this single mom thing on my own. I'd made up my mind, and it's hard for me to walk it back once I make a decision. I think that's why I always end up in these situations."

"Situations?" I cocked an eyebrow, aiming for levity. "You mean to tell me you've had more babies with random men you've met while crying at bars?"

She gave me a faux glare of annoyance which bowed into a reluctant laugh. "We talked about how it's okay to need comfort and support from someone else. To *want* it from someone else. I just have to allow myself to trust them."

I cleared my suddenly dry throat and tapped my index finger on the table a few times. "Do you trust me, Maggie?"

She didn't blink or hesitate. "Yes. I trust you."

Damn, my ribs really hurt. I rubbed at my sides. This woman, she was so much stronger than she realized, yet so much more delicate too. She covered her pain with smiles and tried so hard to be tough to the outside world, but here she was, opening herself up again for me.

"So..." I offered her a teasing grin. "Does this mean you're all sorted now? No more therapy?"

She snorted. "When you meet my mother, you can tell me if I've had enough therapy."

"See? That's what I like about you, Mags. You put up a good front, but I'm the one who gets to see you." Then I leaned in closer to my phone, all traces of humor gone. "The *real* you."

Her teeth sawed into her bottom lip, and I closed my eyes so I wasn't temped to confess how desperate I was to suck that lip between my own. I still had two more days away from her.

But I didn't have a lot of free time to complain about wanting to be home, because on Saturday, Chris and I attended a party at Ruthie Van Acker's house. She was Chris's castmate from the movie *The Gilded Cage*. They had remained good friends since, and he had his eye on Ruthie for the small but important role of Laurel in *Turning Leaves*.

"Hey, you two. I'm glad you could make it." Ruthie kissed Chris's and then my cheek before pointing to my *No Country for Old Men* shirt. "I love it."

"Thanks my..." I stumbled over what Maggie was and went for the easiest explanation. "My girlfriend designed it."

"Yeah? Are they for sale?"

"She's got an Etsy shop."

"Send me the link?"

"Yeah, absolutely." I immediately had my phone out to text it to her.

"Come on, in the back." Though short, Ruthie carried herself like she was eight feet tall. She swept through her expansive Beverly Hills home.

"Wow," Chris said, and I whistled as we stood at the open back door, taking it all in.

Ruthie heaved a sigh. "I know."

"It's..." Chris frowned for a moment when he evidently couldn't come up with any words.

"Not me." She gestured to the Olympic-size pool, the basketball court, the outdoor living area complete with a bar, fireplace, and rug. Guests idly swam or ate at the table, under the shade. "I can't wait to be rid of it. Get something smaller, more me. Less like...him."

It was no secret Ruthie had recently gone through a rough divorce from her husband, who'd been famous for playing a television doctor and infamous for being caught cheating on Ruthie with his costar. This was her last hurrah before they sold the house.

"I want a cute little contemporary place in WeHo, I think."

Chris jerked his thumb in my direction. "That's where he is."

"In a cute little contemporary," I added.

Ruthie laughed. "Yeah? You thinking of selling."

I shrugged. I hadn't been, but now...maybe.

She didn't give me time to answer because she pointed to the bar, where a young woman poured ingredients into a pitcher, mixing up a blue concoction of some kind. "I have an official cocktail for this party. It's called Adios, Motherfucker." She lifted her champagne glass, filled with the blue drink, topped with a lemon slice. "It's delicious, and I'm going to get wasted. Help yourselves to food, or a bed later if you need to. No drinking and driving," she warned, swaying to the music with her drink above her head. "Turn it up!"

A moment later, Ruthie flung her arm around a friend, both of them shouting the lyrics to "Before He Cheats" by Carrie Underwood.

Chris chuckled. "I better go try to sweet-talk her into this part before she's too shit-faced to listen."

We parted ways, and I grabbed an Adios, Motherfucker, plopping down on one of the plush chairs under the shade. Dozens of people milled around, all vaguely familiar in the way everyone was at these kinds of parties, but I didn't have it in me to make small talk today, so I tugged my cell phone from my pocket.

> What are you up to?

MAGGIE

> I just got back from a walk, and why are you
> texting me? Aren't you at a party?

I took a sip of my Adios, Motherfucker and grimaced. "Jesus. Adios, liver."

> Yeah.

MAGGIE

Why aren't you mingling?

Most everyone is in the pool or drunk.

MAGGIE

Why aren't you?

Because I don't feel like doing anything but talking to you.

MAGGIE

Who is there?

MAGGIE

Take pictures!

I'm not taking pictures.

MAGGIE

Let me live vicariously through you. Take a
picture.

I snapped a photo of myself stretched out in the chair, holding the blue drink.

MAGGIE

OMG Are you wearing my shirt!??!

Yeah, got a bunch of compliments on it.
Ruthie wants to buy one.

MAGGIE

Shut your gorgeous face up right now!

Swear on our baby.

She sent a bunch of crying face emojis.

MAGGIE

Do you think she'd take a picture wearing it?
Post on social media?

I can ask her to. I'm sure she would.

MAGGIE

I can't believe you're hanging out with a
bunch of famous people right now and you're
texting me. Go do something important.

I rubbed my fingers over my jaw, exhaling an exhausted breath. My job here, on this trip, was completed for all intents and purposes. I was ready to go home.

I'd rather hang out with you.

It took a while for her to get back to me.

MAGGIE

It's a good thing I live at your house, then. You
get me 24/7.

The thought of her waiting for me had my heart speeding up, and I gulped down the blue liver-killer to slow it.

MAGGIE

Now stop texting me and go have fun.

Fine.

I put my cell phone away and joined Chris in convincing Ruthie to sign on to our movie. After a couple drunken sing-alongs of Kelly Clarkson, Ariana Grande, and Justin Timberlake, she finally said yes.

Sunday morning found me hungover, while Chris had gotten up for a workout. Afterward, he joined me on the deck outside the living room. "What're you doing out here all broody-like?"

I laughed into my coffee. "Enjoying the view."

He dabbed at his face with his T-shirt. "And brooding."

"I'm thinking."

"'Bout what?"

I polished off my coffee, set the mug on the floor then folded my arms on top of each other. "I'm thinking about what I want to do with this house."

His eyebrows rose so high, they disappeared under the brim of his baseball cap. "You mean you want to sell it?"

"Maybe."

"After you gave me so much shit for selling our place here?"

"That was before I understood."

He slapped his hand on his thigh with a guffaw. "Mister you-can-have-it-all-and-be-bicoastal-because-it-won't-be-a-problem-to-split-your-life-between-two-places is finally understanding you can't have a family and move back and forth all the time?"

Years ago, when Chris and Bronte were still figuring out their lives together with him acting and her teaching, I thought it obvious. They could divide their time between the two coasts. And at first, Chris and Bronte did try, but they quickly learned it wasn't so simple. And now that they were trying for a family, it made no sense at all for them to have two homes.

I didn't truly get it. Until now.

Sure, it made sense for me to have multiple properties before. I had traveled enough to warrant them, but I was about to have a child in a few months. I wasn't going to be jetting off. I didn't want to.

"I could keep this place," I said, weighing the option. "But how often would I really be here? It'd be good to have a place to stay when I am here, or you," I added with a tip of my chin to Chris, because whenever he needed to be in LA, he stayed with me. "But, on the other hand, I could sell it and buy a bigger place in New York or somewhere else… Give my kid a house with a huge yard and a swing set."

"You could do that here too, if you wanted," Chris said after a moment, and I agreed.

"Exactly. I'm considering a lot of options."

"What does Maggie think?"

At that moment, my phone buzzed in my pocket with a phone call. "Speak her name and she appears."

Chris backhanded my shoulder. "I'm gonna shower and pack up. Tell her I said hi."

I nodded as I brought my phone to my ear. "Hey, Mags."

"Hi. I was calling to check in on you. I could barely decipher your drunk texts last night."

"Remind me never to drink anything the color of a Smurf."

She let out a breathy laugh that had a chill running down my spine. "What time do you get in tomorrow?"

I rubbed at my eyes. "Around six, but by the time I take the train home, it'll be closer to eight."

Her hum sounded like she didn't quite like that answer. "Are you going to be able to sleep on the plane?"

"Yeah, I'm used to it. I'll get a couple hours in," I said like I wasn't counting down the minutes until I would see her again.

"That's good. When are you leaving for the airport?"

"Soon," I told her, even though my flight didn't leave until almost midnight. Chris was taking a much earlier flight into Philly, so I used my nervous flyer of a friend as an excuse to get to the airport hours ahead of time. Really, I was dying to get home to Maggie. No use waiting around here.

"I miss you," she said after a moment, her voice so quiet I wasn't sure I heard her right. But then she repeated it. "I miss you a lot."

My chest ballooned, and I could probably float back across the country on those words alone. Instead, I cradled my phone with my hand, as if it would bring me closer to her. "I miss you too, sweetheart."

When she didn't speak again, I lowered my voice, imagining I was with her now. How I would take her in my arms, speak my words into her mouth. "It's always been hard leaving you, but this trip... It's been the hardest yet. I hate being away from you."

I couldn't be positive, but I swore I heard a sniffle, and my heart broke. Because I knew the front she put up and how much courage and trust it took to admit her feelings for me. It wasn't easy on her.

"I hate it too," she said after a while.

"I'll be home soon," I told her, and if a person could hear a smile, I did.

When we hung up, I showered and changed, haphazardly throwing everything into my carry-on, my heart on a fishing line being reeled back in to Maggie.

When I finally arrived in Brooklyn, rumpled and wet from the rain and jet-lagged from not having slept on the plane, too anxious, I dropped my bag on the floor. "Mags?" I tossed my keys on the table. "Maggie."

I heard her footsteps upstairs before she called, "Hey!"

Then she was at the top of the steps, and I was stalking toward her, saying, "Careful, careful," as she sped down to me. I caught her around the waist when she leaped at me, sending me back to the wall, laughing. "What a welcome."

With her nose against my throat, she inhaled, her arms banded around my neck. "I missed you."

"I missed you too."

"I didn't realize how much I would until you left."

I kissed her hair and carefully set her down, coasting my hands up her back to her shoulders. She smelled so good, like her shampoo and fresh cotton and a little bit like my laundry detergent. "I'm home now."

She towed me even closer with my jacket clutched in her fists. "Wes?"

"Hmm?" I cupped her jaw.

"Can I tell you a secret?"

My gaze lodged on her mouth when she bit into her lip. "What is it?"

She dipped her eyes to my throat, her voice a whisper. "I've been sleeping in your bed."

I laughed, loud and immensely pleased at her secret. "Okay."

"Can I keep sleeping in your bed?" she asked, lifting her face to mine.

My grin dropped, the insinuation of her question sending my pulse into overdrive, my blood pumping south. "Of course."

Then she pressed up onto her toes, and that was all the invitation I needed. My lips were on hers, my fingers threading into her thick hair. I pivoted, pressing her back against the alcove, and when she opened her mouth on a gasp, my tongue stole into her mouth. Now, *this* was home.

Her round belly pushed against my stomach, and I curled my hand around it, breaking away briefly to ask, "How do you feel?"

"Good."

"Good," I murmured against her lips. I knew I should go slow, carry her upstairs to bed and take my time, but I couldn't wait.

It had been weeks, *months*, and now that I had her flush against me, I couldn't bear to wait even a minute longer. I had to feel her.

"I missed you." I unfastened the buttons of her shirt, exposing the white camisole underneath. I tugged the top down, licking the valley of her cleavage. "I missed you so much," I said against her skin, and she held me to her as I palmed the heavy weight of her breasts. She moaned, her nipples tight, and that sound alone had me nearly delirious.

I fell to my knees, kissed her stomach, and lifted the soft cotton of her camisole. Her jeans had no zipper, and maternity pants were my new favorite invention. I had them down and off her legs in seconds, followed swiftly by her underwear. I smelled her arousal and trailed my nose along her pubic bone, under the curve of where she'd started to swell. Then I kissed the juncture between her thighs.

"Yes, Wes, please."

I pulled back slightly when her legs trembled. "I will. I'll make you feel good, but I don't want you to fall. Hold on to me."

She nodded, and I gently nudged her legs apart. I licked up her slit, the first glorious slide of my tongue over her heat, and she let out a sound I'd never heard from her before, a long, drawn-out groan. Like she'd been anticipating this exact moment, my mouth on her pussy, and all her tension was escaping her body.

"Sweetheart, you need to hold on to me," I reminded her, steadying her with my hands on her hips. "Pull my hair if you have to. I don't care." I pressed a smile to her inner thigh. "I'd like that."

She followed my direction, and I rewarded her with a drag of my tongue down the crease of her hip. "Good girl."

Her laugh was cut off by a gasp as I curled my tongue into her again, and this second taste was better than the first. I was slow at first, teasing and grazing her, but as soon as she tightened her hold on my hair, her head falling back against the wall with a thump, I gave in to my craving to feast on her. Easing one of her thighs over my shoulder, I held her open to my mouth, while still making sure she was safe in my arms as she balanced on one leg.

I sucked at the bud of her clit until her legs shook, and I raised my head to make sure she was still okay. When she whimpered from the loss, I dipped my middle finger inside her. She was so wet, practically dripping down my hand. Licking her flavor off my lips, I asked, "You know how much I love this, Maggie?"

She met my gaze, her eyes wide behind her glasses, and shook her head.

"I want to do this for hours." I crooked my finger, working it until she was panting. "You gonna be a good girl and come for me?"

She didn't answer, instead closing her eyes and dropping her head back once more.

"I've missed this so much," I said against her tender flesh. She was the only woman I wanted for the rest of my life. Here on my knees, worshiping her, this was what I wanted. Forever.

"Come on, Mags, let me hear you." Then I licked her again, sucking at her, pressing my finger against the spot to make her coil with unreleased energy. She was so close. I added a second finger and lapped at her with quick, short strokes of my tongue until, finally, she spasmed, falling over the edge. She was beautiful. And perfect. And so fucking made for me.

I eased her leg down, holding her upright with an arm around her hips while I kissed and licked her wetness from between her thighs. When her breathing audibly slowed, I stood, smiling at her rosy cheeks and bright eyes. I could feel my own cheeks warm, my skin flushed with desire for her.

With her jaw between my palms, I kissed the corner of her mouth. "Hi."

She giggled, a little like she was drunk, her hands around my wrists. "Hi." Her eyes drifted down to the watch I wore, her freewheeling grin dropping instantly. "Shit. I'm going to be late."

"Late? For what?"

"I have an appointment to get my blood taken."

"For what?" I studied her more closely, examining every inch of her face. "What's wrong?"

"Nothing." She ducked under my arm to pull up her pants. "Standard glucose test to make sure I'm not diabetic. I have to get an extra one since I'm a *mature mother*," she said with air quotes. She slid into her shoes then grabbed her purse, a scarf, and jacket. "We'll finish this when I get home?"

"Continue it," I corrected.

She smiled into a kiss, then waved out the door. "I'll be back in an hour."

With her gone, I wiped the smirk off my face along with her taste as I smoothed my palm over my mouth before heading upstairs for a shower and quick nap.

Except that nap was interrupted by a phone call. "Mr. Isaacson, my name is Melinda. I'm at nurse at HLN Diagnostics. Margaret has you listed as her emergency contact. She passed out, and we—"

My heart dropped clear through my stomach. "I'm on my way."

CHAPTER TWENTY-THREE

Maggie

I swallowed another bite of the peanut butter cracker while the daytime talk show hosts on the television above my head made Halloween-themed candy apples.

"Here's some juice."

I accepted the small container with a thanks to the nurse.

"We called your husband. He's on his way."

"Oh, thank you, but he's not..."

She left before I could tell her that, number one, Wes wasn't my husband, and, number two, he didn't need to come here. I was fine. I only needed a snack and some juice to pep up.

This was the first time I'd ever had an issue after getting blood drawn, and it didn't take an MD to diagnose why. I hadn't drunk much water this morning, too busy being swept up in Wes's homecoming, and I'd run out of the house without my emotional support water bottle. Between the dehydration and the overheated, cramped subway, not to mention hoofing it through the rain to the diagnostic center, it was no wonder I felt a bit woozy after they siphoned off a couple vials of blood. When I stood to leave, my legs wobbled. Three steps later, I'd fallen into the wall for support and my vision went black.

Next thing I knew, I was being helped up off the floor by the receptionist and two nurses.

But I felt perfectly fine now.

"I'm here for Maggie Levendoski. Is she okay? Where is she?"

I spun around at the sound of Wes's panicked voice. They could probably hear him next door at the falafel place.

"This way," the receptionist said, and I watched from my perch on the chair as his eyes tracked side to side until they landed on me, his entire face falling.

"Oh my god, Maggie." He towed me into him, crushing me to his chest. "Are you okay?"

"I'm fine," I mumbled into the lapels of his jacket.

"We wanted to make sure she had someone to take her home," the receptionist said.

"But I'm fine, really," I repeated when Wes gripped my face between his hands, his brow pinched in concern. "This has never happened before. I got a little light-headed, that's all."

A nurse took the receptionist's place next to us, explaining, "We gave her crackers and juice to get her sugars back up. It's not entirely abnormal to feel a little faint after this test because of the solution or not being able to eat prior, but we have made a note for your doctor in the system."

"Is she all right?" Wes asked, and I rolled my eyes. I was right here. He didn't have to ask someone else if I was all right.

I tried to wiggle out of his grasp, but he refused to let me go. "I feel fine now. I think I was dehydrated."

He scowled at me. "You haven't had any water? Why not?"

I tried to answer, but he lifted his attention to the nurse. "Do we need to call the doctor? Should she get checked out?"

"I'm fine, Wes."

"Maggie will feel better with some rest and food." The

nurse smiled at Wes then at me. "And make sure you keep drinking water. Take it easy, okay?"

He slung my purse over his shoulder—because obviously I was too weak to carry it on my own—and wrapped an arm around me. "Come on. Let's get you home."

"Wes." I struggled in his vice grip. "I can walk on my own."

He ignored me. "I drove, parked right out front."

"You drove?"

"I wasn't leaving public transportation in the rain up to chance." He produced an umbrella and held it over my head for the few steps I had to walk to the car, which was parked in a loading zone.

"You could have gotten a ticket."

He grumbled while helping me into the car, even as I elbowed his hand away. "You're being ridiculous."

His mouth puckered as he gripped the headrest behind me and smacked his other hand on the console, completely boxing me in. "You think I'm being ridiculous now? Wait until we get home, and I force-feed you vitamins and pour water down your throat."

Then he slammed the door shut and jogged around to the other side, speeding off like we had robbed a bank. As he drove, he curled his hand around my thigh, fingers pressing into my skin. It wasn't a possessive touch, but it was hard, like he wanted to keep me right where I was.

I stared at the side of his face, with his jaw firm and mouth in a tight line. I didn't understand why he was so upset. "It's not that big of a deal."

He didn't say anything, his silence filling up the car, and I sighed, folding my arms across my chest. This man could really be a stubborn ass when he wanted to be.

A few minutes later, he removed his hand from my leg to parallel park the car in front of the house, and when I started to unbuckle, he ensnared my hand. "It's a big deal, Maggie. Me getting a phone call that you passed out is a *very* big deal." He let me go after a moment and pushed his hand through his hair so it stood on end. "I had no clue what happened. It was my worst fear, so, sorry not sorry, I'm freaking the fuck out."

Now that his angry façade had dropped, the annoyed rigidity of my muscles subsided, and I reached for his hand. "I'm okay. I promise. It was a perfect storm of not eating and then rushing out so I forgot my water."

"Rushing," he repeated so low I had trouble hearing him. His eyes flicked out the windshield, his throat working on a swallow. "I made you late to your appointment."

"But it was worth it."

He brought his eyes back to my face, frowning at my flirtation. "Why didn't you drink this morning?"

"I don't know." I lifted one shoulder. "I was..." I waved my hand between us. "I was excited you were coming home and not really paying attention to anything and... I don't know. I didn't drink any water. But it's fine. I'm fine."

He nodded a few times like he was arguing with himself, and I expected him to say something, but he didn't. Only let go of my hand and opened his door to get out of the car. He held the umbrella and helped me out but still didn't say anything.

I assumed once we were back home he might relax, but he radiated even more tension. "Hey," I said when we hung up our jackets, "do you want to go upstairs?"

His brows drew together. "Are you tired? Do you want to lie down? That's probably a good idea."

"No." I slowly traced my fingers up his arms, willing him to catch up. "You promised we could pick up where we left off."

"Maggie." His tone wiped the smile right off my face. "You need to rest. You heard the nurse. You need to take it easy. I'm going to make you something to eat."

"Bu⸻"

He gripped my biceps, gently nudging me away. "What happened this morning..." He dropped his chin toward his chest. "I wasn't thinking. We need to be careful. *I* need to be careful." His shoulders lifted on an inhale, and he picked his head back up, meeting my gaze with watery eyes. "You are too important to me to be so flippant about your health. This baby is everything to me. I should have been in better control of myself."

"You didn't do this to me. You had⸻"

"I should have checked on you. I should have made sure you had enough to drink. I should have gone with you to the appointment. And even though you weren't supposed to eat, I should have made sure⸻"

"Stop." I broke away from him, throwing my arms out at my sides. "Look. I'm fine. Perfectly healthy, okay?"

His scrutinizing gaze swept over me, from the top of my head to my toes and back. Then he pivoted to the kitchen. "Soup and grilled cheese sound good for lunch?"

"Yeah, fine," I grumbled.

"It'll be ready in a few minutes. Sit down and put your feet up. I'll bring you your water bottle."

I made a face at his back but couldn't do anything about his sour mood now, so I tossed myself down on the sofa and hoped once I ate, he'd feel better about the whole thing.

CHAPTER TWENTY-FOUR

As the pat of butter sizzled in the hot pan like my nerves, I struggled not to stab the bread with my knife. Then I added a bit more butter just for the hell of it. Maggie could stand to eat some extra calories after this morning.

I cursed myself again for being so stupid. For losing control with her when I was supposed to be the one to support her, take care of her. Instead, I fell to my baser instincts, more concerned about making her moan and feel her orgasm on my tongue, and where did that get her? Passed out.

"I'm going to get changed," she called from the living room. "Don't worry. I think I'll be able to make it on my own."

"Smartass," I mumbled and turned the heat down on the pot of soup.

She was lucky she *only* passed out. That she didn't hit her head, or... Christ, any number of things could have happened to her, let alone the baby.

I bunched my fists a few times, hoping to rid myself of the buzzing sensation in my fingers. When I'd gotten the phone call and heard Maggie's name, it was all I could do to keep myself together. It felt like I hadn't been able to take a breath the whole way to the testing center until I laid eyes on her. Only then did my lungs function again.

And for her to be so casual about it? As if her being sick or in pain didn't cut me in half. Didn't she know she was the most precious thing in my life? If something ever happened to her, I wouldn't know what to do with myself. After almost forty years on earth, I had finally found my other half. I couldn't lose her now.

Minutes later, I had the grilled cheese and soup served up on the table, along with water and a mug of tea, and we sat across from each other.

She pulled her sandwich apart, blowing on it for a few seconds. I watched with rapt attention as she bit into it.

"I'm eating. You don't need to babysit me like I'm going to throw it up on the table."

I scowled at her.

"You don't scare me."

"Well, you certainly scared the shit out of me."

She swallowed a bit of tomato soup from her spoon. "I didn't mean to."

It wasn't her fault she passed out; I understood that. Yet, I couldn't shake the lingering fear of what could have happened. I wasn't able to find any good humor to even start a conversation, so we ate in relative quiet with Tony Bennett crooning softly from the speaker in the corner.

After we finished eating, and Maggie drank all of her tea and most of her water, I cleaned off the table, stopping Maggie when she tried to help. "I'll get it."

"I'm okay." She lifted up her nearly empty bowl. "Really. I can carry it to the sink."

Without a word, I took her plate and bowl and piled her utensils on top. Even though I could see she was okay, and the logical part of my brain informed me I was being too overprotective, I couldn't quit. It was as if someone had flipped a switch in me, and I didn't know how to go back. I'd follow her around all day, every day if I had to. Stick an IV in her arm to make sure she had enough liquids. Cool her off with a fan and hand-feed her grapes while she lay on the couch.

I turned to her after closing the dishwasher. "Did you want anything else to eat?"

She shook her head, her lips wrapped around the straw from her water. I was half tempted to glue that goddamn bottle to her palm so she never went anywhere without it.

"How about something cold? Ice cream? Or a popsicle?"

She wrinkled her nose. "Do we even have any?"

"I could run out and grab some."

"No, I'm full."

"Are you sure?"

"I'm positive." She stretched her arms behind her back. "I'll watch TV since that's all I'm allowed to do."

She stood up from the table, her T-shirt so worn I could see her nipples pebbled underneath, and memories from hours earlier flooded my brain. The taste of her on my lips, the feeling of her soaking my fingers, how she trembled when she finally came, and I blinked them all away, slapping the dish towel on the counter before trudging after her to the living room.

"Are you going to be my shadow all day?" She plopped on the sofa, extending her legs.

"All week, maybe all month too."

"You're taking this a little too far, don't you think?"

"You're lucky I don't get an extra-large BabyBjörn and carry you around on my chest."

She rolled her eyes, though she didn't bother tamping down her smile. I grabbed the remote, and she bent her knees so I could settle on the other end of the couch. "What do you want to watch?" When she shrugged, I flipped through the streaming services. "You've never told me what your favorite movie is."

"*Dirty Dancing.*"

"I should have known." I found the movie and played it before settling against the cushions. "Nobody puts Baby in the corner."

"Except for you."

I slanted my gaze to her, grabbed one of the pillows to lightly smack her with it then put it in my lap. "Come here." She didn't move, so I tapped on it. "Lie down. Take a nap." When she still didn't move, I exhaled a long breath and dropped my head back to frown up at the ceiling. "I am sorry I'm overreacting, but can you cut me a little slack?"

After a few seconds, I felt her shifting next to me, and I brought my attention to her face, washed of makeup, slightly dark circles under her eyes. She was tired, even if she didn't want to admit it.

I gently curled my hand around her throat, sweeping my thumb along her jaw. "Can you blame a guy for going a little out of his mind when his heart is ripped out of his chest?"

"I didn't rip it out."

"Yes, you did." I tangled my fingers in her hair. "The night we met. You've been carrying it around in your pocket ever since, and I was afraid I'd lost it forever when they called me."

Her lips quivered, her eyes going a little watery behind her glasses. Honestly, it was like she didn't know. I kissed her forehead. "Don't do it again."

"I'll try not to."

"Good." I urged her down, positioning her head on the pillow. I spread a blanket over her legs then combed my fingers through her hair as Baby began her opening voice-over. Maggie quoted it right along with her, and I laughed.

"I'm not the only one who can't be quiet during movies."

She blindly reached for my hand when I stopped stroking her hair. "Keep petting me, and I'll be quiet."

"I'll keep petting you even if you talk through the whole thing."

She shimmied her butt, finding a more comfortable position, and stuck her fist under her chin, not hiding a yawn.

"Feel good?" I asked, one hand in her hair, the other sliding under the blanket to massage her ribs.

Her eyes drifted closed for a few seconds before looking up at me, all sleepy. "Feels amazing."

It wasn't long before she was asleep. Me too.

CHAPTER TWENTY-FIVE

Wes

"Are you nervous?" I whispered, taking hold of Maggie's hand.

"No. Are you?"

"Not at all." More on a knife's edge, like a cat trying not to fall into a bathtub. I'd had a lunch with two producers in from LA, and even Naveen and Terrance told me I was acting weird and jittery. I couldn't stop fidgeting with the cutlery.

The nurse and Maggie exchanged pleasantries as we strolled down the hall of her OB-GYN's office, the walls lined with photos of babies and families. Most of the doors were closed, and I idly wondered how many physicians were on staff. After Maggie had passed out last week, I had pestered her for days until she finally called the doctor to follow up and find out if she was indeed "fine."

I had stood right over her as she'd spoken to the nurse and explained what had happened, and when she hung up, she'd thrown me such a scowl of ire, a lesser man might've crumbled. But I'd merely kissed her forehead. "Thank you. Makes me feel better."

"I'm so glad *you* feel better," she'd snapped as she stomped up the stairs.

"You want salt and vinegar chips?" I'd called after her. "I got you a big bag."

"Yes, of course I want salt and vinegar chips!"

Maggie had mostly vacillated between being annoyed at me and appearing as if she wanted to strip me naked. At times, like in the mornings when I would roll over in bed and she was there, I had trouble not giving in to those pleading brown eyes. But I just couldn't get over that phone call and the feeling of being lost at sea. It was seconds, and yet it was my whole life too.

She was my whole life.

I wasn't immune to her. Maggie was gorgeous, wearing my hoodie basically every day now. My dick twitched at the sheer sight of her sitting on the couch in her plain black leggings and no makeup. I wanted her all day, every day, fantasized about putting my face between her legs for hours, once again sliding into her. But every time I allowed myself to touch her, I remembered sprinting into the blood center and the fear coursing through me. Then all I could do was hold her, safe and warm in my arms, kiss her head, and tuck my face against her neck to sleep with one hand on her belly.

"Here we are," the nurse said, yanking me out of my reverie of Maggie's naked body when she opened the door to a room with an exam table and an ultrasound machine in the corner, as well as some other equipment lined up along the wall. The nurse grabbed a Velcro cuff, and Maggie removed her coat and scarf.

"Blood pressure is good," the nurse said absently and marked it on the chart. "Any changes or issues since the last time we saw you?"

Maggie shook her head. "Usual ache and pains."

The nurse nodded. "It's only the ultrasound today, so unless you need to see the doctor, I'll send the tech in."

"All good," Maggie said, and the nurse smiled.

"She'll be right in."

Maggie was halfway through the pregnancy now, her stomach like a soccer ball, and she started to bend over, but the angle of the table made it seem like she was in pain.

"What? What's wrong?"

"Nothing. My sock is stuck under my heel."

I stooped down in front of her. "I'll fix it."

"I can get it."

I swatted her hands away. "I know you can, but let me do it. I need something to do besides wait around."

"You *are* nervous," she said in amusement as I untied the laces of her sneaker, slipping it off to pull her sock back up her heel. "You should wear different shoes. I don't think you get enough support. Might be why your back's been bothering you so much."

"Or it might be because I'm growing a monster baby that will turn out to be eight feet tall like you."

"Six five." I stood up to my full height, blocking her sight of anything but me because I knew she liked how tall I was. "How old are these sneakers?" I asked since most of the time, she slipped them right on. They were threadbare and no longer white, more ash gray.

"I don't know, but they're my favorite."

"Where'd you buy them? Old Navy for ten bucks or something?"

"Exactly. We need to discuss this controlling thing you have going on—"

"Worried."

She narrowed her eyes, although she couldn't hide the way her lips pursed as if trying to stifle a grin. "Domineering."

I leaned into her space, a low sound rumbling from the back of my throat. If only she knew how domineering I wanted to be with her. How I barely kept myself in check around her.

She placed her hands over mine on either side of her hips. "I know you're nervous, and it's okay. It's all going to be okay. Women have been having babies for millennia."

"And you know how many have complications? You know where this country falls in maternal mortality rate?"

"Maybe don't tell me about the latest article you've read on mortality rates right now," she said, and I hung my head, mumbling an apology.

I was dumb to mansplain birth complications to her, but my heart was in my throat, and I couldn't stop the churning in my mind about this appointment. She scraped her fingernails over my scalp a few times. "We made a human together. Crazy, right?"

I met her eyes, and her grin helped to loosen the tight knot in my chest. Her fingers scratched along my unshaven jaw, and I nuzzled into her palm, soothed by her touch. "I hope they look like you," I said, cupping the back of her head. "You're much prettier than me."

"I hope they get your organizational skills."

"I hope they get your talent."

"And your patience," she added.

I kissed her once on the lips. "Our baby will be perfect."

Then I took her face between my hands like I had wanted to do for the last week and swept my tongue into her mouth. Her answering whimper might as well have been a gunshot in the quiet room, and I tightened my hold on her, coaxing her lips wider. I craved more of her sounds, more of her pleasure, but a knock at the door sent me lurching back.

"Good afternoon!" the gray-haired tech chirped, and I swiped a palm over my mouth as Maggie squirmed on the exam table. "My name is Lynn. How are we today?"

"Good," Maggie and I both said, our eyes clashing over Lynn's head as she wheeled the ultrasound machine over.

"Okay, we're here to check on the baby's growth today, make sure everything looks good. Did you want to know the gender?"

"Yes, please," Maggie said.

"Okay." Lynn lowered the lights. "Let's get to it."

Maggie lay back, pulling her shirt up, and Lynn tucked tissue paper into the top of Maggie's jeans, lowering them down her abdomen before squirting some gel on her skin. "This'll feel warm." She pressed the wand onto Maggie's stomach and hit a few buttons. "All right. There's baby."

Without taking her eyes off the screen, Maggie held out her hand, and I was at her side immediately. I bent down, kissing the back of her hand, smudging away a tear from her eye as Lynn rambled around positioning and organs. It was a blur of black and gray, arms and legs, lungs and heart, and then Lynn pressed a button so a heartbeat echoed in the room.

Maggie's eyes shot to mine. "Our baby."

"Not an alien," I said, earning a watery laugh.

"Thank god."

Lynn called our attention back to the screen. "There's the face. You got a little thumb-sucker. See that? The fist at its mouth." She took a few more pictures then glanced at us. "Ready to find out if it's a boy or a girl?" She moved the wand over to the other side of Maggie's stomach. A minute later, Lynn pointed to something on the screen. "You got yourselves a boy. A healthy and big baby boy."

I honestly didn't care one way or the other, but hearing it had my eyes stinging. "Healthy," I repeated.

While Maggie's eyes were wet, her mouth flattened in mock scorn. "And big. Your baby boy is stretching me to my limits."

I kissed her forehead, temple, mouth. "I'm sorry."

Lynn checked a few more things then powered down the machine. She wiped the gel off Maggie's stomach and handed over an envelope full of photos, but it was difficult for me to pay attention to anything she was saying with the image of my son fresh in my mind and Maggie's glow lighting up the dark room.

"Congratulations and take care." Lynn flicked on the lights and left the room.

As soon as Maggie sat up and tugged her shirt back into place, I crushed her to me, one hand in her hair, the other tight around her waist. "Sweetheart, if you thought I was bad before, you're gonna hate me now."

CHAPTER TWENTY-SIX

Maggie

Two days later, I scooped up some of my frozen yogurt, making sure to snag a piece of brownie as Vivienne sat across from me, twirling her spoon in the air. "I don't get it. What do you mean, he won't touch you? Didn't you say you're sleeping in the same bed?"

"Yeah, and he touches me, but it's like a parent to a child or something. He hugs me and rubs my back and kisses my forehead, but that's it."

"Forehead kisses are the best kind of kisses," Vivienne noted.

"Agreed, but I thought we were going to...you know."

She shook her head.

"Have a lot of sex now," I whispered so the little kids at the next table didn't hear.

She covered her hoot of laughter with her hand as she tossed her head back, and I barreled on. "When he got home from his trip, he had this look in his eyes. It was like he was feral for me, and now he treats me as if I'm made of glass."

"Oh yes, okay. Now I get it. David was like that when I was pregnant with Henry. He was so afraid he was going to hurt me or the baby."

"But Wes wasn't like that…at least, I don't think he was." I leaned in toward my friend, my volume low when the kids next to us screeched. "Sex wasn't really an option until now. I was trying to sort myself out."

Vivienne swallowed a spoonful of her yogurt. "Sort through your hang-ups with your ex?"

"Yeah, and Wes was so patient and flirtatious the whole time. He wanted me. He dropped to his knees he wanted me so bad, and now he's treating me like…like I've got some Victorian wasting disease and he's trying to nurse me back to health."

"Wasting disease?" She shook her head in amusement. "Listen, all you need to do is seduce him. Show him you're not some porcelain doll. You're a woman with needs."

"Yes." I thumped my fist on the table, already planning my attack. "I am a woman with needs."

At home, Wes was working at the dining room table, and he stopped momentarily to smile at me. "How was yoga?"

"Good."

"Went out with Vivienne?"

I nodded. "I'm going to grab a shower."

"All right. Let me know if you need anything," he said, exactly as I knew he would.

Ten minutes later, after I got my hair and skin all soapy, trying to position myself in the most alluring pose I could find, imagining how the light might reflect off the water running down my skin, I yelled for Wes. "I need you!"

He was upstairs in a flash. "What's up? Are you okay?"

"Yeah, fine. I forgot to get a new razor. Can you get one for me? In the bottom drawer."

I heard him riffling around in the small cabinet.

"Anything else?"

"No, just the razor."

He stuck his hand in, behind the curtain without moving it. I pouted but grabbed it and flung the curtain open with the other. In the process, water sprayed over my head, sending shampoo right into my eye.

I sucked in a breath at the sting and shoved the heel of my hand into my eye socket.

"Are you all right?"

"Fine," I bit out. I was supposed to be seducing him, not making him get that nervous twitch in his voice. "I'm fine."

I wiped my face clear of water and shampoo and blinked my eyes open to find Wes holding his hands out, ready to catch me. "I'm fine!"

His gaze never even drifted below my neck, and my boobs were right there. I knew he loved them. He'd told me so multiple times.

"Are you sure?"

"Oh my god, Wes!" I snapped the curtain closed. Obviously, I required a different seduction plan.

Thursday, I wore a matching bra and panty set, feigning the need to go get laundry from the basement. Wes stopped me. "Let me get it."

I was braving near nakedness, even though stretch marks crawled along my breasts, lower belly, and hips, and I ignored my plunging self-esteem for him to not even take a peek? The man was insufferable.

Friday, we handed out candy to trick-or-treaters, and I sat close to him on the porch as we shared a blanket. He draped his arm around me, and I nuzzled into his shoulder, tipping my chin up, our breaths mingling together in the cold autumn air. I swore he was going to kiss me, he even lowered his head a fraction of an inch, but when I skimmed my fingertips over his neck to the back of his head, he stilled.

"You're freezing. Let's get you inside."

He grabbed hold of my hand, wrapping his warm fingers around mine, and kissed the center of my palm. Yeah, it was cold, and, yes, I *might* have been freezing, but if he took me upstairs, he could warm me up with body heat.

As I lay in bed that night, with Wes fast asleep next to me, I texted Vivienne.

Either I'm hideous or he's turned into a monk.

VIV

Still no P in V?

Nope.

I bit the corner of my lip. Maybe this was how it was going to be for the next few months. Torture. Absolute torture.

I give up.

———

Two weeks had passed since Wes had started acting like a maniac. Piles of books had shown up overnight. Each day, a new package arrived, and he'd cleared out the third room upstairs for the nursery.

"You know we have months until he comes right?" I asked, sorting through Wes's closet for another hoodie. He lounged on the bed, his laptop open, as he texted someone, probably one or both of his parents. All four of us were on a text thread now, Abby, Jeff, Wes, and me. I had also been added to the larger family text chain that included Dani and her husband, Colin.

"Yeah, but his room still has to be painted—"

I whirled on him. "Do. Not."

He lifted his gaze, one eyebrow arched. "What?"

"I am painting his room. I'm going to do a mural."

"You can do the mural, but I don't want—"

"Wesley Louis Isaacson." I advanced on him with a hanger. "Do not tell me I cannot paint my own son's room."

He wrestled the plastic hanger from my white-knuckled grip. "We can hire someone to do it. You can do the mural after."

"Absolutely not. I am painting."

He curled his hand around my neck, and for fuck's sake, he *knew* I couldn't say no to him when he did that. "I want you to do a mural. It'll be beautiful and the best present you can give to our son, but let someone else come and paint his room in a few hours."

My shoulders dropped when he massaged the tight muscle at the base of my spine. He tenderly kissed my neck, barely a brush of his lips, not enough. Not nearly close to enough. "I'll take you to Home Depot this weekend. We can spend as long as you want looking at color swatches."

"And then get Chinese food?"

He wore a predatory smirk, knowing he'd caught his prey. "Of course."

"Fine."

"I'll get someone in to paint the room this week." He kissed my forehead. "What do you want from the closet?"

"Something comfy to wear."

He unzipped his Chapman University hoodie, the one that was probably twenty years old and coming undone at the seams, and held it out for me to slide into. Then he zipped it up over my belly and yanked the strings to tighten it around my neck. "Good?"

"Yeah. Feels like nothing fits me anymore."

I hadn't expected him to drop his hands down my back and cup my waist, and I squeaked out a surprised gasp, but right when I assumed he would lower his head and kiss me, he didn't.

Instead, he tapped my hip and sank down to the mattress once again. He stretched out his legs and typed something on his computer. "My mom was asking about a shower. Are you having one?"

"I, uh…" I toyed with the edge of his sweatshirt. "I don't know. Usually someone else who is not the parent plans it, but…" I swiped my hand over my hair and fixed my glasses on my nose.

Wes froze, his fingers above the keyboard, and I could practically see the cogs moving in his brain. "You haven't talked to your mom or sister about it?"

I shrugged. I'd sent them the photos from the ultrasound, to which they'd responded with felicitations, and that was it. Well, besides the ever-exciting invitation of **Can we expect you home for Thanksgiving?** from my mother.

I hadn't responded yet.

I padded over to the bed as Wes worked. He replied to an email and logged a meeting into his calendar. "Painter will be here next Tuesday." He turned to me. "What's that face for? You literally agreed to it a minute ago."

"No. I know. I did. It's not that. It's…" I took a deep breath. "My mom asked if I'm coming home for Thanksgiving."

He waited for me to continue.

"Do you want to come home with me?"

"If you want me to."

I nodded, and he offered my hand an encouraging squeeze. "It'll be weird. My family's not like yours."

"I'm excited to meet them," he said, and I huffed.

"I'd temper that. It'll be mostly silence or my mom lighting into me about something or other. Dad'll be half in the bag by the time we get there. My sister will sneer at everything and everyone."

Imagining what was waiting for us in my childhood home had me cringing, but Wes brought my hand to his mouth, kissing my palm. "I will be there. No one will say shit to you this time around. I won't let them."

He kissed my hand one more time before letting go, and my heart threatened to beat out of my chest at the sincerity in his promise. At a moment when I wanted to throw myself at him, show him how much I appreciated him with my lips and hands, he went back to typing away on his computer.

I inhaled a shaky breath, ignoring the ache deep inside needing release, and stood up. "I'm going to work for a bit."

I made my way out of his bedroom, which I supposed had become my bedroom since I had slept there every night. And yet, it was nothing like I'd assumed it would be. With each passing day, he was sweeter to me than the day before, but his eyes barely lingered on me. At least not in the way I hoped they would.

Before, his attention used to sometimes fix on my mouth, and he'd absently lick his own lips, though he always held back because that was what I'd wanted. But now that I wanted him to touch and kiss and caress me, all his fervor was gone.

Sometimes I saw flickers of it, when I'd catch him staring or when his fingers drifted down my leg, yet it was gone as soon as I noticed. And every inch he pulled away might as well have been a mile.

I closed the door of my bedroom and settled on the bed, reaching for the vibrator I had hidden away at the bottom of the nightstand. Lately, it'd been getting a lot of use, yet even the alleviation of an orgasm didn't seem to help.

Maybe I was hormonal, a little overemotional, but between the stress already building about seeing my family and not being able to connect in the way I wanted to with Wes, I was one big ball of anxiety. Our parenting class didn't help either.

CHAPTER TWENTY-SEVEN

While Maggie had been quiet all night, I hadn't thought anything of it until we arrived home and she immediately marched to her room. Usually we hung out and watched a movie or something, but she trudged right upstairs and closed the door. She never closed her door anymore.

Hell, she was never in her room anymore.

She only kept her clothes in there, which was illogical to me, but I was operating on her timeline. If she wanted to move them, she would.

I got ready for bed and sank down to the mattress, reading a *Variety* article on my iPad. A few minutes later, I heard Maggie shuffle into the bathroom, followed by running water. Nothing out of the ordinary.

Except a few minutes later, when the water had already been shut off, I heard no other movement.

"Hey, you all right?" I called.

A few seconds passed before she answered. "Fine."

She didn't sound fine, and I walked down the hall to knock on the closed door. "What's going on?"

On the other side of the wood, she sniffled and cleared her throat. "Nothing."

"Maggie."

"Go back to bed."

"No. I can tell something's wrong." When she didn't respond, I put my hand on the knob. "I'm coming in."

"No."

I opened the door, and she whirled on me, her dark eyes rimmed with red. Her glasses lay discarded on the sink, her hair was down and tousled. Even though she was angry, she was still the most beautiful woman I'd ever seen.

"You don't understand what the word *no* means anymore?"

"Not when you're upset."

She turned her back to me. "Leave me alone."

"Is that really what you want?"

She hunched over, allowing me to see myself in the reflection in the mirror. My brow narrowed in confusion and frustration when she said, "It doesn't matter what I want."

I moved behind her, skimming my hands down her arms to where her fingers white-knuckled the sink. "Of course it does."

She breathed out an irritated sound.

"What do you need?" I kissed her head. "How can I help?"

"I..." She lifted her face, her watery eyes briefly meeting mine in the mirror before dropping again, and I couldn't have that. I gently spun her around, but her attention stayed down on my bare chest then sank lower to my cotton sleep pants. After a moment, she folded her arms and shot her gaze to the shower.

"What's wrong?"

"I thought..."

"What?" I shoved my hand through my hair. "Come on, Mags. You're killing me here."

"You're killing me," she mumbled, and I rolled my eyes at her petulant tone.

"Tell me the problem so I can fix it."

"You won't."

"Yes, I will," I said, my voice rising in exasperation.

She moved her jaw back and forth like she was chewing on her words, and I wished she would spit them out already.

"Are you not feeling good? Is it your back or ribs?"

She shook her head.

"Then what? What is it?"

She darted her eyes back to my face. "It's you!"

"Me?" I stepped back from her. "What did I do?"

"Nothing." She huffed. "You have done nothing."

I sat on the edge of the tub and scrubbed my hands down my face. "I don't understand why you're upset."

She dropped her gaze to her bare feet on the floor, all of her sudden bluster gone. "Tonight, one of the dads in the room asked if it's okay to..."

I filled in the gap for her. "He asked if it was okay to have sex with his wife."

She nodded, her nose crinkling when she sniffled.

"Can you connect the dots for me because I'm having trouble?"

Her toes wriggled on the tile. "Am I... Do you still..." She bit into the corner of her lip as she lifted her chin back up, her shoulders drooping. "Do you still want me like that?"

"Like that?" I blinked a few times until my brain caught up to her meaning. Then I stood up with as much control as possible and slowly stepped in front of her, using the tip of my index finger to force her chin up. If I touched her with any other part of my body, I might lose all control in my insistence to prove I still wanted her *like that*. "You think I don't want you?"

The infuriating woman shrugged. As if every one of my cells wasn't on fire for her.

"You think I haven't wanted you every second of every day since we met?"

Her throat worked on a swallow, and I was tempted to wrap my hand around it, feel her pulse, taste her skin, but I kept myself as still as possible.

"You think I don't dream of you naked? That I don't wake up every morning wanting—needing—you, and the only thing that helps is getting out of bed before you do, so I can run until I'm too exhausted to come home and tear your clothes off?"

Her eyes were wide and a little wild, and I lowered my mouth to hers, speaking my words against her lips. "You are all I think about. Your smell, your taste, your body, there is nothing about you I don't like. Do you understand? I want you all the time."

Then I took her chin between my thumb and index finger and pressed one kiss against her mouth. Her arms finally dropped from where they'd been folded over the top of her stomach, and she held on to my waist. I wrapped my other hand around her hair, holding it so she had to meet my gaze, listen to what I had to say. "I've only *just* been holding back from rolling on top of you every day because I'm afraid of hurting you. What happened after I came home from Los Angeles, it will never happen again. It can never happen again."

She panted through sweetly parted lips, and I was desperate to taste them but had to get the rest out.

"I didn't realize how you were feeling. If I knew I was hurting you, I wouldn't have been so careful." I huffed a self-deprecating laugh. "Or as careful as I want to be." I let my hand on her chin drag down to the base of her throat. "These past few weeks have been torture for me. Tell me what you need, and I'll give it to you. Whatever it is." *Put me out of my fucking misery*, I didn't say, but maybe she could read my mind because she raised a brow.

"You honestly don't know?"

"I want to hear you say it."

Her shoulders rose on a deep breath. "I need you, Wes. I need to feel you."

I didn't hesitate to kiss her the way I had wanted to for what felt like centuries, with my hands tight around her head and neck, holding her in place so I could take what I wanted. I licked into her mouth, and she shivered against me, the stiff peaks of her nipples rubbing against my chest. I wanted to howl at my own stupidity. In trying to protect her, I had made her feel like she wasn't all my dreams come true.

"I'm sorry." I dragged my teeth down her jaw. "You are everything I want. All I want."

She bowed back slightly, though with her belly, there wasn't very far to move. "I thought maybe you weren't attracted to me anymore."

Clearly, I was being way too cautious with her if I had let it get this bad. "Let's go." I took hold of her hand and led her out of the bathroom and into *our* bedroom. "Tomorrow, we're moving your clothes in here. Tonight, you'll be lucky if I let you sleep before midnight. Come here."

I urged her arms up so I could remove her T-shirt. Her breasts were full and heavy, so much more than when we'd first met, and I bent to suck one of her dark nipples into my mouth. She gasped my name, her fingernails biting into the skin of my shoulder.

"You're so sensitive."

She hummed an agreement. "Hormones, I guess."

Releasing her nipple, I trailed my thumb over the wet skin and moved to her other breast, licking and sucking at it until she was writhing in my grasp. "Think I could make you come like this?"

"I-I don't…"

I straightened, taking her mouth again while my fingers traced continuous circles around her nipple, and she shivered in my grasp. "I think I can," I said, sucking at the skin below her ear. "I think I could get you to orgasm doing just this." Then I gently twisted the hard tip, and she sucked in a breath. "Again?"

She nodded, and I bent to flick at her other nipple with my tongue. Her fingers combed into my hair, tugging at the roots and holding me to her. "Oh god, Wes," she moaned, her thighs rubbing together, and I was tempted to tease my fingers between them, but I held on tight to her waist as I kept my other hand on her breast. I wanted to make her come as many times in as many ways as I could. Alternating to the other side again, I scraped my teeth over her, and she let out a sweet little whimper. "Oh please."

Squeezing the heavy weights in my hands, I pushed them together, licking down the valley I'd made then pinched the peaks until she shook. "Come for me," I rasped, breathing over her glistening skin, and her mouth dropped open on a silent moan as I tenderly twisted her nipples. When she cried out, I smiled into the soft pillow of her breast. "That's it."

Then I sank even lower, mapping kisses in a line down her stomach. I knew she was self-conscious of the stretch marks, and I kissed those too. On my knees, I wrapped my fingers around both of her wrists, urging her to place her hands on my shoulders. "Hold on to me."

When she followed my direction, I hooked my fingers around the elastic of her pajama pants and tugged them down, helping her to step out of them so she was left in her under-wear. In the low light of our bedroom, I couldn't see all of the imperfections she sometimes complained about, but even if I could, I wouldn't care. She was beautiful, with her thick, dark hair and those lips. And she was carrying *my child.*

With a reverent touch, I skimmed my palm around her stomach and down her hips. "You're so gorgeous. I thought so that night in the bar. But now..." I pressed my mouth to her lower stomach, right above where her underwear lay. "Even more so."

I dropped her panties to the floor, and she stepped out of those too before I guided her down to the bed. I took my time kissing and massaging her ankle and calf, but when I nuzzled her thigh, she jerked away.

"I'm ticklish there."

I drew my teeth over her soft skin, and she wrenched her leg away again with a soft whine. "Don't."

I laughed against her skin then gave her other leg the same treatment, rubbing the muscles I knew were getting more and more sore with each passing week. After one last kiss to her thigh, I positioned her higher on the bed and set a pillow behind her back.

"I want you to watch me," I told her. "See how much I love this. How much I love you."

Her jaw dropped at my words, but I was too busy guiding her legs over my shoulders to ease her into my confession. It was my fault she'd become insecure in herself and our relationship. I had a lot of making up to do.

Using my thumbs to hold her open, I licked up her center then lifted my gaze to her while I sucked and nibbled. She didn't break eye contact with me, even as her hips jerked.

"I guess I need to do this every day," I said, sliding my middle finger into her. "I don't mind. It's my favorite thing, loving you."

"Wes." Her eyes watered as she reached out her hands,

tugging me down, and I latched back on to her, licking up her sweetness until she was wriggling beneath me. I crooked a second finger into her, working them so she threw her head back to the pillow, her orgasm barreling down on her *and* me. It was too quick, too frantic, and I made it up to her with the next one, placing sloppy, openmouthed kisses along her thighs as I circled my wet fingers on her swollen clit. She moaned, her legs tensing, but I didn't speed up or touch her harder like she asked. I wanted to stretch this one out, make it last, remind her I was in this for the long haul. I wasn't going anywhere.

"Please," Maggie whimpered, canting her hips closer to me.

I nibbled her drenched skin. "Please, what?"

"Please make me come."

"I love hearing you beg."

Her skin prickled with goose bumps at my words, and I adored how she responded to me, needed my reassurance, because I loved giving it to her. Loved being the one to make her feel this way. I languidly stroked my fingers in and out of her. "You're mine."

"Yes," she breathed.

"Say it."

She met my gaze once again. "I love you, Wes. I'm yours."

I ignored my instinct to crush her with my body and instead spoke the words I knew she craved. "You're such a good girl for me," I rasped, and she whined. "I'll take care of you. Don't worry."

I licked at her, wedging my shoulders to open her legs more so she couldn't close them reflexively. As she peaked again, she fisted the bedsheet in her hand, every part of her tensing as I felt her climax against my tongue, until she relaxed little by little, first her feet and legs, then hips and fingers.

Finally, she lifted her head, her cheeks red and eyes dazed, and I wiped at my mouth before crawling over her. "I told you

I'd take care of you." I pressed a kiss to the corner of her mouth and temple. "Always."

I yanked my pants down and off my legs and gripped my cock. It was hard as iron in my fist. "Now give me your mouth."

She sat up and took my length between her perfect lips, wetting me with her even more perfect tongue, but after a few moments, I backed away, gently rolling her to her side. "I need to be inside you. It's been forever."

She agreed with a hum, reaching her arm over her head, pulling me down to her shoulder. I nipped at the slope of her neck and lined myself up at her entrance, thrusting deep inside her in one easy movement. She sighed, her head going lax against the pillow, and I sucked on her throat as I lifted her leg, granting me more room to rock into her.

She moaned, pressing her ass back against me. "Feels so good."

I didn't have words to respond, my pleasure stealing the last of my cognitive abilities. It had been months, but it might as well have been decades. Maggie was warm and wet and making my favorite sounds. She was everything. My heart and soul. My most treasured love and agonizing fear. I didn't think I believed in soul mates, but knowing how it felt to be without her, I was certain she was my other half.

I curled one arm around her neck and collarbone, squeezing her breast, drifting my other hand down between her legs, paying attention to that sweet little bud at the cleft of her sex.

"I love you," I told her, and she tipped her face to me, her mouth open and hungry for mine.

"I love you so much," she said, breathless, her skin hot and damp, and I toyed with her nipple, sucking on her throat. "I think... Oh god." I could feel her starting to fall apart again, heat pulsing around me, pulling me over the edge with her. "I think I knew from the beginning."

My agreement was lost on a low moan as my own release took me soaring, and when I finally came back to earth, out of breath and lying on my back, Maggie turned into my side, kissing the middle of my chest. I smiled up at the ceiling. "We should have been doing that the whole time."

She nuzzled her nose against my pec. "Wasted opportunities."

"Don't rub it in." I laughed, curling my hand around the back of her head. "This is how it should always be."

She mumbled something I didn't quite catch as she wrapped her arm around my waist and yawned against my shoulder. A minute later, she was asleep.

And *this* was how it was going to be.

CHAPTER TWENTY-EIGHT

Wes

I parked the car across from the little two-story house with white siding in need of a good power-wash, but from how Maggie described it, I'd expected it to be a lot worse for wear. Then again, it wasn't the house she struggled with; it was the people inside it.

She twirled a lock of hair around her finger. "My sister's here already."

"Theresa," I said, reminding myself of their names. "Her husband is Corey, and their kids are..." I drummed my thumb against the steering wheel. "Julie and...Nate?"

"Noah."

"Hey." I took hold of her hand, forcing her to stop fidgeting. "We'll get through it. It'll be great."

"Yeah." She refused to meet my eyes even as she nodded. "Great."

I tipped her chin up. "What's our code word for when you want to leave?"

She quirked a brow, thinking for a moment, then tugged on my gray cashmere sweater. "Sweater weather."

"Perfect." I motioned down to my clothes, worried I was a bit overdressed. Although I wasn't about to show up to her parents' house in a T-shirt and jeans. "How do I look? Should I lose the jacket?"

She dragged her hand down my shoulder, over my blazer. "You look hot, as per usual. How did I end up with someone who dresses like this, while I wear leggings and sweatshirts?"

I plucked one of the ruffles of her green dress. It was a rare occasion when she wore anything that wasn't spandex or cotton. "I like you in leggings and sweatshirts."

"I wish I were in leggings and a sweatshirt now, but then my mom would be all, *You couldn't even find something nice to wear for one night,*" she said in a nasal voice, which I supposed was an imitation of Sandy Levendoski.

"You look beautiful." I brushed my hand over her hair. "I haven't seen you without your glasses in weeks. I almost forgot what you look like without them."

"Like a different person?" She leaned into me, aiming for a kiss, and I obliged her, teasing my tongue along her bottom lip before pulling away.

"Like the night I met you." When the worry lines between her brow refused to move, I smoothed the pad of my thumb along her eyebrow. "I love you, you know."

"I know." She finally gave in to a smile, taming my own nerves.

"Come on." I nodded toward the house she'd grown up in. "We got this."

With the reusable shopping bag filled with flowers and the two pies Maggie had baked in one hand, I followed her inside.

The man who I assumed was Mr. Levendoski was seated in a plaid recliner, his attention on the football game. He wore jeans and a T-shirt, and I tried not to feel self-conscious about my dress pants and leather shoes. Two teenagers slumped on the couch along the wall, their eyes glued to their phones, and

Maggie stepped into the middle of the small but tidy living room. "Hey, everyone."

"Hey, Margaret," her father said, then threw his hand out to the television. "Oh, come on! That's holding!"

She glanced over her shoulder to me, her eyes already weary, and I wrapped my arm around her waist for support. "This is my boyfriend, Wes."

"The guy who knocked you up, huh?" Mr. Levendoski brought his beer to his lips, assessing me. It would've been a lot more intimidating if his speech weren't already slurred by alcohol.

"Dad," Maggie chided, but he shrugged, uncaring.

I held out my hand. "Nice to meet you, Mr. Levendoski."

"Well, since you're the father of my grandchild, I suppose you could call me Dale." Then he shook my hand. "You like football?"

"I catch a game from time to time."

"Wes was at the Super Bowl last year," Maggie said, and Dale coughed on his swig of beer.

"No shit. How'd that happen?"

I didn't know how much Maggie had divulged to them about what I did, so I avoided telling him about the box seats with Chris. "I got tickets through my work."

Dale's mouth tipped down as he studied me more thoroughly, but as soon as the commercial ended and the game returned, he didn't seem to care anymore.

Maggie bent to hug her niece and nephew. "How are you guys?"

They both mumbled something that sounded like "Good."

"How's school?"

"Terrible." Julie's lip trembled. "My boyfriend broke up with me."

"I'm sorry," Maggie told her niece. "Breakups are always hard."

Julie ignored the sentiment and stomped off.

"This is Wes," Maggie informed Noah, who spared one quick glance up from his phone.

"Yeah. Hey. I'm Noah."

"Nice to meet you," I said, although the kid was already back in his own world on his cell phone game.

"Happy belated birthday." Maggie tossed him an envelope. "Don't spend it all in one place."

That got Noah's attention, and he ripped it open, finding a Visa gift card for fifty dollars. He jumped up and hugged Maggie. "Thanks, Aunt Maggie!"

"I didn't know what fourteen-year-olds are into now."

"Money. We're into money."

I muffled a laugh, and Maggie pinched her nephew's side, which he playfully pretended to be hurt from before he flopped back down to the sofa, resuming his game.

Maggie hung up our coats in the small hall closet on our way to the little dining room, directly off the kitchen. Corey stood in the corner, and Maggie introduced us.

"I'm staying out of their way," he explained, his eyes flicking toward the kitchen.

"Well, you make a nice statue," Maggie told him, and he slanted her a chagrined half smile, as if he was afraid she was going to tattle on him for hiding away.

She did no such thing as she took the pies from me and made her way into the kitchen. "Hi, Mom, Theresa."

Theresa, with the same thick, dark hair as Maggie but cut short above her shoulders, tipped her chin at Maggie, preoccupied with mashing potatoes. Their mother huffed. "Finally. You're late."

With her eyebrows slanted behind a pair of glasses, Mrs.

Levendoski didn't appear very happy to see her daughter, and even though I knew all about her contemptuous personality, I didn't expect her to be so aggressive right out of the gate. Maggie hadn't been home in a long time; I'd figured there would at least be a pat on the back.

I slid my hand between Maggie's shoulder blades. She was tense under my palm. "I'm sorry we're late," I said. "It's my fault. I didn't fill up the tank before we left, so we had to stop."

Which wasn't a total lie, but I was taking a bullet for Maggie. Between baking and being unable to decide what to wear, she was the one who'd made us late. Though not by much—fifteen minutes, at most.

"You're Wes," Mrs. Levendoski stated like it was an accusation.

I handed her the spray of flowers from the bag. "Thank you for having me, Sandy."

Although she seemed to flinch at the use of her first name, she didn't correct me. "It's nice to meet you." She tentatively took the flowers then turned to her daughter. "And you're looking...big."

"Thanks." Maggie clucked her tongue, her hands dropping to her sides. "I guess."

"I only gained twenty pounds with you and your sister."

Maggie opened her mouth, maybe to defend herself, but I wasn't going to make her do that. She'd been doing it long enough. It was my turn now.

I pulled her into my side, smiling broadly. "I'm keeping her well-fed, don't worry. Wouldn't want you to think she's malnourished."

"Certainly not." Mrs. Levendoski gestured to Maggie's stomach. "The more you gain, the harder it'll be to lose."

I toggled my gaze between the three women in the kitchen and noted their physical differences. Maggie was taller and more full-figured, even without being pregnant, and next to me, she ran her hands over her hips and thighs. I couldn't stand that she was insecure.

"Maggie knows her weight isn't important." I arched my brow in challenge. "As long as she and our baby are healthy, that's all that matters." There was no way Mrs. Levendoski could argue against that point.

Sandy pressed her hand to her flat stomach. "Yes, well…" She let out a sigh, like she couldn't be bothered to continue the conversation anymore. "The table is already set, Maggie," she said pointedly, "so why don't you find somewhere to put these?"

Maggie took the flowers from her mother and searched for a vase in the back of the cabinet underneath the sink.

Her sister finished up with the potatoes. "I'm Theresa, by the way."

"Nice to meet you," I said, meeting Maggie at the sink to fill the vase with water while she trimmed the stems.

Theresa wiped her hands off on a dish towel and stretched her neck to pin Maggie with a sharp stare, on the other side of me. "I haven't heard from you in a while."

Maggie's brow crimped. "I haven't heard from *you* in a while."

"I'm busy with work."

"Me too."

"I started on nights at the ER." Theresa propped her hand on her hip, her head tilting, and I didn't know if I was supposed to referee this game or if I should hide away weapons, including the glass vase. I moved it aside, to the corner of the counter.

"Okay. I'm sorry, but texting you isn't really at the forefront of my mind right now." Maggie pointed to her belly. "I kinda got a full plate at the moment."

"Most women can handle being pregnant. What's your problem that you can't multitask?"

Maggie pivoted around to reach for my hand. "I multitask fine. Maybe I don't want to call or text to hear you on your high fucking horse."

Theresa huffed as their mother hissed, "Language, Margaret. Why can't we get through one dinner together without you cursing?"

Maggie pulled me out of the kitchen, but right as she moved to sit down at the dining room table, her mother poked her head around the doorframe. "Get in here and carry the vegetables to the table."

I squeezed her knee. "I'll get it."

"You're our guest," Sandy said to me as I swept by her to grab the green beans and sweet potatoes.

The three Levendoski women were armed and dangerous with their words, but with the speed at which they threw their darts at one another, I couldn't keep up. I needed to slow it down, give them time to cool off. "And it's my pleasure to help."

My second trip was for the gravy and mashed potatoes. "Maggie was up this morning making the pies. I can't wait to try them. She's an amazing baker," I told Sandy, offering to take the turkey off her hands and setting it down on the table. "But I'm sure you know that. She made a three-tier cake for my birthday."

Her mother didn't acknowledge the statement, and Maggie leaned into my side, whispering, "Sweater weather, sweater weather, sweater weather."

"It's not so bad," I said with a kiss to her temple. We hadn't even eaten yet, and I hoped once everyone had a full belly, they'd chill out.

"It's about to be," Maggie muttered as Sandy called

everyone to the table, and Dale exchanged his empty beer bottle for another. He was the last to sit down.

"Couldn't we find a bigger table, for Christ's sake," he grumbled. "Margaret can barely fit."

This table could comfortably seat six . Stuffing in extra people left no elbow room, let alone enough space for Maggie, who was seated at the corner, the wooden leg between her own.

Sandy thumped her hand on the table. "It's Thanksgiving. Can you cut taking the Lord's name in vain for one day?"

Dale swallowed down about half his beer in one gulp then saluted her. "My apologies. I didn't know Jesus was at the table with us to be offended."

"We need to say grace." Sandy made the sign of the cross and sped through the prayer before carving the turkey, carefully setting slices on everyone's plates.

"No phones at the table," Theresa reminded Noah, who tried to hide it under the table, next to me.

Dinner was silent, intermittently broken up by the scraping of utensils or Dale saying something like, "Scoop me out more of the sweet potatoes, will ya?"

It was incredibly awkward. And got more so when Sandy broke the silence. "So, what are your plans for the baby?"

"Plans?" Maggie repeated.

"When are you baptizing him?"

Maggie glanced at me, but I shrugged, caught off guard by the question. This conversation was full of land mines, and we had to tread carefully.

"I don't think we're going to do that," Maggie said after a while.

"What do you mean?"

"Wes wasn't really raised in a church, and his dad is Jewish. Besides, I—"

Sandy set her elbows on the table, pointing her fork at me. "You're Jewish?"

"No. My stepdad is, but he's really more secular than anything, and my mom never converted."

"So, you don't have any religion?"

Dale's utensils clattered to his plate as he stood noisily from the table. He snatched another beer out of the fridge and made his way back down the hall, muttering, "You and your fucking religion. Never saved us anything."

Sandy ignored her husband and stared at me, waiting for my answer. "I believe in God, but I wouldn't say I'm religious."

"But if you don't baptize your baby, he'll live in purgatory," Sandy informed me, one hundred percent serious.

"Purgatory isn't a thing," Maggie said.

"Limbo, it's where all souls go who can't get into heaven."

Maggie blew out a slow breath, and much to my surprise, Theresa stepped in. "Mom, the Church doesn't really teach that anymore."

"Still." Sandy waved her hand in the air. "You're not going to baptize him, so what? You'll raise him without any religion?"

"We haven't talked about it much," I said, finding Maggie's hand under the table to give it a reassuring squeeze. "But I promise you, we will think about it."

"You aren't even married."

Maggie sighed. "Lots of people have kids without being married, Mom."

"Lots of people aren't you," Sandy snapped. "I raised you better than that." She grabbed her plate, stamping away from the table to the kitchen, and I heard "The Imperial March" in my head.

Julie and Noah immediately rescued their cell phones from

their pockets, and when Theresa reached for them, Julie scooted away. "Brayden texted me. I have to text him back."

Before Theresa could say anything, her daughter scurried away from the table, her head down as she hastily typed away on her cell. Noah followed. "Duane's going to the movies tonight. Can I go?"

Theresa's elbows clunked on the table as she rubbed her temples. "Fine. Your dad will drive you. I have to go into work later."

Sandy heaved yet another sigh from where she stood by the sink, her voice rising so everyone in the house could hear. "I spent all this time making this meal, and no one can even sit for twenty minutes. Everyone is running everywhere. Why do I do this to myself?"

Although Theresa didn't pick up her head, I caught her eye roll as Maggie poked at her turkey.

"That's six! Finally!" Dale cheered from the living room.

Sandy filed out of the kitchen, through the dining room to the hall. "The television is so loud. No wonder you're going deaf. Turn the volume down!"

The volume stayed where it was. "I can't hear a goddamn thing over your constant squawking!"

Sandy muttered something about "All I do for this family," as she circled back toward the kitchen, and Maggie stood up, trailing her.

"I really wish you wouldn't say things like that, Mom."

"Things like what?"

"That you raised me better than this. I'm not doing anything wrong. I'm having a baby with the man I love."

Sandy huffed out a sardonic laugh. "The man you love? That's what you said about Brian and about that boy in high school, who smoked cigarettes."

"Scott," Theresa supplied, and Maggie raised her palm to

her sister in a *What are you doing?* sign. I didn't understand why Theresa fueled the ongoing conflict between her mother and sister.

"You go from one guy to another," Sandy said, her hand flapping above her head like every guy Maggie had ever been with was floating in the air.

I clenched my fist to keep from snapping my dinner plate in half. I had to stay calm for Maggie.

"I do not go from one guy to another," she bit out. "I was married to Brian for six years."

"And you ran right into him." Sandy gestured in my direction.

I sprung up from the table, ready to let loose, but Maggie was already speaking. "Why can't you be happy for me? For once?"

Dale's voice cut in. "Hey! Shut up in there!"

Sandy stabbed an indignant finger through the air. "You want me to be happy for my daughter to have a baby out of wedlock?"

"It's not 1950 anymore. Lots of people do it."

"So, I should be happy you're like every other person sleeping around?"

I now fully understood the mistake I had made by underestimating how much damage could be done over a dinner. "Hey, whoa, there is no need to—"

"I'm not sleeping around!" Maggie shouted. "And even if I was, that doesn't give you the right to be so judgmental!"

Sandy threw her hands up. "How am I being judgmental?"

Maggie's gaze coasted around the kitchen, her eyes landing on me, and I knew she was seconds away from losing it. I reached out my hand to keep her steady. She blinked twice then faced her mother once again. "You're accusing me of things you think are bad. It's like you're purposely trying to make me feel guilty about my decisions."

"Well, I'm not going to baby you. You're an adult. You can make whatever decision you want to." Sandy flicked her long index finger between Maggie and me. "It doesn't matter what I think. If it did, you wouldn't be flitting around, wasting your life. What happens when it doesn't work out with this one? What are you going to do with the baby? You think you can support a child with your pictures?"

Maggie inhaled a shaky breath, and that was fucking it. I was done. "That's enough, Sandy—"

"Mrs. Levendoski!"

"Quit your yapping!" Dale yelled.

"Mrs. Levendoski, you may not like me or the choices your daughter makes, but there is no reason to be so abusive."

"Abusive?"

"Yes. You're emotionally abusive."

"You don't get to come to my house as a guest and accuse me of things!"

I kept my voice low and even but a knife's edge. "And you don't get to insult Maggie in front of me. I don't care if you're her mother, the president of the United States, or Jesus Christ himself, I will not stand by and listen while you break her down like you've been doing her entire life. She wanted to come today to introduce me to her family, but as far as I'm concerned, we should have stayed home. Maggie is *my* family now, and I will protect her from whatever and whomever tries to hurt her, including you."

"I have never in my life been talked to so rudely before!"

Dale appeared in the doorway of the kitchen. "What the hell is going on?"

Sandy placed her hand on her chest, like she was the victim. "Maggie's boyfriend is insulting me. In my own home."

When her husband didn't move, she threw her hand out. "Aren't you going to say anything?"

I turned to Dale, who finished the rest of his beer before throwing the bottle so it smashed in the sink. Maggie jolted, and I placed a hand on the back of her head, tucking her closer into my side. I needed to get her out of here.

"I can't get any fucking peace and quiet in my own goddamn home. Get the hell out of here," he said in our direction.

"Gladly." I narrowed my eyes on him and then Sandy. "Enjoy your pies. It's the last time Maggie will give you anything."

"All she's ever given me is headaches," Sandy said, but it was immediately followed up by Dale saying, "Oh, will you shut up for once in your life."

With our coats in hand, I hustled Maggie outside and opened the car door for her. "I'm sorry. I'm so sorry."

She tried on a smile, but it wavered. "It's okay."

"It's not okay."

She lifted her hand to her cheek, but I was already there, wiping her tear away.

"Let's get you home."

As I drove, I found some soft rock station on the radio but kept the volume low, so Maggie wasn't left alone with her thoughts since I wasn't in the right state of mind to think or speak clearly about what happened. Especially with her sniffling next to me. I wasn't a violent guy, but I would have thoroughly enjoyed burning that house to the ground, leaving no evidence of Maggie's lingering pain brought on by her family.

I white-knuckled the steering wheel, but once we were on the highway, I relaxed with every mile. My shoulders lowered, my jaw unclenched, and eventually I was able to find my words. "How you doing over there?"

She shifted in her seat, facing me, and I chanced a glance in her direction. Her nose was red, eyes swollen and bloodshot, lips puffy. Fuck the house. I'd burn the whole goddamn world down.

"Mags, I wish—" I couldn't even finish my sentence because she broke down, this time in loud, long sobs that racked her body. She bent over, a high, keening noise leaving her with every hiccupped breath.

At the first opportunity, I pulled over to the shoulder and parked the car before digging around the console for tissues. I handed them over and unbuckled my seat belt to turn and gather her in my arms. "Don't cry over them. They don't deserve it."

"I'm..." She wiped her face. "I'm c-c-crying be-because no..." She blew her nose. "No one has ever stood up for me before."

When she finally caught her breath and wiped her eyes, a mixture of amazement and hurt crossed her features. I felt them etch into my own frown. Hurt that Maggie had lived so long with those assholes for a family and amazed that this wonderful, loving, funny woman was so surprised anyone would stand up for her.

Because there was nothing I wouldn't do for her.

"I can promise you two things." I linked my fingers with hers and kissed the back of her hand. "I will always stand up for you, no matter what." I settled our locked hands in her lap. "And I will always listen to your code word from now on."

That got a laugh out of her. "I love you."

"Sweetheart, you have no idea."

CHAPTER TWENTY-NINE

Maggie

Back at home, Wes ushered me into the kitchen, where he opened the refrigerator. Neither of us had eaten much. "What are you hungry for?"

I leaned against the counter, bone-weary. "Nothing."

"You want a sandwich?"

I shook my head.

"Want to order something?"

"Really, I'm not hungry."

He let the door shut and came to stand in front of me. "What can I do for you? Tell me what to do because I need to do something. Anything."

"Hold me."

His mouth curled into a relieved smile as he pulled me to him, directing my hands up to his neck. "Alexa, play 'Maggie May' by Rod Stewart." He looped his arms around my waist, holding me as close as possible with my belly between us, swaying gently in rhythm to the song. "How's this?"

Being in his arms was more than enough to calm me down, put the world back on its axis. "Perfect."

He hummed along with Rod in my ear, slightly off-key, and I tightened my grip on him, fingers playing with the hair at the nape of his neck. He let out one of his delicious groans and held me closer if that was possible, tracing the tip of his nose up my throat. His kiss was soft behind my ear, sending goose bumps over my skin.

"You still feel tense," he said, his hands pressing into the muscles along my spine. He rubbed at my sides, massaging my sore ribs, and soon I was dead weight. I felt his laughter rumble in his chest, his breath against my ear as he hoisted me up like a rag doll. "How about a bath?"

"Mmm. That sounds good."

He steered me upstairs to the bathroom, where he deposited me on the closed toilet lid, then dug through the cabinet. I didn't often take a bath, but I still had some of the fancy stuff stowed away for the rare occasion. He raised the jar of pink salt above his head like a trophy. "Here we go." He sat on the edge of the tub, testing the temperature of the water before plugging the drain and adding the salt. "Nice and warm."

Then he stood me up, removing my cardigan, dress, and tights, taking a long moment to stare at me in my bra and underwear. His nostrils flared. "I hope you don't believe your mom. You're perfect no matter how much weight you gain or lose. You know that, right?"

I nodded, though I absently traced the stretch marks on my lower abdomen. He pushed my hands away and knelt down to the floor, kissing the jagged lines marring my skin, no matter how much oil and lotion I rubbed on them. With his thumbs hooked around the elastic of my panties, he dragged them off my legs, his fingertips gliding back up my thighs as he stood to unclasp my bra so it, too, fell to the floor.

He gazed down at me with such concern, I would cry if I had any tears left. That this man would be so painstakingly sweet to draw me a bath with the perfect temperature and handle me with kid gloves, providing me something so simple and yet so rare, I didn't know how to pay him back.

But then again, that was the point, right?

Love wasn't about IOUs or check marks in a column. It was about supporting and caring for those you loved. It was helping someone into a warm bath and massaging their sore muscles without asking anything in return. Love wasn't something to be earned or traded. It was given freely and without limitation.

That was what Wes showed me. Unconditional love.

As I sank into the water, Wes crouched on the floor next to the tub, rolling a towel up to put behind my head.

"Thank you."

He lifted a shoulder, not understanding.

"Thank you for this, too, but I meant thank you for what you said."

His chest rose on a long inhale, his eyes drifting up to the tiled wall behind me. After a minute, he dropped his hand into the water, cupping some into his palm to drop it over my bent knees. He did that two more times before he said, "Whatever you decide to do about your parents, your sister, if you want to be in contact with them or not, if you want to see them or not, I will support you. Just know I don't expect you to say thank you."

"Even if I murdered someone?"

"I'll get rid of the body."

I caught his hand as he once again brought it up to spill water down my legs. "Even if you don't expect it, I'm going to tell you because I am so grateful."

He leaned forward to smooth hair back from my face, his fingers lingering by my temple. "You are the only thing that matters." He drew a wet line down my jaw as his gaze landed on my mouth. He traced my lips with his thumb, color rising high in his cheeks as familiar fire lit his eyes. His hand glided down my throat, between my breasts, to my stomach. "You and our baby, you're my family, and I will always protect what is mine."

Mine.

I sat up to capture his mouth in a kiss, but he barely let my tongue dip into his mouth before he gently urged me back down to the water.

"Let me make you feel good," he said, his palm curving around my breast. They were so big now, it felt good to be in the bath, alleviating some of the pressure from my back and shoulders. "Lie back. Close your eyes. Relax."

I did as I was told, settling against the tub, letting my head drop down to the towel.

"That's it. Now open your knees." When I did, he brushed his lips against my ear. "Good girl." He kissed the corner of my mouth. "I love how responsive you are to me."

I didn't have time to answer him, tell him it was because I trusted him, before his fingers were between my thighs. Barely a minute passed and already I was gasping his name. "Oh god, Wes..."

"I'm here." His lips ghosted over mine. "I'm here."

With his fingers plunging into me, he coaxed my mouth open like he couldn't get enough. A splash of water hit my collarbone as he moved, angling his hand under the water to press the heel of his palm against my clit, grinding down as his fingers worked inside. Encased in the warm water, the usual spark of heat didn't flood my veins. Instead, reaching my peak was like being wrapped up by a soft blanket, a slow and steady compression until it consumed me, my limbs loose and heart soaring. The only sounds were my echoing breaths and the occasional swirl of water.

I kept my eyes closed even when I heard the familiar snap

of a cap and squirt of body wash. A moment later, Wes's hands were on me again. He rubbed the arches of my feet and ankles, massaged my calves and skimmed his fingers up my thighs and hips, smoothed his fingers over the still swollen and tingling skin between my legs before brushing over my belly and breasts. He lifted each of my arms in turn, skating his soaped-up hands from shoulder to wrist then pushed his thumbs into the circle of my palm. He even kneaded my fingers.

After he finished his ministrations, he gently trickled water over my throat and collarbone until I opened my heavy-lidded eyes to him. "Feel better?"

I mumbled some kind of affirmative, and he chuckled, extending his hands to help me up. Once I was out of the tub, he wrapped a thick towel around me.

"I'm so relaxed I feel like I could pass out right now," I said, reaching for my toothbrush.

He grabbed his own and passed the toothpaste off. "I have nothing to do the next couple of days. You want to have a movie marathon?"

I nodded as I scrubbed my teeth.

"You've never seen *The Godfather*, right? We could—"

"Aren't they each, like, three hours long?" I wrinkled my nose. "For every *Godfather* we watch, I want to watch a Meg Ryan-Tom Hanks movie."

"You've got yourself a deal, Maggie May."

I started to smile, but the sudden kick in my belly had me frozen.

"What?"

"I..." I stared at my stomach. "I think... I think the baby moved."

"*What?*" He threw his toothbrush down and placed his hand over my bump. For the next two minutes, neither of us made a sound, waiting for the baby to kick again. But when he didn't, Wes sulked. "I can't feel anything."

"I'm sure he'll move again," I said, and his eyes met mine, wide and a little frantic.

"What did it feel like?"

"Like…" I poked his abs. "That."

"You think it was his finger?"

"No." I snorted. "I doubt I could feel his finger. It was probably an elbow or a foot or something."

He placed his hands at the ten and two position, waiting patiently for something to happen, while I put my toothbrush away and swiped on some moisturizer. Even after I finished my nighttime routine, he remained unmoved. A soldier on guard. I laughed. "Come on."

With his hand in mine, I led him down to our bedroom, where I threw on a T-shirt and comfy pajama pants and settled into bed. Wes stripped down to his underwear and slid next to me under the covers, placing a gentle hand on my stomach. He scooted down a few inches, his face right next to my belly button as he said, "Hey in there."

I couldn't help but giggle, it was so similar to the night we met, when he told my ovaries to "buck up."

"What are you doing?" he asked the bump. "I had your mom all relaxed until you kicked her, you know."

I combed my fingers through Wes's hair, tugging on a few strands. "I am relaxed. You're the one who's up in arms."

"I'm trying to look cool in front of our son, if you please."

"Sorry, sorry."

He huffed and dropped his attention back down, moving his palm two inches to the left. "What's your favorite thing to eat? Your mom's really into anything with a lot of salt, but I'm more of a sweet than savory guy myself." When there was no movement, he nodded. "Savory then, like Mommy. Okay."

I bit back my growing grin as I continued to toy with his hair.

"How 'bout movies? I read you can hear in there, so which ones do you like? You must have a favorite."

Again, there was nothing.

"We're going to watch *The Godfather* tomorrow. It was directed by Francis Ford—oh my god!" He jerked back. "He moved!"

I laughed. "I know."

"He moved," Wes repeated, his voice cracking with emotion. He blinked a few times and stroked my sides and across the swell of my belly. "I love you, buddy. I love you so much already, and I don't even know you yet." He sniffed and bent closer, his lips grazing my skin with each of his words. "When you finally get here, we're going to hang out all the time. You and your mom, you're my favorite people."

As if the baby understood, he moved again, and Wes exhaled an audible breath before grinning up at me.

"I think you're one of his favorite people too," I told him, and he crawled back up the mattress to lie next to me.

He kissed my forehead, temple, jaw, chin, and, finally, my mouth. "I love you."

"Love you too," I said, turning on my side so he could line up behind me. He wrapped one arm around my neck and the other around my middle, his knees bent behind mine.

"I think he's going to really like *The Godfather*," he whispered, and I barked out a big laugh.

"If you say so."

Behind me, his chest rumbled with a contented sigh, and he placed one more kiss to my neck. "Can't wait to find out."

CHAPTER THIRTY

Wes

"Ladarius, Laertes, Laik with an I or Lake spelled like the water, La—"

"Wait, wait, wait, go back." Maggie held up her fork. "Laertes? From Shakespeare?"

I tilted my head. I'd never paid much attention to those units in high school. "Uh, sure?"

We were in the baby's room, leaning up against the wall opposite of the mural she'd just finished. To celebrate, I had ordered Greek takeout and opened up our big book of baby names to resume the pursuit. "It's in Hamlet." She speared an olive. "I wonder if people actually name their kid Laertes. Feels like *a lot.*"

I nodded in agreement and continued. "Lam, Lance, Landis, Langley, Lanton—"

"I don't know about an L name. That letter isn't speaking to me."

"Nothing has been speaking to you." I closed the book, placing it between us.

"Because it's hard to name a person you haven't met yet. What if we settle on Langley, and he comes out looking...not like a Langley?"

"What does a Langley even look like?"

She pursed her lips. "Hipster mustache and bow tie?"

"You're right." I stole one of her olives. "Langley is out."

"Hey! If you wanted olives, you should have ordered your own."

"They're not on the menu," I told her. "I know you've been hungry for them lately, so I asked for them to put extra on the side."

She pouted. "You're sweet to me."

I kissed her cheek and poached another olive before digging into my gyro and fries. "You did an incredible job," I said, tipping my chin to the mural as I chewed. The jungle scene was more whimsical than realistic, but that was Maggie's style. Perfect for a baby's room. "You should be a professional artist or something."

She filched one of my fries. "I'll consider it."

She had worked on it for about two weeks and probably would have finished it earlier if I hadn't badgered her to help. But after the first day when I'd come home to find the stubborn woman was up on a ladder, painting the top portion, we'd gotten into an argument. I eventually wore her down to agree to wait to do the top until I was around to make sure she didn't fall from the ladder. Then I thanked her with an orgasm.

It was a pretty good deal for me.

"How was yoga class today?" I asked.

"Good. Me and Viv talked about getting together for dinner with you and David."

"I finally get to meet the famous Vivienne, huh? Let's do it." I wiped my hand off on a napkin and pulled my phone out of my pocket when it buzzed. "It's my mom." I answered with, "Hey, Mom. Maggie's here too," and put it on speakerphone.

"Hey, Abby."

"Oh my god, Maggie! The picture you sent of the mural is adorable."

Next to me, Maggie smiled down at the phone. "Thank you."

"Honey, you are so talented. I can't wait to meet you in real life and give you a big squeeze."

"Not too big. I'm like a blueberry. I might pop."

"I can't make any promises." My mom laughed. "I wanted to let you know we booked our flight and hotel, so I was—"

"Hotel? You and Dad could stay here," I said.

"No. You two need your space. We're going to make a long weekend out of it, maybe see a show," she explained, referencing their visit in January for the baby shower. "We're going to fly in on Friday and leave on Monday."

I raised my brow at Maggie, silently asking a question before I voiced it. "You want to come over Saturday, spend the day at our house?"

"We were going to invade anyway, but it's always nice to be invited. Now, listen. While I have you on the phone, Maggie, I got the invitations. So whenever you have the guest list finished, email it to me, and I'll get them all sent out. We'll want to do that in the next week or so, especially with the holidays coming up. Mail might be slow."

Maggie slid a weary gaze to me. After the Thanksgiving fiasco, she had said she didn't even want a baby shower, but my mother would hear none of it. After I described a little of what had happened, she'd promptly called Maggie herself to talk. I'd eavesdropped from my spot in the hall, listening to Maggie's side of the conversation. And though she did try to say she didn't want one, as usual, Abby Isaacson got her way. When I had asked Maggie what my mom had said to convince her, she'd responded with a watery smile and an echo of my mom's words. "Every new mother deserves to be celebrated and given gifts to take the burden off her."

So, Mom immediately took the reins and—along with Bronte, who derived most of her pleasure in life from planning any and everything—made all the arrangements. All Maggie had to do was register for what we needed for the baby and make a guest list. Registering for gifts was easy; we did it together in one afternoon.

It was the invite list that was proving difficult for Maggie.

"I'm sorry," she said, "I'll get it to you soon."

"No problem, hon. You have a thousand things going on, so don't stress about it."

Maggie bit into her bottom lip, nodding absently as her focus drifted to the mural.

"All right, Mom." I took her off speakerphone and lifted it to my ear. "We're eating dinner, so…"

"How's she doing?"

"Good."

"Really?"

I stuffed a fry in my mouth as I watched Maggie dig back into her dinner. "Mm-hmm."

"I know you don't want to talk about her when she's sitting next to you, but my heart breaks for her. Give a kiss to the baby for me."

"I will."

"Love you."

"Love you too," I said then hung up and swiftly bent over to kiss Maggie's stomach. "From Gogo." Then I curled my hand around Maggie's neck and towed her to me, kissing her mouth. "From me."

She offered me a reluctant smile.

"Don't stress," I reminded her.

"I know."

"You are, though. I can see it." I smoothed my fingertip over the crimped lines between her brows.

She batted me away. "Those are my wrinkles. Next you'll be pointing out my gray hairs."

"I like your gray hairs."

"You're so rude."

I kissed her once more, and we both tucked in to our food.

"Where does Gogo come from anyway?" she asked after a few minutes, and I shrugged.

"I think when Dani got pregnant, my mom said she wanted to be called Grammy or something like that. But when Aiden started talking, Gogo came out and it stuck. Suits her, I think."

"She is always on the go." Maggie turned to me. "You're lucky to have her as your mother."

It wasn't so much the way her words came out almost too quiet to hear, but how her coffee irises amplified to dark pools, crestfallen and so unmistakably full of disappointment. I wrapped an arm around her shoulders. "I got really lucky, but she's your mom now too. Whatever you need, she'll be there for you. My mom, dad, sister, and me, of course, you've got all of us now." I kissed her temple. "You're stuck with us."

She heaved out a sigh. "I guess I'll try to tolerate it."

I smiled against her hair. "Thank you. I know it's a hardship."

She tilted her head back for a kiss, which I happily indulged. "Let's move on to the M's."

"M's is it." I opened the baby name book once again. "Mabon, Mabrey, Mac, Macario, Macey…"

CHAPTER THIRTY-ONE

Maggie

With Christmas right around the corner, it seemed all of New York was lit up. Twinkle lights hung from every window and door, shops displayed tinsel and trees, and even the occasional busker was dressed as Santa Claus. Wes and I didn't venture into Manhattan together all that often, but Vivienne had made reservations at a new Italian eatery in Tribeca. A gust of wind plowed through the street as Wes escorted me inside, the immediate warmth of the restaurant keeping the worst of the cold at bay.

Before I could even remove my scarf, Vivienne waved from her spot at the bar. I took Wes's hand, leading him to my friend. We hugged, although our matching belly sizes made it more and more difficult with every passing week.

"I'm so glad we could do this," Vivienne said, after introductions were made between Wes and her husband, David. "And I'm so glad to be able to eat here. I heard they have this delicious goat cheese ravioli."

"Mmm." I rubbed my hand over my stomach. "I'm starving."

A moment later, the hostess led us to the table. The place was packed, and I struggled to squeeze between some of the patrons, repeatedly apologizing and asking to be excused. Finally settled, with Wes at my side, I pointed at Vivienne's heels. "I don't know how you do it."

She lifted one slender shoulder, her cream sweater dress hugging her figure perfectly. "I don't get dressed up all that often, so I like to."

"Me too, but I struggled to do heels even before I was pregnant."

Vivienne was due in about two months, and she didn't show any signs of swelling, unlike me, who had three months to go and felt like a water balloon.

David lazily stroked his wife's neck. "Never quite gave up the fashion life."

At Wes's quirked brow, I explained, "Viv went to school to be a designer."

"Yeah, then he blew all those plans away." She jerked her thumb at David, who caught her hand.

"Hey, I never said you should quit."

"Somebody had to make concessions for us to be together," she said, though there was no malice behind it. In fact, with how the two smiled at each other, it was quite obvious they were both blissfully happy.

Under the table, I placed my hand on Wes's thigh, and he toyed with my fingers and knuckles. "Seems like it worked out, though."

Vivienne and David both nodded at Wes, and we chatted amiably about David's executive position at his accounting firm, and Wes described a little bit about the filmmaking process, including some plans for *Turning Leaves*. By the time we finished our main course, David and Wes were talking like they'd known each other for a few years instead of an hour. Which was good, because if it were up to Vivienne and me, we would be doing this a lot more. At least once our babysitters were lined up.

After we finished up with the check, Vivienne pulled her phone from her purse. "Maggie, I told you about Henry's friend, right?"

"Yeah. Sara?"

David chuckled. "Oh god. His girlfriend."

"Girlfriend?" Wes asked. "Henry's what? Five?"

"Four," David said. "Kid's got game, what can I say?"

"Look." Vivienne held her phone so Wes and I could see a picture of Henry and Sara, who held up Wonder Woman socks. "He wanted to buy her something for Hanukkah."

"Oh my gosh." I cooed. "That's adorable."

"Her mom asked me what she could get Henry for Christmas."

"That's commitment," Wes joked. "Basically engaged."

Everyone shared a laugh, but I squirmed in my seat, needing to use the restroom. The third trimester ushered in the inconvenience of having to pee every hour.

"Before we leave, I'm going to run to the bathroom right quick," I told Wes, scooting my chair back, bumping into someone behind me. "Oh, I'm sorry. I didn't mean—Amber?"

There she was, my ex-best friend of fifteen years.

"Maggie," she said, her dark, perfectly plucked brows rising in surprise over her green eyes. Then, as her gaze dropped down to my stomach, she let out a derisive snort. "Didn't take you long to move on, did it?"

I lurched back as if she had slapped me in the face. "Move on? What—I don't—what are you talking about?"

She pointed her long, blood-red fingernail at my belly. "So much for how distraught you were over the divorce and how you couldn't get pregnant. You were crying to me all the time." She rolled her eyes. "Guess that was a lie too."

"A lie?" If Amber had stabbed me in the back with a knife, it would have hurt less. "I have *never* lied about anything. You were my best friend. You know how upset I was for so many years."

Behind her, I heard Vivienne and Wes exchange words about who this woman was, but I was too wrapped up in the sparring match to comprehend anything else.

"We were best friends, so imagine my surprise when I come to find out you were using my brother—using me—for money."

Sure, I enjoyed the perks of being friends with Amber, but I never once asked for anything besides help in being set up with her brother. Since *that* had worked out so well, I was glad it was the sole thing I had ever asked of Amber.

"What the hell are you talking about?" My voice rose above the din of the restaurant, earning annoyed glares and flashes of confusion from those dining around us. "How could I use either of you for money? Brian left me with nothing. The prenup made sure of that."

"Good thing too," she sneered, and the man with her cleared his throat. He undoubtedly wanted to get the situation under control, like I supposed Wes was trying to do by depositing my coat around my shoulders.

"You are...awful." I was at a loss for words. I didn't like calling other women names, but Amber was a callous bitch if I ever met one. "Just, like, awful."

"Eloquent as ever," she said with a roll of her eyes.

"I don't know why you think you still need to try to hurt me. What good will it do you now?"

She rotated more fully around in her chair, as if she was a second away from jumping up and getting in my face. But that wasn't Amber's style. She'd much rather use her words sparingly, keep her tone low and light, like it was no skin off her back. "You were always so sensitive. Of course you'd think I planned to be here at exactly this moment to—" she lifted her fingers in air quotes "—hurt your feelings." She huffed. "Get over yourself."

I pressed my fingers to my chest. "*You* telling *me* to get over myself is laughable. You treated me like a lap dog and sent me out to pasture when I no longer served your purpose. I thought we were friends. I thought we loved each other, but really, you only ever loved yourself and how I made you feel."

She spun around in her chair, evidently not willing to hear anything else I had to say, but I wasn't about to let my ex-best friend off that easy. I slid my coat on, took hold of Wes's hand, and gave a nod to Vivienne, letting her know I would be leaving. Once I delivered parting words. "Unlike you, Amber, I know what it feels like to be loved for myself and not my money or looks. So, you can take your self-righteous bullshit and fuck right off with it."

A few stunned gasps from patrons sounded around us, but I paid them no mind as I pivoted to Wes. His mouth stretched in a wide, proud grin, and he wrapped his arm around my shoulders, shepherding me out of the restaurant. We burst out of the doors and into the cold night air, with Vivienne and David following close behind.

"Incredible!" Wes hooted. "You were incredible. It was like the perfect ending to a movie. I couldn't have planned it better myself."

"Who was that?" Vivienne asked.

"My ex-best friend and sister of my ex-husband."

She let out a long "Oh" in understanding, and I blew out a foggy breath as I paced a few steps back and forth. My blood pulsed so fast, my skin heated so much, I didn't even need to button my coat. I wondered if this was what mothers felt when they lifted cars off their children, and I held my hands out in front of me as if fireballs were about to shoot from them. "I feel like I could chop down a tree, rip something apart with my bare hands."

David cheered me on as Wes laughed. "Bet you could, you badass."

"And you know what?" I glanced between Wes and Vivienne, finally free of guilt and obligation. "I'm not going to invite my family to the shower. If they can't love me for who I am, then fuck them too. They don't deserve to have any cake pops."

Vivienne clapped. "Well said."

Wes hauled me in for a tight hug. "I'm so proud of you. Seeing you stand up for yourself is amazing."

"Feels good too."

He kissed me then gestured to Vivienne and David. "Now let's go find some cake. Dessert's on me."

"Oh wait! I have to pee first!"

CHAPTER THIRTY-TWO

Maggie

I was still getting ready by the time the doorbell rang. "They're early," I called from the bathroom, unplugging the hair-dryer. "I'm not even dressed yet."

Wes poked his head into the bathroom, his stare lazily roaming over me in the reflection in the mirror. When he finally met my gaze, he gave me one of his contented smiles and lifted his shoulder like he couldn't help it.

But I rolled my eyes. If I didn't fully appear the size of the barge, I certainly felt like it.

When he started toward me, I brandished my brush like a weapon. "Hands to yourself. Go answer the door, your parents are waiting."

He swatted my butt. "So full of sass this morning."

"Don't be cute." I pushed him away. "I'll be down in a minute."

I heard his soft chuckle down the hall as I waddled back to our bedroom to pull on leggings and a long maternity top. With a quick check in the mirror, I made my way downstairs to meet Wes's parents. Abby spied me first and squealed, practically throwing herself at me.

"Honey, how are you? You are glowing! This hair, it's so

lush. Must be from the vitamins. Or is it always so long and thick? My god, look at you! Can I touch the belly?"

Unsure what to answer first, I slid my hands around my stomach, appreciative that Abby at least asked first. "Sure, you can touch the belly."

She grinned and oh-so gently laid her palm on the top of the bump, leaning down to whisper, "Hello in there. This is Gogo. I can't wait to meet you." Then she stood up and circled her arms around me for one more hug. "I told you I was going to squeeze you."

I didn't pop like a blueberry, much to my relief, and I accepted Jeff's one-armed hug. He was tall, though not nearly as tall as Wes, with a head of dark hair and a golden tan. He wore pressed slacks and a button-down, and I speculated that was why Wes was always dressed similarly. Because he learned it from his dad.

"Nice to meet you in person, Maggie."

"You as well. Thanks for making the trip up. Even in this weather."

He waved my words away. "It's nice to get away from the heat sometimes."

"Right into the tundra," Wes said as he marshaled his parents to the dining room where he had set up our takeout lunch.

"I wouldn't miss your shower even if there was a blizzard." Abby took a seat next to me. "I would've put on snowshoes and cobbled a team of sled dogs together if I had to."

She squeezed my hand, and I had to blink back the stinging emotion in my eyes. "I really..." I cleared my throat when my words wobbled. "I really appreciate that."

"Any chance I have to see my children and grandchildren, I take it. And that includes you now."

I knew how big Abby's heart was, but after the last few

weeks, full of confrontation and a lot of soul-searching about what I deserved from the people in my life, it felt like finding a rainbow after a storm. She was my sign that everything would be all right. And I hugged her once more before we all dug into the food.

"So what did you decide about the LA house?" Jeff asked, stabbing a couple pieces of lettuce from his salad.

"I'm selling it to Ruthie Van Acker."

"Oh, she's the one from the movie, right?" Abby peeled a garlic knot apart. "Didn't you send me a picture of her wearing one of Maggie's shirts?"

I twirled spaghetti on my fork. "Yeah. She's been posting a lot of my stuff. It's done wonders for my business."

"That's great to hear. I'm so happy for you."

"Mags can't keep up with orders anymore," Wes informed them. "We talked about hiring an assistant, especially for when the baby comes."

Abby placed her hand on the table. "If you ever need any help, I am here. I will get on the next plane. In fact, should I make arrangements to come?"

"Honey," Jeff said quietly as Wes laughed.

"I think we'll be okay, Mom."

"If Wes and I need help, you will be the first call I make," I told her, and I meant that. I trusted her implicitly. After all, she raised Wes, and he was the best person I knew.

"So, back to your house," Jeff said. "What are you doing with that money?"

It was also obvious where Wes got his business sense from.

"We'll sign all the closing papers in the next few weeks, and then I'm looking into buying some space to make into a sound stage. The company can have an official office, and we can rent out the stage when we aren't using it."

Jeff nodded. "Smart."

"I want one address," Wes went on with a confident smile my way. We had talked about possibly moving to Los Angeles, but living on the West Coast held no appeal for me, and Wes promised he was just as happy living in New York as he was there, so it was an easy decision. "I may still take a few trips out a year, but once Chris and I open up the office here, it won't be necessary."

"Sounds like you got it all figured out." Jeff winked, a proud father. "Good for you, kid. Good for you. I know you two didn't have an easy start, but I'm happy you've been able to work it out." Then he turned to me, his dark eyes shining. "From the moment my son told me about you, I knew you were something special to him, but you're also special to us, to Abby and me. We're here for you always."

"Thank you," I said, my voice barely above a whisper, overwhelmed once again by how caring and kind the Isaacsons were.

"Now." Abby wiped her mouth with a napkin. "Have you decided on a name yet?"

Wes and I caught each other's gaze and burst out in laughter. Because, "No."

"Absolutely not," Wes said.

"But we know, for sure, it's not Langley."

"Or Rhodes."

"Or Bruno."

"Or—"

"Okay." Abby held up her hand. "I get the picture. I guess I'll have to wait to personalize the baby blanket."

"He might be a year old before we decide," Wes said, and I couldn't disagree. I couldn't pick a name out for a person I hadn't met yet. But what I had decided on was my first meal after the baby was born.

"I told Wes I'll need him to sneak in sushi and champagne to the hospital room."

Jeff cut into his chicken Parmesan. "Excellent way to celebrate."

"Maybe after a few glasses, you'll come up with a name," Abby suggested.

"Maybe," I echoed, then Wes tipped his head to the side, his mouth curling into a teasing grin.

"What about Moët?"

"For the champagne or the name?"

"Both?"

I tossed my balled-up napkin at him, and the four of us spent the next few hours sharing more laughs and hugs than I had ever hoped to imagine.

CHAPTER THIRTY-THREE

Chris, Dad, and I set up camp at a pub down the street to have some wings and a beer while Maggie and her friends celebrated with the baby shower at a Brooklyn winery not far from our house. It was a small affair. Maggie ended up inviting a little over a dozen people, including Abby, Bronte, Vivienne, and my sister. But that was what Maggie wanted.

She'd been in a good mood all morning, humming along to Rod Stewart as she got ready. She hadn't even minded me sitting on the tub, watching her, my hand caressing her thigh while she curled her hair and applied makeup. My mom informed me all I had to do was show up at the end for some pictures and carry all the presents home.

If only all of my duties as a dad would be that easy.

When the three of us showed up to the private room, Chris immediately headed for the cake pop tower, snagging a handful of treats, while Dad proceeded to corner the server to ask about the different bottles of wine. I was sure he'd be flying back to Florida with a case or two.

"Hey, sweetheart. Have fun?"

"I did, thanks for asking," Dani said with a shove to my shoulder. I palmed her face and kissed Maggie's temple.

Her cheeks glowed pink. "It was perfect. We didn't play any games."

"Well, that was your number one rule," I said with a laugh, tipping my chin to Bronte, who was attempting to pull Chris away from the desserts to help load up the car.

"Your mom really is amazing to plan this for me."

"You're amazing to let her take over. She's—"

"A lot," Dani offered from her seat next to Maggie, who smiled between me and Dani.

"She's exactly enough."

"Let's see if you think that in another few years," Dani said, though it was all in good fun since I was aware of how Dani talked to our mother more than I did.

"Speak of the devil. Hey, Mom." I stood up from where I was crouched next to Maggie. "How'd it all go?"

"Wonderful. Wonderful. Go stand over there with Maggie." She held up her phone. "I want to get a good one to put in a frame at home."

Following her direction, I held Maggie close, one arm around her back, the other resting on her stomach as she dropped her head to my shoulder.

"Gorgeous. You two are gorgeous together." Mom snapped a few shots then kissed us both on the cheek. "Where's your dad?"

"I think I saw him walk that way—" I pointed out of the doors, toward the restaurant "—with one of the servers. He had a bottle of wine in his hand."

"Oh god. He better not be buying any. We still have three cases from the trip we took to the winery in North Carolina."

As she paraded away with a grouch, Maggie tucked her face into my chest to stifle her giggle. I kissed her head. "I'll pack up all the gifts if you want to head out soon."

She nodded and headed off toward a trio of women chatting at the other side of the room, so I grabbed a few gift bags and boxes from the pile on the table. With Chris's help, we Tetrised everything into my car in no time, while Bronte had the room cleared out and leftovers boxed up.

"I can't thank you enough." Maggie hugged Bronte. "This was great."

"Good. I'm glad you're happy. You got so many cute things for the baby."

"And your gift was so generous," Maggie said, referring to the laundry basket full of detergent, cleaning products, Tylenol, baby wipes, nursing pads, and some other little self-care items for Maggie. Inside the envelope was a gift card for Uber Eats. She really did think of everything.

Bronte waved her hand. "You guys will need it."

"Well, we appreciate it. Thank you." Maggie hugged Chris too. "Let's get together again soon. Wes has to go to LA for a couple days to pack up the house, but maybe you can come up one last time before the baby arrives."

I placed my hand on her side where our kid often liked to elbow her. "One last hurrah."

Chris nodded as Bronte smiled. "You let us know when, and we'll be there."

After another round of hugs, they headed out, leaving Maggie and me to find my parents. They were up at the front arguing over wine, and I helped Maggie bundle up. "Hey, we'll see you two at home?"

"We'll be there in a bit," Dad said, handing over a credit card as Mom tapped her foot impatiently.

We shared a grin as we walked out hand in hand to go home, where she changed into comfy clothes while I brought everything inside. Mom and Dad showed up twenty minutes later, spending some time before they needed to go back to Manhattan for dinner reservations.

"*Schitt's Creek* in bed?" I asked, locking the front door behind my parents.

"Yes, please. I'm exhausted."

We still had to get all the presents put away, but we could do that another time. All I wanted to do right now was cuddle Maggie under the covers. But of course, as soon as everything was calm, her family struck.

Her cell phone buzzed from where she had it charging on the nightstand. "It's my sister."

I didn't say anything as Maggie held the phone in her hand like a grenade. After a few moments, she answered it. "Hey."

I turned down the volume of Moira's wine commercial, and I could almost hear Theresa on her end of the phone call, saying something about the baby shower.

"But why would I want to invite you? We haven't spoken since Thanksgiving, and it's not like you seem to care about the baby."

I gave Maggie's leg a squeeze, a silent signal of encouragement. After she had stood up to Amber last month, she was resolved. She didn't want anyone in her life who made her unhappy. It was a mantra she kept repeating, even inspired a few stickers about toxic people. "I want people in my life who will bring our baby joy, not bring us down."

And it made sense to me. She was a lot less stressed out without the gray cloud of her family hanging over her.

Except now, with her sister on the phone, I could see Maggie's color rising, feel her tensing under my hand.

"Well, no, I—" Maggie was cut off by her sister, and I leaned in, hearing something about Sandy.

"She screamed at me and my boyfriend, Theresa. I don't want that kind of behavior and anxiety in my life. I don't deserve it, Wes certainly doesn't deserve it, so don't call me and tell me Mom is upset, like I should do something about it."

Maggie crossed her legs, her fingernails leaving little half-moons on her palm. I rubbed my hand along her arm, hoping to relax her.

"I don't care," Maggie said after a minute of listening to her sister. "I need to do what is best for me. I'm sorry you're upset, I really am, but if you want to be involved in my life, you can't play into Mom's game. You can't pretend you want to be my sister and then turn around and talk shit about me to her. You either support me or you don't."

"Oh, don't be so ridiculous," I heard Theresa snap, and I shook my head, my teeth grinding so hard my jaw felt like it might lock in place.

"I'm not being ridiculous. I'm setting boundaries, something that has taken me a long time to learn. I would love to have a relationship with you. Hell, I'd love to have one with Mom too, but I will not be made to feel bad every time we talk. So, I am not going to put myself in situations where that will happen."

Theresa said something I couldn't hear, but whatever it was had Maggie moving off the bed, facing away from me. And then I could swear I heard her sniffle, and I leaped off the mattress, placing my hands around her shoulders.

"Whatever. I don't care. If she wants to be done with me, she can tell me herself instead of sending you after me." Then Maggie hung up the call and threw her phone on the bed.

I hauled her into me, rocking her gently as she found her breath. It was a long time before she lifted her head. I straightened her glasses and smoothed away her worry lines. "What happened?"

"My mom saw the pictures I posted on Facebook. She's pissed she wasn't invited today. Apparently so is my sister. But I don't understand why. She said we're family, it doesn't matter if we fight." She frowned. "But, like...yeah, it does. I wouldn't invite anyone else I was always fighting with, so why would I invite them?"

"Exactly," I said. Just because they were family didn't mean Maggie needed to put up with their traumatic bullshit. She had for long enough.

"My sister said I'm being selfish. *I'm* being selfish."

"No." I cupped her face between my palms, bending my knees so we were eye to eye. "You're doing what is right for you and for our baby."

She darted her gaze away to the wall behind my shoulder. "My mom said she's done with me."

"Yeah? Well, you're done with her," I bit out, yet even as I said it, I knew it wasn't true. While Maggie had been able to put her foot down about her shower with her family, I knew she still yearned for their approval. I wasn't sure she would ever give up on it. Then again, how did you completely walk away from the people who were supposed to love you unconditionally?

I kissed her forehead. "I'm so sorry, Mags. This was supposed to be a good day for you."

"It was."

"But now..."

She sniffled and reached for a tissue. She blew her nose then sank down to the bed. "Can you pet my head?"

"That you even have to ask..." I mumbled in playful outrage. "Come here."

I stretched out next to her as she shoved the body pillow under her belly. She'd bought it after Vivienne suggested it might help her to sleep. So far, it had. Then I snuggled up behind her and combed my fingers through her hair. She never made it through the next episode, her soft snores alerting me to her sleep, but I kept stroking her hair anyway.

"You'll be up to pee in an hour anyway," I whispered

against the back of her head. "And I'll have to start this whole process all over again." I smiled to myself, even though she couldn't hear me. "But that's okay. It's one of my favorite things to do, loving you."

CHAPTER THIRTY-FOUR

Maggie

At the blare of Wes's alarm, I groaned and rolled over. It wasn't easy. With a month to go, I was swollen, huge, and over it. Next to me, Wes curled his hand around my hip.

"Morning." His voice was coarse with sleep, his breath hot against my neck.

"I know what you're doing," I said, blinking my eyes open to find him staring down at me.

"What?"

"You're trying to seduce me."

"Seduce you?" He tilted his head back with an annoyingly arrogant laugh. "Sweetheart, I think I did that a long time ago." He added a little rub to my belly.

"I mean, right now. You and your growly morning voice."

He hummed against my temple. "Is it working?"

I sighed, not answering, and he ground his hard cock against my thigh. "Wes."

"Now look who's talking? You saying my name like that is seducing *me*."

I threw my arm over my head, inadvertently causing my shirt to ride up. "I don't feel very sexy right now."

"But you are." He nibbled at my ear.

"No, I'm not. I'm hot and moody and ready to get this thing out of me," I said, flailing my hand at my stomach.

"We haven't had sex in so long. In over a month."

"You keeping track?"

"My right hand is." He smoothed his palm up to my breast.

"You better get used to it. I can't imagine we'll feel like it once the baby gets here."

"Exactly." He rolled my nipple between his fingers. "So let's do it now."

"You have to get to the airport."

He bent to lick my throat. "Yeah, so send me off with a going-away present."

I snorted.

"It wasn't a no." He sucked on my pulse point, his hand trailing over me, urging me to turn on my side. "But I'd really like to hear you say yes."

Even though it was the middle of February and winter still lingered outside, I had taken to wearing a loose cotton nightgown to bed, often needing to get up multiple times to use the bathroom at night. Plus, elastic waistbands were just plain uncomfortable. So, it was easy for Wes to slip his hand into my underwear as his teeth scraped over my jaw.

"What do you think? Could I get you to beg?"

My breath shuddered when he pushed his finger into me.

"I think you missed me," he murmured against my neck, fingers plying me open. "I know it's been hard for you lately. I know you're tired, but this pussy needs attention."

With each of his rasped words against my skin, I eased farther back against him. My joints ached, and my belly was so big I could barely bend over to put socks on. I hadn't felt the desire to be with Wes. But now that his hands were on me, drawing out goose bumps along my flesh as his fingers pressed gently inside me at a steady pace so that my hips rocked back for more, I *needed* him.

"Come on, sweetheart, let me hear you say it." He dragged his fingers back out to circle my clit. "You're so wet for me."

I moaned softly, stretching my neck so he would kiss me there. He pressed his fingers back into me at the same time he curled his other arm around me to pluck at my painfully hard nipples, alternating between them until I gripped his forearm. "Please. Please."

"Please what?"

"I need you inside me. Please, Wes."

His hand left me for only a few seconds as he pushed my underwear and his pajama pants off, then his fingers were between my legs again. "See? You missed me. You missed this," he said as he lined up the head of his hard length at my entrance, not yet pushing inside, and I whimpered. "Hm?"

"I did." I reached for him, gripping his thigh, trying to spur him on. Still, he didn't move. "I need you. Please." When he stroked up my slit once, twice, three times without ever entering me, I turned over my shoulder. "Stop teasing me."

He smirked then thrust inside, his fingers back to circling me, teasing where our bodies met in a gentle but sure rhythm. "I've got you."

And he did. Not just now, but always.

He kept each jut of his hips shallow so we barely rocked together, but it was enough to knead the spot inside me that had my heart racing and eyes fluttering closed in pleasure. His fingers worked over me, his mouth on my neck, his teeth grazing as he spoke soft words into my skin about how much he loved me, how much he craved me, how I felt so good, and it could have been three minutes or three hours, I wasn't sure, until my muscles coiled and released with an orgasm. Wes followed closely behind, grunting quietly against my shoulder.

"Now, I can get on the plane," he said, and I huffed out a laugh. He caressed my hip before patting it. "Let's go shower."

"Together?" I let myself be pulled up out of bed as he nodded. "We both won't fit."

"Yes, we will. Come on."

I shook my head but followed him down the hall anyway, where he turned on the water and tugged my nightgown off. He helped me step into the tub, and we both barely fit in with my stomach bulging out between us.

"Okay, so maybe we think about renovating the bathroom, expanding it." He squirted some shampoo into his hand and massaged it into my hair. "We'll probably need it anyway if we're going to have more than one kid."

"More? We haven't even had one yet."

He aimed the showerhead to rinse my hair. "Yeah, but it might be nice, right? Have a playmate for each other."

"I never played with my sister." I soaped up as Wes finger-combed conditioner through my strands.

"Well, your family notwithstanding, I think siblings get along for the most part."

"I guess," I said, thinking about how it might be nice to have more than one. I had always wanted at least two, but with how my life had zigged and zagged, I was surprised to even be pregnant with this one. "Let's put a pin in this conversation until he is at least breathing oxygen."

"Okay." Wes grinned and finished washing me before moving on to himself.

"You know I'm still perfectly capable of bathing myself."

"I know, but I like doing it. Besides, I'll be gone for five days. I need to——"

I gasped, cutting off his words, my attention on the floor of the tub.

"What?"

"I think..." I lifted my head, meeting his gaze. "I think my water broke."

"You think?"

We both stared down at where the spray of the shower washed away any evidence of what might have happened. But there had been a very distinct feeling of a plug being pulled out from inside me and a rush of liquid. "I think it's *still* breaking."

He blinked at me a few times, his eyelashes clumped together, and I could tell how he grappled to make sense of this. "But you've still got a month to go."

I curved my hands around the bottom of my stomach as if I could keep the baby inside.

"I assumed sex bringing about labor was an old wives' tale," he said, and I pinned my thighs together as if that might stop the fluid from gushing out of me.

"I don't—"

"Wes! Stop analyzing and get me to the hospital!"

"Right." He shook his head a few times. "Right. Okay." He pivoted from right to left, clearly at a loss for what to do with the loofah still in his hand. "Yeah. Hospital. Okay."

I sighed and flicked the faucet off before carefully stepping out of the bath to grab a towel, leaving Wes muttering to himself about how this was possible. My normally cool, calm, and collected boyfriend was suddenly completely inept at putting one foot in front of the other. It was endearing. Maddening but endearing.

"Come on, Wes. We have to go."

He ran in circles, half finishing tasks like brushing his teeth and sending text messages. "We didn't even get to pack a go bag yet. Doesn't this kid know he has to cook longer?"

"I think he must not have checked the calendar."

"Don't joke, Maggie."

I laughed, nudging him out of the way so I could snag a

sweatshirt from the closet. "It's completely fine for a baby to come any time after thirty-six weeks. I'm sure you must have read that somewhere."

"At this moment in time, I can't remember a goddamn thing from any book." He shoved random items of clothing into a duffel bag. "Charger! We need a phone charger." He skidded to the nightstand, where he grabbed the charger but put it right back down to pick up his cell phone again. "I need to text my mom, Ruthie, tell her I'm not making it out. I could do that on the way to the hospital."

Then when he noticed me struggle to put my sneakers on, he darted over. I slid my hands around his face, stopping him from kneeling on the floor in front of me. "I am fine. I will put my sneakers on if you go back over and pick up the charger to put in the bag and finish packing, okay? I love you, my sweet darling man, but if you don't start to pull it together, I will go to the hospital and have this baby by myself."

"Mm-hmm. Okay. Yep. Got it." He squeezed his eyes shut, took a deep breath, and when he found my gaze again, he beamed. "We're going to have a baby today."

"Yes, we are."

He threw an arm around me and laid a big, wet kiss on my lips before straightening up, his cool, calm, and collected personality back in place. "You finish getting ready. I will pack the bag and text my family. I'll make a list and take care of all the rest later."

I curved my palm around his jaw. "I hope he has your self-assuredness."

"But your bravery in a crisis."

"Don't get too ahead of yourself there. I'm keeping all my panic locked up tight for now." I toddled down the hall toward the bathroom.

"There's nothing to panic about. You're only going to push a nine-pound watermelon out of you. No big deal."

"Don't make me laugh." I shoved a towel down my pants because what the actual fuck? Was there supposed to be so much fluid? It never stopped coming out of me. "I've already got enough liquid pouring out of me, I don't need anymore."

"Don't worry. I read that's totally normal."

This time, I laughed. "Of course you did."

CHAPTER THIRTY-FIVE

Wes

It wasn't normal for labor to take so long, I knew that. There was only so much time after someone's water broke in which they had to have the baby, or else... I couldn't remember the *or else*, but I knew it was bad.

"You're doing great," I said, tucking a lock of loose hair behind Maggie's ear because she was starting to get nervous too. We'd been here for more than eight hours, although the doctor assured us the baby was healthy and there should be no problem when he finally decided to come out and see the world. Yet with every passing hour, Maggie seemed more and more exhausted.

"I'm not feeling well," she told me for the second time in the last few minutes, and I didn't know what else to say. The nurse explained it was normal to feel nauseated during labor, so what else was I supposed to do besides offer her ice chips and rub her tense muscles?

"I know, Mags, I know. I'm sorry."

"We're going to start pushing as soon as the doctor gets back," the nurse informed us since she had been in a minute ago to check Maggie's progress.

"But I feel like I'm going to throw up."

The nurse grabbed a pan and handed it to Maggie as I helped her to sit up. She swayed, and I stabilized her with an arm around her shoulders while the nurse studied the beeping lines and numbers on the monitor next to the bed, her brow furrowed. She pressed a button that set off a code blue alert, and my own heart spiked. "What's happening? What's going on?"

Before I could get an answer, the doctor and a second nurse flew into the room, and I gripped Maggie's hand so hard I worried I broke a bone or two, but I wanted to keep her close. Keep her safe.

"Wes…" Maggie moaned. "My chest… It feels like…" Her hold on my fingers went slack as her eyes fluttered closed, and my heart sank to the floor.

"What's going on?"

The medical staff started speaking a language I couldn't translate.

"Cardiac arrest…"

"C-section…"

"Embolism…"

"Maggie!" My whole entire world shrank down to this one moment, and I felt it slipping away. I bent down, shaking her hand. I hadn't read anything about this. I didn't know what to do. "Maggie, sweetheart, open your eyes. Maggie!"

Another nurse, this one younger and male, gently pushed me backward as Maggie's bed was wheeled away. "Your wife needs an emergency cesarean. She's going into cardiac arrest, most likely because of an amniotic fluid embolism."

"Amniotic fluid…" Fear clutched every cell in my body, and the only thing I could think was "My wife…"

"Come with me," he said, "and I'll get you suited up to see your son."

"Is she going to be okay? Is my baby going to be okay?"

"We will do everything we can to make sure they are." Then he tugged me down the hall, thrust some scrubs into my hands, and less than a minute later—or maybe an hour later, I couldn't be sure since time had ceased to exist once Maggie's eyes had closed—I was ushered into the OR, where the doctor was working on cutting our son out of Maggie. She lay on the table, didn't even flinch or move, as our baby cried out. All at once, relief and a new wave of fear washed over me.

"He's a healthy baby boy," a gray-haired female nurse said, taking the screaming little guy to wrap up. "We will take him down to get checked out. Does he have a name?"

"My...wife and I... We were going to name him together." Then I blinked over at where Maggie still lay there, like a corpse, her skin ghostly white, her red glasses missing, and hot tears stung my eyes.

"She's hemorrhaging," the doctor said to the nurses around her, and I lunged toward the table, but someone caught me, towing me away.

"We need you to come with us, sir."

"No. Maggie." I fought against them. "Maggie!"

My world was getting smaller and smaller by the second.

The young nurse was back, his arm across my chest. "We will take good care of her."

"Promise me," I croaked. "Promise me you'll bring her back to me."

"I can't..." He looked tortured, how I felt. "I can't promise you that, but I can promise we will do everything we can to help her. Go be with your baby right now."

I was escorted out of the OR and down the hall, where the gray-haired nurse explained how they would make sure Baby Isaacson's vitals and organs were all good. "Though with how he's screaming, I don't think you have anything to worry about."

"He's not premature?"

"As long as his lungs are fully developed, he will be fine." She assessed my baby from top to bottom and marked some things down on a chart then placed him in my arms. He wore a blue cap on his head and a band around his foot, which matched the one on my wrist. The same one on Maggie's wrist.

Maggie.

"Do you have family who can come be with you?" the nurse asked, and I drew my son closer to me, taking in his pink skin and dark eyelashes. He had a head full of dark hair like his mother.

His mother.

I cleared my throat, but I couldn't unclog the terror stuck there. Tears leaked from my eyes as I pressed a kiss to my son's forehead, his skin so soft and warm, and I didn't know whether to rejoice or fall to my knees in despair.

How could everything be so wrong and yet so right?

"Here, let me..."

I hadn't realized I'd slumped against the wall until the nurse took the baby from my hold, transferring him to the little plastic crib. And that was when I let out a howl of pain, giving in to a cry like I never had before. On the floor, I hooked my arms over my bent knees and dropped my head, tears wetting my sweatshirt, the same sweatshirt Maggie had worn the day before.

I had promised her I would always take care of her, and now she was in a room by herself, dying.

I couldn't imagine what the doctors were doing to save her from a hemorrhage. Of course, logically, I knew what that meant, but I couldn't think rationally. I kept picturing the worst-case scenario, the love of my life covered in blood and medical staff unable to stop it.

I sniffed and hiccupped, trying and failing to take a deep breath and calm down.

Scrubs appeared on my left side, a gentle hand on my back. "Let's get you up off the floor."

The nurse led me to the doorway, where she passed me off to another nurse, who sat me in a chair in the hall with a cup of water. I could barely see, my vision blurred, eyes stinging, but I pulled my cell phone from my pocket and called my mom.

She answered with a hearty, "Is he here?"

"Mom," I cried.

"Oh god, honey, what is it?"

"I need you. I need you to come here, please, Mom."

"Yes, of course. What's going on?"

"Maggie… She's…" I couldn't get it out, but I didn't have to.

"We will be there as soon as we can. I'm going to call your sister. She'll be there tonight. Hang on, honey, we're coming. Sit tight. I love you. I love you so much."

I disconnected the call and crumpled against the wall, another wave of uneven breaths not making it to my lungs, and I felt like I might pass out.

"Put your head between your legs," someone ordered. "Breathe in through your nose and out your mouth."

I did as the person said, folding in half. It took a minute, but I was finally able to lift my head and see straight. Yet another nurse was next to me. "I'm going to walk you back to your room. Once you're settled, we will bring your son in there with you, okay?"

I followed her back down the hall to the room Maggie had been in minutes or months ago.

"How is she?" I asked, unable to help myself.

"I don't know. You'll get an update as soon as the doctor is able."

I wiped my hand over my face then whispered my thanks. My cell phone buzzed with a text.

CHRIS

How's it going? You hanging in?

I didn't hesitate to call him. I couldn't be here alone. It would be a while before Dani could drive up from Delaware, even my muddled brain recognized that. And I couldn't sit here, in this room, with the bag I'd haphazardly packed for Maggie and her cell phone staring at me, like those inanimate objects were waiting for her to come back too.

"Hey, man," Chris answered.

"Hey. I need you to come here. Can you come here?"

"Where? The hospital?" His laugh trailed off when I didn't make a joke.

"Yes. I need…" I rubbed my fingers in my eye sockets. "I don't know if Maggie…" I cleared my throat and tried again. "Something happened. She had an embolism."

"Is the baby…?"

"He's fine, he's healthy."

"Fuck." Chris mumbled something to someone, probably Bronte, then was back on the line. "We'll be there as soon as we can."

I nodded to myself and hung up, shoving my phone back into my pocket to wait.

Wait for my friend.

Wait for my family.

Wait for Maggie to come back to me.

CHAPTER THIRTY-SIX

Wes

Seconds or seasons later, a nurse arrived with the baby. I peered down at the tiny creature, the one who had given Maggie so much trouble, poking and prodding her, and I reached out my hand to hold his hand.

His little fingers curled around my index finger, his eyes barely opening as he yawned.

"Tough day for you?" I whispered. "Me too. I don't know what I'm going to do if..."

I couldn't think it, let alone say it.

"I have to be honest," I told my son, "it's hard to have you here and not your mom. It's confusing. Probably for you too, huh?" I kissed the baby's cheek. "I love you, and I'm sorry your first moments here aren't better."

I sat down, keeping my baby close, and shut my eyes.

———

The older pediatric nurse with gray hair came back into the room, smiling kindly at me before she held out her hands for the baby. "I'll take him down to the nursery and bring him back in a bit. The doctor's here to talk with you."

I passed off my son, and she placed him back in the plastic cart to wheel him out of the room as the doctor walked in, followed by the younger male nurse. I couldn't remember their names when all I cared about was Maggie.

"How is she?"

"Margaret has lost a lot of blood," the doctor said. "We had to do a transfusion, but she's still losing too much. Often, when a person has an amniotic fluid embolism, the uterus doesn't contract like it normally would have after delivery. We think the best way to stop the bleeding would be to remove it completely."

I rubbed the heels of my hands against my eyes. "I don't understand."

"I know it's a lot to comprehend right now, but we need to work fast. Time is of the essence. AFE is rare, and it is even rarer for a woman to survive."

I swallowed down the ash in my throat, coughing a few times. "She's not going to survive?"

"The mortality rate is high, so we need to act now. We think the best course of action is a complete hysterectomy."

The room spun, and I threw my hand out to the chair, trying to stay upright. "You want to take away her chance to have any more children?"

"We want to give her the best chance of surviving, Mr. Isaacson."

I bent to put my hands on my knees. When was it we had talked about having more kids? This morning? Yesterday? Last week?

Maggie's dream was to have a family, and now she was lying helpless in a hospital bed, at risk of losing not just future children but her life.

And I would lose everything without her.

"I need her to make it," I said in a voice that sounded

nothing like mine. I wiped the tears on my face. "Do whatever you have to. I need her. My son needs her."

"We will give you an update as soon as we have one." The doctor offered me a swift nod and strode out of the room, while the nurse stayed. He offered my shoulder a squeeze.

"I know it's hard. I'm so sorry you're going through this, but I would have made the same decision in your shoes."

I wiped my face and blinked a few times. "Thank you."

He gave me a sad smile before heading out of the room, leaving me alone once more.

I'd waited my whole life for Maggie. I couldn't lose her now.

"I'm scared," I said to the empty room, her voice echoing the words of her favorite movie in my head.

I'm scared of walking out of this room and never feeling the rest of my whole life the way I feel when I'm with you.

Then I dropped my head into my hands and prayed.

———

A knock sounded on the door before it opened, and I lifted my attention from where I'd been staring into space.

"Hey." Chris shuffled into the room with his arms open wide for a hug. I stood and accepted the embrace, though I didn't have the strength to return it. "We're here for you. Whatever you need, we're here for you."

When we broke apart, it was Bronte's turn to wrap an arm around me, saying, "We love you."

I still couldn't answer.

"We brought you dinner," Chris said. "You probably don't feel like eating, but you need to keep your strength up."

I sat back down with the paper bag in my lap.

"It's soup and a sandwich. I figured it would be easy for you to stomach."

At this point, nothing was easy. Nothing mattered, not hunger or thirst or exhaustion.

"Is this him?" Bronte asked, leaning over the crib, where the baby slept. The nurse had brought him in a while ago, or maybe a moment ago. They had fed and changed him, and he'd been asleep ever since. "Do you mind if I hold him?"

I shook my head, and Bronte tucked him safely in the crook of her elbow as Chris positioned a chair up next to me. He patted my knee but said nothing.

And for a while, I didn't either.

The tick of the clock on the wall and occasional soft sound from the baby were our soundtrack.

I dragged a sweaty palm over my mouth and days' old stubble. "I, um...I called my mom. She said she was going to tell Dani to come. I think I should probably update them."

Bronte carefully handed the baby over to Chris. "I'll take care of it."

"I should contact her family too. I don't know..." I picked up Maggie's phone, staring at the picture on her lock screen. It was of the two of us at her baby shower.

Bronte knelt down in front of me. "I can call them if you'd like."

I sniffled. "She needed a transfusion and hysterectomy. They said it's a slim chance to save her, but they had to do it."

"Maggie is strong," Chris said. "She'll pull through."

"What if..." I covered my eyes. "What if she doesn't?"

Bronte pulled me in for a hug, her arms wound tight around me as she let me soak her shirt. When she finally pulled away from me, her own cheeks were wet with tears. "Do you know the passcode for her phone?"

"It's 0320, his original due date."

Bronte plugged in the numbers, unlocking Maggie's phone. "I'll be in the hall." She kissed me once on the head. "Try to eat something."

I peered at the clock on the wall, fighting the fog in my mind to recognize we'd arrived at the hospital this morning around eight, and it was past six now. I hadn't eaten all day. I opened the paper bag and unwrapped the sandwich to pull a piece of the crust off. It was like woodchips in my mouth, and I dropped the sandwich back into the bag before facing Chris and my baby.

"You and Maggie have a perfect little kid here," he said, like he knew I would lose it at any moment, and handed him to me.

I settled my son against my chest, taking comfort in the weight of him, his shallow breaths, the almost inaudible whines. He was perfect. Like Maggie. "Thank you for coming all the way here."

"You know I would never pass up an opportunity to drive fast."

That actually drew a small yet pathetic laugh from me. At one time, Chris was known for drag racing and had gotten in some trouble. The worst was when he got behind the wheel after a few drinks and smashed up his car. He was lucky to be alive.

And now he was sitting next to me, while I hoped to avoid my own tragedy.

"I couldn't... If something happens, I didn't want to be alone."

"I know." Chris scooted his chair closer so it butted up right against mine, and he draped an arm over my shoulders. "You're not alone. No matter what happens."

I blinked at the prickle in my eyes and nuzzled against my baby's shoulder. No matter what happened, I had my son, this one perfect tiny human Maggie and I had created together.

"One of the nurses called Maggie my wife. I didn't correct him."

"Well, when you guys get out of here, you can make her your wife, for real."

Chris was so confident to say *when*, and I wanted to believe all three of us would walk out of this hospital, me, Maggie, and our baby.

We had to.

———

By the time the medical team—two doctors and a nurse—came back into the room, Dani had arrived with coffee and doughnuts, and Bronte had called both sets of parents to inform them of what had happened. She'd said Sandy was stunned into silence, but Bronte relayed the information for the hospital in case she wanted to make the trip.

"Mr. Isaacson," one of the doctors said, and I stood, my sister following, her palm between my shoulder blades. Bronte stayed seated, holding my baby, while Chris was on the other side of me, a centurion, with his arms crossed and dark eyes regarding everything from under his baseball cap.

Seeing the room full, the lead physician lifted his hand in introduction. "I'm Dr. Hubbard, the attending, and this is Dr. Park, the resident. As you know, Margaret suffered an amniotic fluid embolism and required immediate surgery. I believe Dr. Park explained why we needed to completely remove her uterus."

I nodded, folding my hands to keep the trembling under wraps.

"The survival rate for a catastrophic event like this is usually below twenty percent—"

I brought my fist to his mouth, worried I might vomit.

"But we were able to stabilize her. She received well over one hundred units of blood—"

I reached out instinctively for my sister, needing the support in case my legs gave out.

"And there are always risks and possible complications with a surgery like a hysterectomy—"

My nausea transformed into immense, painful relief. My heart pounded in my chest.

"The recovery time will not be insignificant, especially mentally and emotionally—"

"But she is going to recover?" I asked, nearly delirious at this point.

"Yes, she will."

It seemed like everyone around exhaled audibly along with me, and I crouched down, covering my face with my hands as I cried. I didn't think I had any tears left, but I couldn't stop the deluge of gratitude that tracked down my cheeks. The doctor continued to explain further testing and monitoring, though I didn't—couldn't—pay much attention, thankful my sister was there to ask questions and get the answers I would need to understand later.

After a few minutes, the team exited the room, and Dani sank down to the floor, hugging me.

"She's going to be okay," she repeated over and over, my face buried in her neck. This time, I was the one crying, the one in need, the one who needed to be reassured, and my little sister was there. "A nurse is going to come get you in a few minutes to see her, so let's get you up and looking a little less wrecked, huh? You don't want to scare her away with snot all over your face."

A hysterical chuckle bubbled from my throat as she towed me up. She passed me a few tissues, and Chris handed me a water and a sandwich. "Now that you know she's okay, you gotta put something in your system."

I swallowed down a couple gulps of water, followed by half the turkey sandwich. Then I hugged my sister and friends and kissed my son, who was still in Bronte's arms.

"I'm going to call Mom and Dad and update them," Dani said. "They'll be here first thing tomorrow morning."

"And we're staying until they kick us out," Bronte told me since visiting hours were coming to a close.

"I can't thank you guys enough for being here," I said as a nurse appeared in the doorway.

"There was no way we weren't going to be here for you. Now, go see her." Dani all but shoved me toward the nurse.

"Get your happy ending," Chris added, and I tossed my hand up in a wave, a smile taking over my face for the first time in what felt like decades.

It would be a long time before the credits rolled on this story.

CHAPTER THIRTY-SEVEN

Maggie

Everything was heavy, weighted like I was filled with cement. Even my eyelids.

"Come on. Come back to me, sweetheart."

My throat bobbed on a moan, stirring from a dreamless sleep that tried to pull me back under, but the warm press on my forearm had me working hard to wake up.

"There you are."

Wes's warm blue eyes were there, red-rimmed though unblinking, a soft smile carving his features. His skin was pink and blotchy, his jaw unshaven, hair a mess.

Although none of it made sense.

I couldn't quite grasp reality through the haze of sleep.

"You don't know how happy I am to see you," he rasped, his voice raw.

I attempted to lift my arm but the tangle of wires kept my fingers from reaching his face, and he leaned down, granting me easier access. When I finally traced the pads of my fingers over his cheek and jaw, he closed his eyes, holding his hand over mine, keeping me there.

"What—" My voice cracked, and I tried to clear my throat

of the pieces of glass that had cut it up, to no avail. "What happened?"

He didn't answer, his lip quivering.

"Wes."

He was slow to lift his eyelids, and when he did, he bent to kiss my temple. "I was scared I'd never hear your voice again." He rested his forehead on mine. "Scared I'd never see you again."

Another long moment passed before he moved away, staring down at me like it was the first time. Like I was his kryptonite. "It's so good to hear you say my name."

"Wes, where's the baby?"

He tucked strands of hair behind my ear. "He's here, in the hospital room with Dani, Bronte, and Chris. He's so perfect."

I swallowed but my mouth was dry, and I smacked my lips.

"The nurse said you can have water when you get back to the room. You're still in recovery from the surgery."

"Surgery?" I scanned down the length of my body, covered up by white sheets. While my big bump was gone, my stomach was still distended. I pushed against the thin mattress, attempting to sit up, and Wes hit a button to help me, moving the bed upright by one degree.

"Better?"

I nodded. "What happened? I want to see the baby."

"You will. You will," he assured me, running his hands along my shoulder and collarbone like he was checking to make sure I was real, and panic surged through me.

"Wes, what happened?"

"You..." He licked his lips, his attention dropping to where his hand covered mine. "You almost died. You went into cardiac arrest and had a cesarean to get the baby out. What you had, it's called an amniotic fluid embolism. Some of the fluid got into your bloodstream and…" His brows furrowed in pain. "Most people, they don't survive."

I didn't know it was possible to feel immense euphoria and fear at the same time. I was here, in this beige hospital room with Wes sitting next to me, his fingers drifting back and forth over my wrist, and yet dread shadowed what I knew was still to come.

"I was so scared." He paused to take a deep breath. "You started hemorrhaging, lost a lot of blood, and…" He cleared his throat, meeting my gaze. "They had to stop it, the bleeding, and to do that, they needed to remove your uterus."

I fought through exhaustion and a pain in my abdomen to understand his words. "They took out my uterus? Like a hysterectomy?"

"I'm so sorry, Mags. I'm so sorry. It was the best-case scenario to get you through it. They came to talk to me, and I told them to do it, to do whatever they had to in order to save you. But, Maggie, I'm so sorry. I saw you lying on that bed, and I couldn't—I knew I would never make it without you. Our son needed you. *I* need you, and I told them to do it. I didn't—"

I lifted my hand to stop his rambling apology. "I won't be able to have any more children?"

He shook his head, and I dropped my chin to my chest, eyes filling with painful tears, my nose stuffy and burning.

"I'm sorry. I didn't know what else to do." He folded my hand between both of his, kissing the back of it. "They said there was a small chance of saving you, and I knew you would hate it. There wasn't anything else to do, and god, Maggie, I couldn't lose you. I'm so sorry."

I sniffled a few times, awareness of the full picture dawning on me. I'd become pregnant and found the love of my life in an untraditional way, but I had planned on doing the more traditional thing with him. Picket fence, dog, two point five children. Except, now that wasn't possible, at least not conventionally.

Then again, I suspected with how Wes and I started out, maybe conventional wasn't ever in the cards for us.

I had nearly died giving birth to our child, and here Wes was, weeping in sorrow for making what was surely an enormously difficult decision. Although, if I had been conscious, I would have made the same one. The alternative was unthinkable.

And I hadn't even met my baby boy yet. I had to stick around a while longer.

"It's all right," I said, carefully moving my arm across to sift my fingers through his hair until he lifted his head. I wiped at his tears. "It was the right decision."

"I love you so much," he whispered, nuzzling into my palm when I smoothed my hand down to his jaw.

"I love you too. Now when can I see our baby?"

He pressed a kiss to the center of my palm before standing to call for a nurse. It was a while until the effects of the anesthesia wore off and I was moved down to the room, where Dani, Bronte, and Chris all greeted me with ecstatic grins and kisses to the cheek, but I couldn't hear their well-wishes when Wes walked over to the crib in the corner and lifted our baby, kissing the bundle before bringing him over to me.

Wes settled him in my arms, and the love for my child hit me like a tidal wave, dragging me under and spinning me around until I didn't know which way was up. I had loved him when he was warm and safe in my womb, and now that he was out in the world, sleeping soundly in my arms, I would give anything and everything to keep him there.

"Perfect, right?" Wes whispered, and my breath stuttered as I reined in my tears. I adored his tiny nose, wanted to bite his round cheeks, and treasured the dark wisps of hair peeking out from under his cap.

"He's got quite a pair of lungs on him," Bronte said, "but once he's asleep, I don't think he'd notice if a tornado tore through here."

"Looks a lot like you, Maggie." Dani stepped toward the bed. "Thank god."

Wes chuckled softly. "My thoughts exactly."

"I snuck down to the cafeteria earlier and got some snacks." Chris gestured to the pile of cookies and chips on the windowsill. "I'm not sure what you're allowed to have, but…"

"Thank you." I coasted my gaze around the room, to our friends and family. "Thank you for being here. For Wes, for him," I finished, staring down at the most beautiful little person in my arms.

Dani placed a gentle hand on my shoulder. "Of course we were going to be here, not only for Wes and for your baby, but for you too."

"I'm so sorry your delivery had such horrible complications," Bronte said, her voice a little weepy. "But I'm so grateful you made it out to the other side. The world is such a brighter place with you in it."

I pulled my attention away from the way my son wrinkled his nose, so similar to me. "Thank you."

Chris hugged Wes. "We're going to head out. Get some rest, and let us know if you need anything." Then he bent to kiss my cheek and offer a soft sweep of his hand over the baby's head. "Take care, Isaacsons."

Bronte followed suit with hugs and kisses, and a "Love you!" to the room.

Dani stayed until well after nine o'clock when the nurses finally informed her she had to leave.

"You want to stay at our place tonight?"

"No, I'll be fine. I'm all hopped up on coffee and sugar. Mom and Dad's flight gets in a little after nine. I'm sure you'll see them soon after."

I squeezed Dani's hand on her way out, which earned me a smile. "I always wanted a sister."

That had my eyes tearing up once again, gratitude overflowing for my found family and the immediate and unconditional support they lent.

"Text me lots of pictures!" Dani exited the room with a wave, leaving Wes and me to stare wide-eyed and shell-shocked at each other.

"Well, this certainly wasn't how I saw this all going."

Wes shook his head, combing his fingers through my hair. "I should've known the night we met, you'd be nothing but trouble."

"And you still kept me around."

He mumbled an agreement against my temple. "I plan on keeping you for a long time."

We sat quietly for a few minutes, simply staring down at our baby, until the nurse came in to change the IV bag, informing me that I would most likely be drowsy from the pain medication, but I didn't want to put my baby down. Not yet.

So Wes sat at my hip, helping me to support him as I drifted off to sleep.

Though it was fitful. Between learning exactly how strong my son's lungs were and the doctors and nurses coming in every so often to check on me, I doubt I slept more than an hour straight at a time. Meanwhile, Wes hovered over me like a vampire, never once closing his eyes. When I had told him to lie down on the little couch and get some sleep, he raised a sardonic brow. "It'll be a while before I close my eyes. Need to make sure you two don't go anywhere."

As Dani had said, Abby and Jeff showed up with flowers,

balloons, and a box of chocolates in hand. After a tearful greeting, Abby swept her arms out for her grandson, swaying him gently.

"What did you name him?" Jeff asked, his head over his wife's shoulder, his eyes on his grandson.

"We didn't yet," Wes said. "It was…" He shrugged, glancing over at me. "It was a hard enough day to get through yesterday. We haven't even talked about his name yet."

Abby frowned, her eyes like a faucet, and she tugged yet another tissue from her pocket to wipe under her nose. "This was all so horrible, but what joy this little guy brings." She gazed down at the baby with that same euphoric expression I imagined was splayed across my own face since seeing him. "Happiness after the storm."

Jeff drew his thumb over the baby's forehead, his dark eyes blinking back wetness. "Asher."

Wes tilted his head. "Hmm?"

"I don't remember much from Hebrew school, but I do remember that. Asher was one of the tribes of Israel. His name means happiness."

"Asher," I repeated, trying the name out on my tongue.

Wes seemed to be doing the same thing. "Asher."

"Asher Isaacson," I said, and Wes grinned.

We spent the morning taking turns holding Asher; however, I had trouble keeping my eyes open. One moment, I was enjoying flavorless hospital Jell-O, and the next, Abby and Jeff had disappeared.

"They went back to our house," Wes explained. "They're going to stay there for a few days until we come home. Mom had a bug up her butt about cleaning and making sure it was pristine."

I gave in to a chuckle and sank back against my pillows even though I'd just woken up from a nap.

"They're going to bring back some clothes and toiletries later. Do you want anything specific?"

"My fuzzy purple socks."

He typed my request into the text thread, but before he had the chance to put his phone away, two knocks sounded on the door. "Come in."

I froze at the first sight of my mother's hair. That brunette bob was unmistakable and unchanging for the last twenty years.

"Mom?"

CHAPTER THIRTY-EIGHT

Maggie

My mother stood in the doorway, her eyes shifting all over the room, her hands clutching the strap of her purse by her shoulder.

Tension corded my muscles. "What are you doing here?"

"You're in the hospital. Why wouldn't I be here?" Her voice was flat, no hint of the usual bitterness or irritation.

Next to me, Wes shifted closer, twining his fingers with mine as he whispered, "I asked Bronte to call her yesterday. I thought she should know what happened."

My eyes didn't stray from my mother as she stepped forward. "I came to see you. See your baby."

"Asher. We named him Asher." I motioned to his crib on the other side of the bed, where he was sound asleep.

She took one more hesitant step. "How are you feeling?"

"Okay, considering."

She rolled her lips between her teeth, maybe holding back an *I told you so* comment or some other caustic remark.

The last thing I expected when my mother opened her mouth was an apology. "I'm sorry for what I said at Thanksgiving."

My eyes shot open wide, despite my fatigue. My surprise

must have been apparent because my mom nodded, her mouth pursed. She stared down at the floor for a minute, and I slid my gaze to Wes, who raised his brow.

"I'm sorry to both of you," she said eventually, and I was grateful when Asher's cry pierced the awkward silence. Wes got up, moving past her without a glance, and picked up our red-faced baby.

"Okay, pal, I got you." He shushed Asher with a slight bounce, and I smiled at the pair, even as I felt my mother's stare boring into the side of my face. Wes changed Asher then passed him to me with a bottle as if he knew I needed to use our baby as a shield, requiring all the support I could get.

I'd tried to breastfeed last night, but it didn't go well, and we decided it would be better for everyone to bottle-feed. It felt like another slice to my motherhood, first losing my ability to have children, and then not being able to provide milk. But Wes had wiped away my tears and reminded me I was Asher's mother, no matter where he got his food from.

My mother moved to the foot of the bed. "He's beautiful. Congratulations." Then she remained there, unmoving and unspeaking. Until I lifted Asher higher up to my chest and reached my hand out to the little table next to the bed. She rushed around. "What do you need?"

"Water."

She grabbed the Styrofoam cup with the straw and brought it to me. "You look well."

"I feel like I've been brought back from the dead," I said once I finished the water.

"I'm glad." At my confused frown, she folded her hands, dropping them in front of her like a well-behaved schoolgirl. "I would hate for the last words I ever said to you to be out of anger."

"So, that's why you're here? You feel guilty because I almost died."

She blanched but recovered quickly, sweeping one finger under her eye. "You're my daughter."

My own guilt niggled under my ribs for not being more receptive to the apology, but I refused to be a doormat for my family anymore. "I am your daughter, which is why it hurt so bad." Wes wrapped a hand over my shoulder, a silent encouragement for me to continue. "I honestly don't know what you want me to say, Mom. I don't know what *to* say."

"You don't need to say anything." She stepped away from the bed. "I came here because I know what it feels like to hold your newborn baby in your arms. I want you to be happy, that's all." She shuffled to the door, her hands back on the strap of her purse. "When the Lord calls me home, I don't want to regret anything I've said, so I'm sorry."

Then she dipped her chin and slipped out the door, and I blew out a long breath. "Well... That was unexpected."

Wes shook out his arms like he was ridding himself of the heebie-jeebies.

I laughed. "Did I say the right thing?"

"There is no right or wrong thing." He took Asher back from me. "You don't owe her anything."

I chewed on my lip. "But...it was weird, right? Like, she basically said she apologized to me because she wants to go to heaven when she dies. Not because she feels bad."

He sucked air through his teeth as he settled Asher on his shoulder, rubbing his back. "Yeah, sounded like it."

"I guess I should be thankful she even showed up."

He huffed. "She should be thankful you didn't throw her out of the room. And I'm sorry I didn't tell you about her earlier. It slipped my mind."

"It's okay." I curled my legs up, wincing at the pain in my abdomen. "I just want to go home."

He wiped his hand over my head, pushing my hair back from my forehead and tapping the edge of my glasses. "I know. Me too, but it's a few more days."

"You can go home. You don't have to stay here."

"You're kidding, right?" He curled his hand around my neck, and I relaxed into the touch. "I'm going to be on you like a bad rash for the rest of my life."

"The rest of your life?"

"Till death do us part, sweetheart."

———

When we finally arrived home four days later with Asher in his carrier, we were greeted by the whole clan. Abby and Jeff, Dani, her husband Colin, and their kids, Aiden and Sadie, along with a welcome home banner, a giant stuffed giraffe, multiple pizzas, and a few sushi rolls just for me.

Wes worried it was too much, but I made myself comfy on the couch and accepted everyone fawning over me, never having to lift a finger, even to retrieve a napkin.

"You're all so sweet to be here," I said, hugging seven-year-old Sadie to my side. "I love you all."

"We love you too," Abby said, having yet to put Asher down. "All the laundry is done and folded in baskets on your bed, the dishwasher is empty, and we stocked your refrigerator, so you shouldn't have to leave the house in the next few days."

"Or weeks," Jeff added, and everyone chuckled.

Wes stood to kiss her cheek. "Thanks, Mom."

"Yeah, thanks, Mom," I said, which had Abby's mouth

quivering with more unshed tears. Then she passed Asher off to Wes and sat down right next to me with a big squeeze.

"Not so tight," Wes warned. "Her stitches."

"It's okay." I could barely wave my hand, my arms pinned to my sides under Abby's hold. Still, I grinned. "I'm okay."

"You're more than okay, honey. I'm so happy to call you my daughter."

And we didn't move from each other's sides for the rest of the day.

The whole crew left around five, taking all their incessant happy chatter with them. Since Abby and Jeff had stayed in our house for five days, they were planning on flying back home to give us time to adjust.

But once the front door was shut and locked and Wes took a seat next to me, I frowned, pointing to a sleeping Asher. "What do we do now?"

"I have no idea."

Then we broke into a fit of exhausted, slightly manic giggles.

Once we caught our breath, I leaned my head on his shoulder, and he kissed the top of my head. "If you want to take a shower, I'll bring Ash with me and put all the laundry away. Then we can try to—"

"Wait. Let's sit here for a few minutes first. I want you to hold me."

Wes sank back into the couch cushions, draping his arm around me. "Sounds good to me."

So we sat, watching Asher sleep.

Until he woke up screaming to eat. Then we figured out real quick what we had to do.

But that was the thing with Wes and me. We would always figure it out.

Together.

Epilogue

MAGCIE

"Of course the flight is delayed," I grumbled, hoisting Asher up on my hip so he didn't run away again. "Wouldn't be February in New York without sleet."

"Gives us time to get a drink."

I lifted my brow, eyeing my ever-brilliant husband. "You're right. Let's go get a drink."

He pressed his palm against my back, steering us to a restaurant in the terminal, where we found a table in the corner. We always sat in corners now. It gave us room to spread out our *stuff*. Everywhere we went, we had to bring the diaper bag, formula, Cheerios, little yogurt pouches, a sippy cup, and at least three of Asher's toys, including his favorite, an insanely annoying stuffed dog that barked and panted. When we had conveniently lost the batteries, Asher cried for two hours straight because his "pup pup" wouldn't work.

Wes flipped over the plastic drink menu. "What do you want?"

"I don't know." I barely glanced at it. "A beer?"

"Want some food too?"

"Yeah. I could eat," I said, holding Asher up on my lap so he could march his chubby legs on my thighs while he giggled.

When the server arrived at our table, Wes ordered for us. He, of course, knew exactly what I wanted without ever having to ask. "I'm going to have a Guinness and the black and blue burger, and my wife would like a Stella and chicken sandwich, please."

Even though we'd been married for about nine months now, it still delighted me to no end when Wes referred to me as "my wife."

We'd had a tiny ceremony in our backyard, almost a year to the day we'd met in June. Chris had officiated it, while Vivienne served as matron of honor. Bronte had decorated, and I wore a white sundress, while Wes wore one of his starched button-downs, the same color blue as his eyes, with the sleeves rolled to his elbows. Abby and Jeff were there, along with Dani and her family and a handful of other friends, including Wes's old pal, Fitz, who was also Bronte's brother. We exchanged vows and rings in the afternoon and then laughed and snacked on our favorite takeout until the sun set. It was exactly our speed, untraditional but full of love.

"Here, let me take him." Wes held out his hands for our son, and Asher happily went, squawking out "Da-da!" over and over again.

Life hadn't been easy once we got home from the hospital after his birth, but Wes and I had made it through to the other side, even if we were a little worse for wear. The medication, therapy, and hiring an assistant for each of us helped. My online merchandise business was booming, allowing me time and money to work on passion projects, like a children's book with Vivienne, about two best friends who can't speak each other's language but learn as they walk through a park, naming animals and plants in both English and French. *Turning Leaves* was in postproduction and was set for a late summer, early fall release.

And best of all, Asher's first birthday was two days away. Abby and Jeff had generously offered to take the whole family, including Dani's, to Disney World to celebrate. But first, we had to get there.

"You are so slobbery," Wes told Asher, who attempted to bite his dad's finger, and I plopped my chin in my hands.

Looking back, I knew I'd loved Wes from the moment we met. We were made for each other, and if that wasn't proof of a higher power, I didn't know what was. That there was someone out there, floating around in the universe, waiting to find the missing piece of their soul to make them whole.

That was what Wes and I were. The missing piece for each other.

It didn't hurt that my missing piece was insanely hot.

The man could change a diaper with his eyes closed and always cleaned up the baby puke since it made me gag.

"What?" he asked when he noticed me gawking.

"Nothing. Just watching my DILF."

He cocked his head. "Yeah?"

"You think Mom and Dad could watch Ash one night, and we could go out?"

"Definitely." He sat Asher on his lap, wrapping one arm around our wiggle monster to keep him contained, then reached out to stroke his thumb along my lower lip. He had that dark gleam in his eyes, the same one I'd become familiar with since he'd first sat next to me at the bar.

I nipped at him, and he sucked in a sharp breath. "It's been a while."

"It's been forever," I said with a laugh because Asher was going through what felt like a permanent sleep regression, needing to be put back down in his crib twenty times a night. We were both so exhausted and barely had enough energy to take off our clothes, let alone spare time for anything more than a quick grope in the mornings after a shower.

He curved his hand over my jaw, his thumb drifting back and forth over my cheekbone, desire and tenderness swirling in his gaze. "I love you, you know."

"I know." I leaned forward and pressed a chaste kiss to his lips but was shoved back with a surprisingly strong hand belonging to Asher.

"Ing! Ing!"

Wes dipped his face down to him. "Buddy, I can't swing you here. There are too many people and—"

"Ing! Ing!"

"I can't. Here, want a snack?"

Asher flung the snack bag of Cheerios away, and I rolled my eyes, picking up the pieces of cereal from the floor as Asher started to cry.

Wes bounced him, trying to satisfy Asher's need to be thrown around all the time. If he wasn't stumbling about with his newly learned skill of walking or being flown in the air, he wasn't happy. He had to be on the move, all day, every day.

Asher's nose wrinkled as he opened his mouth to let out a wail, and because Wes could not just say no to me crying, he also couldn't say no to Asher's tears, he got up.

I snorted a laugh as he stalked outside of the restaurant to find an open space in the terminal to swing Asher. I watched my guys, one giggling in glee as he soared up and down, the other grinning like a fool.

Wes liked to call me his kryptonite. But really, I was at the mercy of my boys. Without them, my life would be bleak. They were my pride and joy, love and laughter, and worth every bit of the pain and wait.

They were everything.

Acknowledgments

Indie publishing is a wild ride. Thank you, reader, for coming along with me.

I wouldn't be able to put out these books if not for the encouragement of my friends, especially Ellis Leigh and Brighton Walsh, and the help of my editors, Libby and Lisa. I'd especially like to thank my street team for helping me spread the work about my books. I'm forever grateful.

If you'd like more information about me, you can find it at: https://sophieandrewsauthor.com.

Sophie Andrews is a contemporary romance author who writes steamy books that will leave you smiling. As a millennial, she's obsessed with boybands, late 90s rom-coms, and will always be team Pacey. When she's not writing, she's most likely trying to wrangle her children or drinking red wine. Or both at the same time.